A DEATH IN BULLOCH PARISH

Also by Nat & Yanna Brandt

Land Kills

Nat & Yanna Brandt

A DEATH IN BULLOCH PARISH

A Foul Play Press Book

THE COUNTRYMAN PRESS
WOODSTOCK, VERMONT

Library of Congress Cataloging-in-Publication Data

Brandt, Nat.
A death in Bulloch Parish/Nat & Yanna Brandt. —1st ed.
p.   cm.
"A Foul Play Press book."
ISBN 0-88150-265-0
1. Journalists—Louisiana—Fiction. I. Brandt, Yanna. II. Title.
PS3552.R3233D4   1993
813'.54—dc20   93-5555
CIP

Text design by Dede Cummings/I.P.A.

A Foul Play Press Book
The Countryman Press, Inc.
Woodstock, Vermont 05091

Printed in the United States of America

In memoriam, to Mootsie

ACKNOWLEDGMENTS

The authors wish to thank Ellen Borakove, Director of Public Affairs, Chief Medical Examiner's office, New York City, and Dr. Leonard Rosen for their invaluable advice regarding medical matters. And our gratitude to Leland Gantt, who read the manuscript and gave us helpful comments and perspective.

PROLOGUE

*H*E HAD ASKED *to be shaved this morning. It was a matter of pride. A lieutenant approached, in his hands a black hood, but he disdained it with a slight shake of his head. That was pride, too—and fear. Fear of darkness. From behind him, the hangman, a civilian, slipped the thick, rough noose over his head and adjusted the knot. The sun, glaring in the mid-winter sky, made him squint. He had already asked which direction was south. He turned that way now, away from where the Union flag flew over the entrance to the fort, as a captain read out loud the charges and sentence. An army chaplain, his hat under his arm, was reading softly from a small Bible, his lips mouthing the words. The Twenty-third Psalm. He had requested that, also.*

Finished with reading the charges, the captain asked whether he wanted to say anything. Again, he shook his head. Anything— everything—he had to say he had said already, or he had written in the letters they had allowed him to send through the blockade to his family in Louisiana. The chaplain was reading louder now, the words coming out in spouts of vapor in the cold air.

The captain stepped back, drew his sword and raised it high into the blue sky. The sun sparkled off it. He followed it with his eyes, then looked away. He trembled slightly, tried to swallow. Hearing the chaplain, he drew erect, his head held up, and began to recite the words with him: ". . . and I shall dwell in the house of the Lord my whole life long." He heard the chaplain's "Amen" and started to echo it when suddenly the planking under his feet gave way, and he fell into the gap where it had been.

ONE

M ITCH CIRCLED THE desks, passing out the information sheet to the students sitting behind the manual typewriters. "For this part of your final, I'm going to ask you to write a news story based on a typical police report of a crime," he said as he tried to pry apart two sheets that were sticking to each other. "A burglary. As you can see by what the officer who wrote up the report said, the family was away on vacation, and it was the third time that the home was burglarized." He handed the last sheet to the student seated alone in the back row and made his way back to the table at the front of the classroom. "Now before you hit your typewriters, I want you to take a few minutes to study the data and come up with questions that you'd ask if you were the reporter handling the story."

Mitch sat on the edge of the table, studying his students as they read the police report. The section of the basic newswriting course that he taught was limited to 14 students, all of them freshmen or sophomores. Eager as they said they were to be journalists, most would change their major by their junior year. By then they either realized that they never would make it as reporters or were turned off by the profession's relatively low pay. Few would make it to his advanced writing and reporting class in their senior year. Fewer still had the ability to become good reporters. Yet those few were worth all his efforts. He nurtured them, helping them to hone their talent, pushing them to follow their instincts, prodding them to pursue a story until they had every fact.

Mitch was grateful for those few students. They kept him going, kept him alert and alive, most of the year, anyway. By this time, the last gasp of the academic year, he usually felt pretty burned-out. Most of the year, particularly to freshmen and sophomores, he spent teaching basic grammar. He often found himself in a state of amazement about the incredibly imaginative and contorted sentence style that many students brought to their work. This had been a particularly trying year after last summer.

"So what catches your eye? What stands out?" Mitch looked around the room. A hand shot up. "Yes, Janet."

"Well, it was the third time the home was robbed."

"We know that, Janet. Go a little further."

"Maybe they ought to be asked why they don't have an alarm system, and what was stolen before."

"Fine, only the first question about the alarm system is whether they have one at all. Don't start with a preconceived notion that the family didn't. Who knows, maybe the alarm was cut off. But you're on the right track by querying the family. What else, anyone?"

"It says here that everything inside the home, even the food that was left in the freezer, was taken. Would you say that in your story?"

"That's good color, Lee. You'll want to give your readers a rundown of that list of stolen items the cop has in the report— the refrigerator, the sofa, all the appliances, the rugs, even the dog food. We've talked about that before in class. Your readers will eat up details like that. But that's not what we want to talk about now."

Mitch peered over his eyeglasses, searching the students for some sign of inquisitiveness, a raised eyebrow perhaps or a quizzical look. "Come on, folks. Use your eyes." Mitch paused. The students looked puzzled. Mitch picked up his copy of the information sheet. "What does the report say after giving the name of the head of the family and the address?"

"It says 'B'," said a dark-skinned young man in the second row.

"And what do you think 'B' stands for, Earl?"

"Black?"

"Now you've got it, and what does that do for you? What does that lead you to think?" Earl shrugged his shoulders. "Tracy, how about you?" Tracy, whom Mitch considered the brightest prospect in the class, had been strangely silent. Usually she was the first to raise her hand, or was so anxious to chime in that she interrupted whoever was speaking. "Tracy?"

The young woman shook herself erect. "I'm sorry, Professor. I have a cold, and my head feels on fire." As if to prove that she wasn't lying, she blew her nose into a wrinkled handkerchief. "I think the first thing I'd want to know," she said, sniffling slightly as she stuffed her handkerchief up the sleeve of her sweatshirt, "is whether there'd been any trouble in the neighborhood. It says here that the home is on an acre-and-a-half plot. That sounds like the suburbs, probably a white suburb." She took out her handkerchief again.

"Go on," Mitch coaxed. "What would you do?"

"I'd ask around, talk to neighbors and the police and see whether there'd been any trouble. I mean, after talking to the family."

"Isn't that stretching things a bit?" asked Earl. "Just because the guy is black, why assume the worst? That sounds like racism to me."

"We're not assuming the worst, Earl, we're checking out a possibility." Mitch took off his glasses and began wiping them with a tissue. "Unfortunately, in the world we live in, some shocking things happen. That's certainly not news to you, Earl.

That black family living in that white neighborhood on Staten Island: Did you read about what happened to their home, how it was set on fire and signs were painted all over their sidewalk? Or, for God's sake, take what happened in Queens recently when those young white guys beat up two blacks, just because they stopped off at a pizza parlor in their neighborhood. As a reporter, you've got to check out that possibility—and seeing that 'B' on the police report should serve like a red warning light."

Mitch turned to the rest of the class. "What else? Who else would you talk to? What else would you do?"

"Check the clips," said Lee. "Maybe the area has a reputation for being prejudiced or something and there've been stories before about it."

"Or maybe there have been other robberies around there," said Earl, "and this one's the latest in a string of them."

"Good. Anything else?"

"Who else could you interview?" asked Tracy.

"I'd try local ministers," Mitch said. "If anyone is concerned with keeping the peace in a neighborhood, it's usually the local priest or minister or rabbi. That's their job in a way." He pushed himself off the table and walked around behind it to stand with his back to the blackboard. "Let me toss another question at you. What if you check out all the sources we've talked about, spoken to the family, to neighbors, to everyone, and come up with zilch. No racism involved as far as you can make out. Okay, when you go to write your story, do you mention that the family is black?"

A half-dozen hands shot up at once, but it was Tracy, one hand up while the other held her handkerchief to her nose, who said first, "No, no way. It's not relevant." The other students with their hands up echoed her.

"Attaway to go," said Mitch. "Their color is a dead issue in a situation like that." He looked at the clock on the side wall. "Okay, you've got 45 minutes left. How about seeing what you can do with the story. Let's say you checked out the racism possibility, and it didn't pan out. So you've got yourself a straight burglary story. Okay, get your typewriters going. There's plenty of copy paper in the cabinet if you need any. And good luck."

"What do we slug the story?" Earl asked.

"Slug it 'Ransack'."

Mitch glanced again at the clock as the students busily began feeding paper into their typewriters. Thank God, he thought, all he had left to do was grade the exams, and he was through. But then, he thought wryly, he would be facing the first day of a very long summer. He had put off a decision about what to do, delaying a commitment to anything. Now here it was the last day of school, and he did not have a single idea in his head.

JACK REED POKED his head around the door. "Still here, Mitch?"

"Come on in." Mitch waved at the slender, balding chairman of the communications department. "I'm just finishing the grading roster." He swept his pen up in a flourish as he finished signing his name, Mitchell Stevens.

"I've got a telephone message for you and thought I'd bring it by in person." Although Jack was friendly and informal, he obviously had something on his mind. Mitch wondered if there was to be another series of cutbacks at the university. He had narrowly missed being "furloughed" during the last faculty restructuring.

Mitch took the note but didn't look at it. "Jack, have a seat. I wanted to see you before I headed out anyway."

Reed dropped into the chair opposite Mitch's desk. He looked around the office. The shelves were bulging with stacks of papers. One pile above a filing cabinet looked on the verge of tipping over and spilling onto the floor.

Mitch followed Reed's eyes. "I know," he said. "It's always like this around exam time. All my students are trying to catch up on their papers. I don't think I've ever read so much drivel in my life."

"No, no, I wasn't being critical. You should see my office now." Reed took a pipe out of his coat pocket and turned it slowly in his hand. "Do you know yet what you're going to do this summer?"

Mitch shook his head. "Not quite. Val wants me to join her in California for her new film, but, hell, I don't know what the devil I'd do out there all day. I can't think of anything more boring than a film shoot. It takes hours just to set up and get 30 seconds that are usable."

"So do some writing." Reed took a pouch out of his other coat pocket and started filling his pipe. "You writer types always have something to fall back on, I hear."

"Oh, really?"

"I'm serious, Mitch. Do some writing. Get your name in print again. I bet it would do wonders for you."

Was this a hint about "publish or perish"? Mitch wondered. Reed was usually more straightforward about such matters. On the other hand, with the budget situation, maybe he was trying to warn him. Mitch thought that as a professional, as a working newspaperman for twenty-odd years, he was immune to the pressure to prove himself. Mitch had dabbled in writing magazine articles since his newspapering days had ended with the demise of the *Tribune*, but he found it difficult to get worked up about the current fads that magazines doted on—Yuppies, new lifestyles, hi-tech mania. He pushed his eyeglasses back on his nose, a gesture he unconsciously made whenever he was anxious or felt protective about his privacy.

"Hey, Jack," Mitch smiled wanly, "am I detecting a little departmental shove here?"

Reed drew the pipe from his mouth. "I wouldn't force you into anything. You know me better than that. Although," he added, turning to face Mitch directly, "I have to admit it looks good for the department to see our guys and gals in print. To be frank, that gets taken into account when budget strings get tightened. It has to be. We're in the teaching-of-writing business, not totally out of the real world, no matter what people think. Especially if you teach journalism, or writing, or whatever you want to call it, you ought to be able to do it yourself."

The two men fell silent, Mitch taking off his glasses and rubbing his eyes, Reed striking a match and holding it above the pipe bowl. As he sucked on the pipe, the shredded tobacco started to glow and smoke. Mitch watched him light up.

"Look, Mitch..." Reed seemed to be fumbling for words. "Look, I'm not trying to pry, not really. But you just didn't seem to have much fun this year. Is teaching getting to you? Look, it's nothing to be ashamed of. It happens to all of us at one time or another."

Mitch looked away. He liked Jack Reed. He was basically a decent man who rarely got involved in academic politics. Still, Mitch felt uncomfortable expressing his true feelings to the department chairman. He certainly didn't want to give Jack the idea that he was teaching just because the *Trib* had collapsed and he couldn't get another newspaper job. And if Reed was under pressure to get his faculty to publish, Mitch had better be careful about confiding in him. God, he hated playing games, and he was usually lousy at it. That's why he had learned through bitter experience and with Val's help to think twice before answering.

Reed paused and then went on, trying to prod Mitch to express himself. "Was it that business in Vermont last summer?— that time you subbed for your friend up in Southborough and got mixed up in those murders?"

Mitch shrugged. He had never gone into detail about the murders or the land development scheme that had prompted them. He had tried to push the entire incident away, but it kept coming back, intruding on his thoughts and occasionally interfering with his sleep. He was still having trouble convincing Val to reconsider building a getaway home in Vermont. Although while he was working there she was calm and supportive, after it was all over she became increasingly haunted by

17

how close Mitch himself had come to getting killed.

"What is it, Mitch? All of a sudden you looked like you were miles away."

Before Mitch could answer there was a light tap on the door and the head of one of his students appeared around the corner. "Whoops, sorry, Professor Reed, Professor Stevens."

"That's all right," said Reed as he got up. "Come on in. I was just about to go anyway." He offered his hand to Mitch. "If you get a chance, buzz me, anytime. I'll be around most of July, running the summer program. We'll have lunch, or if you just want to talk . . ."

"Thanks, Jack, I will if I hang around the city." He shook Reed's hand firmly. "Oh, listen. Will you tell Marcia I'll have this list to her in about half an hour. She wants to post it."

Reed edged himself through the doorway past the student, who smiled courteously at the department chairman.

"Come on in, Earl." Earl Bardun entered, a sheaf of papers in his hand. "I was headed down this way and Marcia asked me to drop these off. She said to tell you she forgot to get you to make out the textbook order for next fall."

Mitch took the forms from Earl. "So what are your plans for the summer, Earl? Are you stringing again for the *Times*?" Earl had been a lifeguard at Jones Beach the previous summer and had written a few sun-and-tan feature stories for the Long Island section of the paper's Sunday edition.

Earl made a face. "I haven't been able to get a thing lined up," he said. "And being a minority doesn't help anymore like it used to, to be honest. With all the cutbacks, we seem to be the first to go—or the last to be hired, as usual. I can't get a job anywhere."

Mitch looked concerned. "I'm sorry. I didn't think you of all people would have a problem, not after having a byline in the *Times*."

"Oh, I can get an internship at *Newsday*, but it doesn't pay a cent. I can't afford to do that. I need to earn some bucks to pay for school next year—or I can't come back."

"I didn't realize things were so serious for you," said Mitch. "If there's anything I can do for you—write a letter of recommendation, a reference, whatever—please let me know." He stood up and shook Earl's hand. "I mean that. You've got the makings of a good reporter. I'd hate to see you drop out."

Earl grinned at the compliment. "Thank you, Professor Stevens. By the way, how did I do on the exam?"

"Get outa here," said Mitch, smiling back. "It'll be posted by lunchtime."

MITCH SAT ON the edge of his desk for a long time after Earl left, staring at the pile of unfinished work. It was a shame that the future of a student like Earl Bardun stood on such shaky ground. He mentally counted up the other minority students in his classes and wondered how they managed. The university was already overcommitted in its financial aid program.

He finally shrugged and started to make order with the exam papers when his eye caught the note Reed had brought. He picked it up. Abigail Cantwell had called. Now there was a name from the past.

Abigail was Tom Cantwell's wife, the man who had taught Mitch everything he ever knew about newspapering. For years, he realized with a surge of guilt, he and the Cantwells had exchanged Christmas cards and that was it. He hadn't seen them since a Pulitzer Prize dinner a year ago at Columbia. It was certainly odd for Abigail to be the one to telephone. Maybe Tom was ill. He'd better call.

Mitch started to fold the note, then hesitated. Was Reed sending him a subtle message about having to write? Was it publish or perish time? Mitch shrugged. He'd worry about it later. Better call Abigail. He reached for the telephone.

TWO

"I'M SO GLAD you phoned, Mitch. I just didn't know who else to turn to. They want me to do something about it now, and how can I when I'm crippled in a wheelchair? If we'd had children—"

"What is it, Abigail?" Mitch interrupted. "I all of a sudden started to get worried when I got your message."

"I'm sorry, Mitch, I'm so upset and everything I don't know where to start. It's Tom, Mitch. He's dead. He's gone."

"Oh, Abigail, I'm sorry, truly sorry." Mitch felt a sudden rush of sadness. "I, I didn't know he was ill. I . . ." He caught himself. "I'm sorry, Abigail. You must have your hands full. What can I do for you?"

"Oh, Mitch, I need someone to help me, and I couldn't think of anyone else to call, anyone who'd care."

"Let's take this slow, Abigail. Start at the beginning. What's happened?"

Mitch could hear the old woman sigh and take a breath. "Tom was in Louisiana. I got a call to say he'd died. Heart failure. They want me to go down to identify him and arrange things. I don't know what to do."

"Now don't worry, Abigail. I'm here to help. Just tell me everything I should know, all right?"

"It happened in Virgil, a small town in the northwestern part of Louisiana."

"What the devil was Tom doing there?" Mitch asked.

Abigail explained that since Tom Cantwell's retirement from the *Brunswick Guardian* two years ago he had gotten so bored with hanging around the house that he'd decided to write a book. "You remember that story he latched onto during the Civil War centennial?"

"That was almost 30 years ago," Mitch recalled. "He had us all doing features during that time. I don't remember specifics about that one—that was Tom's baby. Was there more to it?"

"Tom was never satisfied that he'd done the story justice," Abigail said. "It bothered him at the time, and when he had nothing to do he started poking around into sources and places that he didn't have time to investigate when he was on the paper. Anyway, he came up with some interesting facts and was able to trace the spy's family in Louisiana and the next thing I knew he said he was going to turn it all into a book and off he went."

"He left you alone?"

"He wouldn't do that. He arranged for me to have a nurse's assistant. But I can't ask her to go down there."

"So off he went to Louisiana?"

"Oh, no. Washington. To the National Archives. He spent weeks there. And West Point and the library in New York and the historical society in—"

"Abigail, I don't mean to interrupt again, but maybe you can tell me all this later. Right now I think I ought to get some phone numbers from you so I can arrange things down in Louisiana."

"You'll have to go there. They said so."

"Then I'll go there, Abigail. You don't have to worry about that. My teaching chores are over, so I have time to help you all I can. Let me have the phone numbers, and I'll get back to you when I have something to report."

"Thank you, Mitch. Bless you. And will you come to see me, too? I want to ask you another favor."

"Absolutely."

TOM CANTWELL. Mitch had described him so often to his students. A newspaperman's newspaperman. What a cliché, Mitch realized. But it was true. Cantwell was managing editor of the *Brunswick Guardian* when Mitch, a novice reporter with a minimum of experience on a weekly in Connecticut, went to work there. He had learned so much from Cantwell, sitting at his feet, so to speak, every afternoon after the paper had been put to bed, listening to Cantwell fulminate about local politicians or explain cryptography or complain about the state of writing in newspapers. "Here's a letter I got the other day about the ad I ran in *Editor & Publisher* for a cub reporter, and this guy says he was Phi Beta Kappa and he can't even spell *that* right." Mitch laughed to himself at his recollection of what had happened next. "I'll never forget your letter, Mitch. It was a masterpiece. Here, I saved it." Cantwell had rummaged in a file until he pulled Mitch's letter of application from it. "Your letter got you your job." And Mitch, self-confident after nearly eighteen months on the *Guardian*—he was its star reporter by then—had confessed, softly, "Mr. Cantwell, you hired the wrong person. My wife wrote that letter." And it was true. Val had written it, just as he had written Val's resumé. Neither could sell themselves, but they could sell each other. Cantwell, Mitch remembered, had taken the news with composure. "Well, I never," he'd said, and had burst out laughing.

Tom Cantwell. He wrote the main editorial for the paper each day. It was clear, succinct and always took a point of view without any apologizing or equivocating. God, Cantwell was good. He expected a lot from his staff, but he was no martinet. Mitch and he had hit it off quickly, and developed a father-and-son relationship. Mitch's parents were dead, and even when his father had been alive, Mitch couldn't remember a single moment of tender attention. When Mitch finally moved on to a New York paper—and both he and Cantwell knew it would happen sooner or later; in fact Cantwell had been preparing Mitch for the step without saying so in so many words—the hardest part was realizing that there would be no more afternoon sessions with Cantwell.

They remained friends, of course. Cantwell followed Mitch's career with interest, was proud when he became editor of a major New York daily, and sympathized with him when the paper folded and Mitch turned to teaching. Mitch had continued to subscribe to the *Guardian*, never failing to read Cantwell's daily editorial and to jibe him for every typo he found. By then it was no longer Mr. Cantwell. It was Tom.

"Professor Reed asked me to remind you about your reading list for next fall before you go." Marcia Goodman stood in the doorway. It was hard to look at her as something other than the cliché. She was always smiling, always polite, always efficient. There were moments, hard-to-resist moments, when Mitch wanted to do something so outrageous that even Marcia would be forced to react. It was Marcia who really ran the department from her unassuming desk outside Jack Reed's office. "He said he has no objection to your changing textbooks as long as you and the other professors teaching the basic newswriting sections agree on using the same one."

Yeah, Mitch thought, that would be the day: the day when the others took the lead from him about anything. As the only former working news reporter in the department, he was the outsider and often at odds with his colleagues. Most of the time he didn't let it bother him, and at this moment the last thing in the world he was prepared to contemplate was a fight to the death over a textbook.

"Yeah, sure. But I've decided I'm going to stick with this year's, Marcia, so you can make up the requisition order for the bookstore from my last form." It was a lazy and cowardly decision, and Mitch knew it. Perhaps Tom's death had affected him more deeply than he was willing to admit.

Marcia jotted down a note to herself and started to move away. "Did Professor Reed give you that phone message? He's so absent-minded sometimes," she said as she walked away.

That reminded Mitch that he should phone Abigail and arrange to see her in Brunswick. He had already spoken to the sheriff down in Virgil and told him that he'd be flying down there over the weekend. I ought to see Abigail first, he thought to himself. She needs me. And he realized suddenly, I need to see her.

Mitch lifted the phone from the hook and started to dial the New Jersey area code, then caught himself. I haven't even told Val anything about this yet. She's supposed to leave for the West Coast over the weekend. My being away won't please her, but she'll understand. She knows what Tom meant to me.

THE NURSE'S AIDE, a black woman, wrapped a blanket around Abigail Cantwell's legs and moved to the other side of the porch, where she sat in a white wicker chair and took up two knitting needles and a skein of blue wool.

Mitch sat next to the wheelchair, holding Abigail's hand. She had strong wrists. She still painted, but she tired easily and was prone to fainting spells. She was gutsy, though. She had suffered so many insults and insinuations during the 1950s when Tom Cantwell's liberal leanings had become the target of witch-hunting McCarthyites. That episode had almost cost Tom his job, but the publisher had stood by him, and Tom had felt obliged to stay with the *Guardian*, even after all the turmoil had died down and he had received offers for high-paying jobs in Boston and Washington.

The old woman brushed back a wisp of her gray hair and smiled painfully as Mitch described his conversation with the sheriff in Virgil, Louisiana. "I'll fly down there tomorrow and have Tom's body brought back up here for burial, Abigail. I've already contacted a funeral parlor downtown, so you won't have to fuss with any arrangements whatsoever."

"Thanks, Mitch," she said, squeezing his hand. "All of a sudden, after all these years, I simply couldn't cope. I don't know why. I'm really grateful for what you're doing." She squeezed Mitch's hand again.

"You mentioned a favor yesterday," Mitch said. "What else can I do for you?" Mitch felt a twinge of guilt. There were so many times he had thought of going out to visit Tom and Abigail and something had always "come up." Now, it was too late.

Abigail looked off into the distance at the trees bordering the front lawn. Her husband had planted them more than thirty years ago, and they were still growing stronger and bigger each year. "It's a big favor," she said finally.

"Go on."

"Tom wanted that book so much. You know, he had never written one before. Isn't that amazing? All those words he wrote and never a book. It became a labor of love with him. And he was so excited doing it. I don't think I can remember him ever having so much fun doing something. He'd say to me, 'I'll have a book on a shelf in some library and it'll have my name on it and it'll be there forever. Not like some editorial or news story that gets crumpled up and thrown away the next day.'"

"I don't see what you're getting at, Abigail," Mitch said.

She looked at him pleadingly. "Can you write that book for him?"

Mitch started to say something, but Abigail quickly added, "It would have both your names on it, of course. Tom wouldn't have allowed anything otherwise.

"Mitch," she continued, taking both his hands in hers, "you were really like a son to him. He never put it that way, but he carried you in his heart—as I do, Mitch. I can't think of, or imagine, anyone else doing this. Only you would know what it meant to him."

"But Abigail, where would I begin? It would take me forever just to retrace his steps. I don't know that—"

"He left all his notes, Mitch. I used to help him sort and arrange them in files. It's all there," she said, pointing at the window to the room off the front hallway that Tom used as a study. "And he told me about everything he'd done. I would wheel myself in there and sit there reading while he worked away, and late in the afternoon—" She stopped suddenly. Her eyes went moist.

"Abigail? Don't be afraid to cry," Mitch said gently.

"I'm not afraid to cry, Mitch. I've already cried a lot. It just gets to me every so often when I think how close we were. I'm sorry."

"No need to be." Mitch paused. "Can I think on it, Abigail?"

But as though she hadn't heard him, Abigail went on. "He'd heard about this old lady in Manton—a real old lady, not like me." Mitch smiled slightly at her remark. Abigail was almost 70. "She was in her 90s, practically blind. She'd met and talked to the black slave who went off to the war with the spy. That was before he was a spy, when he was just an officer. You know, all the officers used to take along a slave to care for their horses and do the cooking and such." Abigail glanced quickly at the nurse's aide; the woman was bent over her knitting, trying to undo a snag. "Well, she met the one who'd gone off with this fellow."

"How's that possible?" Mitch asked.

"Tom checked and said it was so. The slave was in his 80s at the time the old woman met him. Can you imagine? Tom found a human link to a man who had died more than a hundred years ago. And he traced the spy's family, too. They had moved downstate after the Civil War. He even identified for them a photograph of the spy; they had a picture of him in a family album but didn't know who it was."

"Now how's that possible?"

"I saw the photograph. It's true." She spoke excitedly, the flood of facts lighting up her face. "The man was hanged at old

Fort Hamilton in Brooklyn, and two men from a Manhattan photo studio had gone to the fort three days before he was executed. The fellow had asked for the photo to be taken so he could send copies home to his family and friends—with lockets of his hair, like they used to do then. A newspaper reporter saw him putting the photos in envelopes addressed to his home on the morning of his execution, and Tom found in the National Archives the pass issued to the two photographers allowing them into the fort to take the picture."

"It sounds fascinating, Abigail. I can understand that Tom must have felt like he was unraveling a mystery. What's there to do other than the writing?"

"I think you'd have to see that old lady again, because I don't know what happened to Tom's notes on that. He said he was going to mail them back to me, but I never got anything."

"Why did he mail his notes?" Mitch asked. "He could have brought them home with him."

"That was just to avoid carrying too many papers around. Tom would ship off a bunch of stuff—his notes, Xeroxes of documents, a book or two that he'd find in a store. It would have been too much for him to carry all that with him on a plane."

"Let me think on it, Abigail," Mitch said. "It's a bit of a tall order. Like Tom, I've never written a book before either."

"You can have all the money from it, too," Abigail said. "I only want to see that Tom's dream comes true, that his name does appear on it, with yours."

"Don't be silly, Abigail, you're going to need the money and I certainly wouldn't think of taking it." Mitch stood up. "Look," he said, stretching his back, "this isn't something we should argue over now. This is not the time for it."

Abigail gripped the wheels of her chair and turned it to face the sun fading behind the distant trees. "I just thought that if you were going to all the trouble of going to Louisiana you might want to take advantage of being there to pick up where Tom left off."

Mitch stood looking down at Abigail. The last rays of the sun struck her face, highlighting her wrinkles. Her enthusiasm about the book had vanished. Creases of sorrow ran across her brow.

"All right," Mitch said finally. "I'll look around while I'm there and see what else needs to be done on the book, but I'm not promising anything, Abigail. It's not a decision I can make right now." Her gaze hadn't changed. "I'll tell you what, though. Run through his notes with me now so I know what I'm up against. Can I stay for dinner?" Abigail's face lit up in a broad smile.

Across the porch, the nurse's aide rose heavily and reached for the handles behind the wheelchair to help Abigail into the house.

"YOU REALLY DON'T mind, Val, really?"

Val turned from the suitcase, a folded blouse in her hands. Without a trace of makeup, her hair unbrushed, she was a striking woman. Whenever Mitch complimented her by calling her feminine, she bristled, accusing him of a nineteenth-century mentality about women. It was a game they played, because she knew that, above all, he valued her intelligence, her talents, and indeed often relied on them. "No, of course not," she was saying. "I don't mind. After all, it shouldn't take you long to straighten out the situation there for Abigail. And then you can fly out to the coast."

"What do you think about my taking on the book? I haven't promised her anything yet."

"That's up to you, Mitch." Val opened her lingerie drawer and stood, pondering what to take with her. "If you want to, do it. You know how we've handled our careers. We do what we like to do. You have, I have. That's the only way to survive in the kind of world we live in."

"You know what bugs me, though?" said Mitch. Val shot him a quick glance. "Reed. Jack is practically saying I ought to get off my butt and write. He doesn't say what, he doesn't say it has to be a textbook, or anything like that. He's just intimating that I should be getting my name attached to something."

"He needs ammunition to defend you, Mitch. You're the only one on staff who's not an academic." Val held up a white cotton sweater. "What do you think, too warm for California?"

"Yeah," said Mitch, ignoring her question, "only I don't like being pushed into something."

"Don't I know that," said Val, putting the sweater back in a drawer. "You're the most stubborn man in the world."

"And you're not?" said Mitch. "Anyway, that's not it. I just don't like being told what to do. I never have."

"So don't do it," Val said.

"But I got to thinking right off that it might be something to keep me busy this summer." And, maybe, it would also serve to put an end to Reed's bugging me about writing, Mitch thought.

"Mitch, I don't want to force you to come to California with me." Val sat down on the bed. "I realize it'll drive you crazy being on the shoot with nothing to do all day. But you don't have to be. There are plenty of sights to take in, museums to go to. We talked about the short trips you could make using L.A. as the base. I just don't like our being apart for so long. And we haven't seen Ken for months now either. And you did promise."

"Let me see what's involved, Val. Ken'll be busy with that summer job he got in Vermont. We'll make a pact to be together for the July Fourth weekend. I'll tell him we'll pay for his flight out to the Coast."

Val made a face. "Look, we can decide this later, Val. Let's take one step at a time. First I'll do what I have to do for Tom there, then we'll see."

"You've just got to make me one more promise, Mitch."

"Just one?" Mitch teased.

"I'm serious, Mitch," Val said, her voice taking on an urgency that Mitch, after twenty-odd years of marriage, realized meant that she was indeed being serious. "I still haven't quite gotten over what happened during those murders last summer. I'm getting funny vibes from this, so you have to promise not to do anything foolish."

"Funny vibes? On a Civil War story? You have to be kidding, Val. What kind of intuition is that?"

"I can't explain it, Mitch, but do you remember that time when Ken was biking in France, and I got a sudden premonition that we should phone him?" Mitch did remember. Ken had been hit by a motorist that day—nothing serious—and hadn't intended to tell his parents until he returned home. Val's intuition—a gut feeling that came out of nowhere—had spoiled that. "Promise me," she was saying, "or, or, or—"

Mitch laughed softly. Val was too honest to make a threat she wouldn't hold to. "Okay, I promise or, or, or."

He sat down on the bed next to her and took her hand. She smiled. Without another word, they embraced. Mitch loosened his grip for a moment and just stared at Val's face, more beautiful now than when they were first married. She had the glowing innocence of a teenager, but now it was enriched by character and as Val, the actress, would say, subtext. He felt Val's warmth, and as he leaned toward her they kissed. Gently, they lowered themselves until they were stretched against each other on the bed, their hands pressing each other closer. Mitch sniffed the skin of her neck. The aroma—her body musk—aroused him. He gripped Val tighter. In response, she pressed her hips against him. His hand moved down her back.

"WHEW." Mitch stretched back in the chair and whistled. There were cups of coffee beside his and Abigail's chairs. File folders were spread across Tom's desk. Mitch's own notes, written on the old copy paper that Tom had still liked to work on, sat on a low table next to the desk.

"Trouble?" asked Abigail. Her legs were paining her, but she hadn't wanted Mitch to stop, so she didn't say anything about the sudden pangs that went through her. Her face showed them, but Mitch had become so wrapped up in the research material that he hadn't noticed the lines of strain.

"No trouble, Abigail, just a lot to digest." Mitch shook his right wrist. He was starting to ache, too. "Tom did a phenomenal amount of research. I'm impressed. I mean, not only did he look into the actual plot and the life of the spy, but he gathered masses of information about the war. I didn't know that Lincoln had lost New York City's vote each time he ran, or that the city was such a center for Southern sympathizers."

"You're starting to sound like Tom," Abigail said. "He was absolutely intrigued by the subject. He said it was his own piece of history. Nobody else had ever written about it."

Mitch picked up a glossy black-and-white print. The man in the photograph was seated, his arms folded in a style typical of the period. His features, except for his eyes, were masked by a beard. Mitch was fascinated by the eyes; they seemed filled with sorrow. The print was a copy of the photo Tom had identified in the family album: Thomas Clay Washburn—a West Pointer and later, when war broke out, a major in the Louisiana Infantry. He had been wounded and captured at Shiloh but escaped into Canada from the Johnson Island Military Prison off Sandusky in Lake Erie.

Thomas Clay Washburn and five other escaped Confederate officers had come down from a rebel headquarters in Toronto in mid-1864 to seize a federal steamer on Lake Erie, steer her to Johnson Island, and free the hundreds of other Confederates, all officers, still imprisoned there. Grant had convinced Lincoln to end the exchange of prisoners that had fed so many troops back into the Confederate armies, so now, more than ever, soldiers—and especially the officers to lead them—were needed if the South was to stop the North. The idea to free all the Confederate officers on Johnson Island was a mad scheme: The prison camp was too well guarded. The scheme failed when the crew aboard the steamer successfully fought off the attack by Washburn and his companions. Crippled by a bullet as he was about to leap overboard, Washburn was captured and brought to New York City for trial. Because he was out of uniform, he was tried as a spy—and convicted. Despite appeals to Washington from the Confederate government in Richmond and from Washburn's mother back in Louisiana, he was hanged just before the war ended.

Mitch's curiosity was whetted, but there seemed to be a lot of work ahead of him. It might take several weeks to get fully acquainted with all the material Tom Cantwell had already compiled. Who knew what else remained to be done? He was looking at what might be a good six months of work, probably more if the writing did not go well. Because he had never worked on a book before, he wondered if he had accounted for the problems that might arise. Was he underestimating the time it might take? Maybe, Mitch thought to himself, I could get the research side wound up this summer. I could work on it while Val is in California. That would be ideal. Tom had himself a good story here—full of drama and action, set against the backdrop of the Civil War.

Mitch broke into a smile.

"What are you smiling at?" Abigail asked.

"It's a great story, Abigail. It's full of action, has drama and meaning, and Washburn is a wonderful character. The whole thing tells a lot about the war and the people who fought it."

"Oh, Mitch, that's just the way Tom saw it, too," Abigail said.

Mitch looked at Abigail, her expression eager and expectant. It scared him. The last thing in the world he wanted was to raise false hopes in Abigail. He must not let his enthusiasm run away with him. He must not let his feelings for her and Tom trap him into doing something he really didn't want to do. Val was right, he was stubborn. He didn't like to be pressured. After all, it was hard enough contemplating doing a book, much less someone else's book. If he were going to take this kind of major step, maybe he owed it to himself to find his own story. He tried to calm Abigail without being cruel. "I'd like to keep open the option of my finishing it for Tom. Let's see what I run into down South."

"I understand, Mitch," she said. "But why were you smiling so? A private joke?"

"No, not private. I just cannot for the life of me imagine what got Val's intuition up. She thinks I might be walking into something dangerous. Hell, the Civil War's been over for over a hundred years. What the devil could be dangerous about that?"

THREE

Mitch glanced at the map on the seat beside him. Virgil should be coming up soon if he hadn't taken the wrong highway out of Shreveport, where his plane had landed that morning. The two-lane blacktop road wound through a forest and over gentle hills. This part of the state was so unlike the Louisiana everybody, including himself, usually pictured. No bayou here, or the feeling of being on the border of a tropical zone. The highest point in the state was near here, snow was not unusual in the winter, and the climate was free of most of the pestilent diseases that had once ravaged New Orleans.

Last summer, driving up to Vermont to take on the editorship of a small town paper for a sick friend, he remembered the rolling green hills and how they gave him a sense of welcome and contentment. Here, the forests of pine were just as green, but Mitch felt wary rather than welcome. He recalled the time— was it 30 years ago?—when he was a high school senior and had traveled by train to look at Baron College in North Carolina. The civil rights movement was in its infancy. There were still prominent signs—"Whites Only" and "Colored"—for restrooms in the train station. He got on a local bus to go to the school and, as he ordinarily did in New York, sat down in the back of the bus—until the driver told him he couldn't sit there, that was for Negroes. Everywhere he went, the demarcation between whites and blacks was evident, except perhaps in the streets. But even when there were no signs, blacks seemed to make a point of getting out of the way of white pedestrians. There was an invisible wall separating the two— a wall covered with common courtesies and pleasantries, with bows of the head and smiles, with a wall of obsequities: "Yes, suh," "No, suh," "Yes'm," "No, ma'am." The entire experience had left a bitter taste in his mouth. He hadn't bothered to apply for Baron.

Rounding a gentle curve, Mitch spotted a roadhouse less than a quarter of a mile ahead on the right, just across from a small, steepled white church. He looked at the car's digital clock: 12:33. No sense putting off lunch, especially if he was on the wrong road.

There were four cars pulled up alongside Chick's, one of them a state police cruiser. The roadhouse was a nondescript, one-story building with neon signs in its windows advertising three different brands of beer—Budweiser, Coors and a regional brew called Bronco. As Mitch pulled in, a red-faced, burly worker in coveralls and a checkered shirt came out of the swinging screen door and got into a pickup truck that was loaded with boards of pine. He gunned the motor into life, tipped his finger to his hat to Mitch and began to back up and turn onto the highway. The truck roared off as Mitch entered the restaurant.

The first thing he noticed was how dark it was inside. No lights were on, and little sunlight came through the windows. The second thing he saw was the large Confederate battle flag tacked on the far wall. Next to it was a newspaper photograph of a smiling young man; it took Mitch a second's thought to recognize him as David Duke. The third thing he noticed was the couple seated at a bare Formica table by a window off to the left: a black man and a white woman. To be more precise, a black policeman and a white policewoman. They had just been served coffee. One was pouring cream into a cup, the other was spooning sugar.

"Anywhere you want." A thin man behind the bar at the far wall waved his arm toward the tables. Two other tables were occupied; three men at one, two at another, were all busy talking and laughing softly. Mitch opted for a table near the police officers. He pulled the cane-covered chair out and sat down. There was a menu tucked between a sugar jar and the salt and pepper shakers. Mitch reached for it and began studying it, deciding even as his eye ran down the page that he probably would be safer with a grilled cheese sandwich than anything in the meat line. And maybe a beer—no, make that coffee. He needed to stay alert. He gave his order to the lanky man, who had ambled over from behind the bar.

Mitch turned his attention to the police officers. Their tan uniforms looked freshly ironed. They had taken off their campaign hats and put them on the seats of the empty chairs at their table. Mitch was pleased to see the match-up—a black and a white, a man and a woman. I've got to get over the stereotypes, he thought to himself. It was easy to live in the past, to let his experience with Baron College blind him to change. He realized that he had expected, assumed, that any policeman he might bump into down South would be a gruff, barrel-chested, big-faced redneck, of the ilk that had used cattle prods, dogs and firehoses to fight civil rights activists in the 60s. He wondered if the change was cosmetic as he got up and walked over to the officers' table.

"I'm sorry to interrupt," he said, looking down at the two, "but I wonder if I'm on the right road to Virgil."

The black officer looked up, a big grin lighting up his face. "You're from New York, ain'tcha?" He thrust out his hand. "I don't get to hear that accent much down here. I'm from up North, too. Clarence Brown." As Mitch shook his hand, Brown continued, "And this is Doreen Gibson, my sidekick."

"You-all are on the right road," Gibson said, extending her hand to Mitch. "You-all got maybe a half-hour more to go—if you don't break the speed limit."

"The road twists too much to do that," said Mitch, grinning.

"Whatcha doin' here?" Brown asked.

"A friend of mine died in Virgil," Mitch said. "I'm arranging to bring home his body."

"I haven't been back in five years now," Brown said. "I'm from Newark."

"Do you like it here?" Mitch asked, wondering if he would get a straight answer.

Brown picked up his meaning. "Newark was no paradise, mister," he said. "I'm no token, if that's what you're getting at. There's been a lot of change down here. Anyway, it's cheaper by far to live here, and I'm close by all my relatives who got left behind."

"They call us the odd couple," Gibson said.

"You wouldn't be so out of place in New York," Mitch said, "but I suppose there are still surprises around here."

"I wish you'd tell my brother Elroy that," Brown said. "I'm trying to get him to join me and my family, but he thinks I live in Ku Klux Klanville."

Mitch gestured with his head toward the Confederate flag on the wall. "He might not believe you if he saw that."

"Well, you can't get away from some things completely—any-where," Brown said. "I won't defend that flag or the people who like to fly it, or Mister Duke. And I'd be the first to admit that a lot of feelings have gotten submerged. But at least some folks are making the effort. We did defeat Duke—give us that. And," Brown added, grinning broadly again, "I'm helping them."

There was the clink of silverware and dishes behind Mitch. Looking over to his own table, he saw the waiter putting down his lunch. "There's my meal," he said, turning back to the two police officers. "Nice to meet you."

Mitch was halfway through the grilled cheese sandwich—the greasy grilled cheese sandwich—when Brown and Gibson left, waving at him as they headed out the door. Mitch put down the sandwich, took several sips of his coffee and stood up, hoping to get the attention of the waiter and pay his bill. The man must have been in the kitchen. Mitch waited a minute, got his wallet out and put three dollars on the table—that should do it, he thought—and left.

Mitch drove off, and a few minutes later spotted a well-worn metal marker announcing that he was now entering Bulloch Parish. Parish, Mitch reminded himself, instead of county, a holdover from the days of the first Spanish and French settlements. Coming out of the forest and into a stretch of open countryside, Mitch could feel the sudden warmth of the sun against his face. He leaned over and flicked the air conditioning switch to high. The change in temperature was barely noticeable. Damn rental, Mitch thought. Just don't break down on me out here.

Another sign was coming up now, a brighter, bigger one that announced:

VIRGIL, LA.
Home of the Virgil Rebs
Pop. 10,342 Christian Souls
WELCOME

And beyond that, a billboard:

Virgil First Baptist Church
"Come ye to me"
Sundays at 9
All Welcome

Not far beyond the billboard was yet another sign, a smaller, circular one for the Rotary Club, which, it said, met every Tuesday at noon at the Reb Bar & Grille. Homes now began to appear, scattered on both sides of the highway, some set back on broad lawns. Traffic signs warned of reduced speed limits. Turning a bend in the road, Mitch saw ahead what a New Englander would call a village green. A statue of a Confederate soldier holding a musket stood overlooking a square surrounded by one- and two-story stores. Behind it was the town's biggest building, the Parish Courthouse, an imposing amalgam of Greek, Roman and Victorian styles. A bronze plaque beside the front entrance announced that the sheriff's office was inside, too.

Mitch pulled into an angled parking space in front of the statue. He hefted his attaché case from the rear seat and opened the car door. Do you lock your car in a town like this? he wondered. He looked around. The windows of other cars were open, so obviously Virgil was not a hotbed of crime. Mitch studied the meter perched on the sidewalk and slipped a dime into it—good for two hours. There was a certain innocence that seemed to pervade the town, something Mitch had experienced once before when doing a story on the Amish in Pennsylvania. But that, he realized, could be merely appearance.

The sheriff's office, according to the little arrow that Mitch could barely see on the plaque, was around in the back of the Parish Courthouse. A little paved sidewalk led to it. As Mitch made his way around the building he became aware of how still everything was. People were walking across the square, going into stores or standing and talking. Cars moved slowly down the street. Birds flew overhead. But the noise was slight, as though it had been muffled. It struck an eerie note. I wonder if I could get used to so much quiet, Mitch said aloud. Startled at the sound of his own voice, Mitch looked around quickly to see if anyone had heard him, but no one seemed to notice.

Mitch walked up to the long counter that blocked the approach to the partitioned cubicles and offices inside the sheriff's office. A middle-aged woman with a beehive hairdo stood up from a desk behind the counter. "Good morning," she said in a heavy drawl. "Can I help you?"

Mitch explained his reason for being in Virgil. "Oh, yes, Sheriff Bochard is expecting you," she said. "You just go right on ahead to his office." She pointed to the only room that was closed off from the rest of the offices. "Just knock and go in."

The sheriff rose as Mitch entered. He was younger than Mitch had expected, in his mid- or late 30s. Tall, stocky. Would be considered handsome if his face hadn't been pockmarked. "Mr. Stevens?"

"Sheriff Bochard," said Mitch shaking the proffered hand. "How'd you know it was me?"

"Sit down, please, sir," Willard Bochard said, waving Mitch into a seat and sitting back in his own chair. His drawl was softer than the receptionist's. "I'm not a whiz of a policeman, Mr. Stevens, but I know a strange face in this town when I see one."

Mitch laughed. "You got me on that one."

"This Cantwell fella," the sheriff continued. "You told me that you're not related, right?" Mitch nodded. "But you know him well enough to identify him?" Mitch nodded again. "All right, then let's not waste your time."

The sheriff rose again and reached for a five-gallon hat that hung from a coat tree. "We'll have to go over to Studley's Funeral Parlor. It's just down the block."

"I've already arranged to have Mr. Cantwell's body flown back to New York from Shreveport," Mitch said as he and the sheriff started to leave.

"Well, this won't take long, and you can be on your way again," the sheriff said. "I'm sorry you had to come all this way for a routine matter, but we try to follow the rules."

"That's understandable, Sheriff."

"Mind walking?"

"Not at all. I'd like to. You look like you've got yourself a nice town here."

"Yup, it's nice," the sheriff said, tipping his hat at two elderly women who walked by them. "Quiet when the loggers are off working in the forest. But watch out come Saturday night when they're in town."

"I might just," Mitch said.

"You staying?" The sheriff stopped. "You only need to look at the man. All the paperwork is done. There's no reason for your having to tarry longer."

"I realize that, Sheriff. It's my choice. Mr. Cantwell was working on a book project and I thought I'd catch up on what he was doing and see if I couldn't finish it for him."

Bochard studied Mitch's face for a moment. "Well," he said finally, "I'm here to help if you want. How long are you considering staying?"

"I'm not sure," said Mitch, wondering if the sheriff's interest was more than routine. "A couple of days just to get my feet wet. I'd like to get to know the area, meet some people who are up on local history, ask them a couple of questions."

The two men were walking again down the street and starting to cross over to the other side. Bochard didn't bother to look whether any cars were coming their way. Mitch noticed that several motorists stopped to let them by without the sheriff raising a hand. Talk about running a tight ship!

"Got a place to stay?"

"The car rental people told me that there was a motel in town, but I don't remember passing it on the way in."

"No, you wouldn't have if you came in from Shreveport," the sheriff said. "It's on the other side."

"Well, I guess I'll stay there," Mitch said. "If they've got room for me."

"They'll have room all right this time of year." The sheriff pointed up the street to a gingerbread house surrounded by a white picket fence. "That's Studley's. I'll tell you what," he continued. "I'll let the mayor know you're in town. His family's been roundabout for practically the whole time the town has existed. Heck, the parish is named after them—Bulloch. He'll be up on history things."

"Thanks, Sheriff, I'd appreciate that," Mitch said as they opened the gate to the funeral home and walked up the path to the front steps.

The sheriff stopped abruptly on the porch. "You know what killed him? Mr. Cantwell, I mean."

"I was told that he died of natural causes, whatever that means," Mitch said.

"Surprise you?"

"I can't answer that, Sheriff. His wife didn't seem surprised. She said he wasn't in good health but he refused to admit it. He had diabetes, heart trouble, you name it. She thinks he probably overdid it and his heart just gave out."

"It surprised me," Bochard said. "I met him. He'd been here, oh, I guess it was a good week or so. He looked healthy to me."

"Well, you never can tell, can you?" said Mitch, wondering again what the sheriff was driving at. "Wasn't there an autopsy to confirm the cause of death?"

"No, we don't do autopsies unless there's something suspicious. The doctor—Doc J. J., J. J. Dexter—signed the death certificate saying it was 'natural causes.' That's about all that was needed."

"Sheriff," Mitch insisted, "you're trying to tell me something and I don't understand what it is. Can you be clearer?"

Before Bochard could answer, the front door of the funeral home opened and a man in his mid-50s, dressed in a dark suit, came out. "I thought I heard folks talking out here. Hello, Sheriff," he said, nodding to Bochard and then turning to Mitch. "Are you Mr. Stevens, sir? I'm Wallace Studley. Come on in."

Bochard started to follow Mitch into the funeral home when a patrol car squealed to a stop at the curb. "Sheriff, Sheriff," a patrolman called, trying to catch Bochard's attention. The sheriff looked back. The patrolman was waving frantically at him. Bochard ran down the steps and ducked his head down at the window. The patrolman spoke excitedly, but out of earshot. "Go," the sheriff said to him, slapping the side of the door and standing back as the car squealed again in a tight U-turn and raced off with its siren screeching.

Bochard came back up the steps. "I have to go. There's a fire out by the cutoff. It's serious—a home."

"Of course," said Mitch.

"Wallace here will take care of you. Let me know if you need any other help." The sheriff tipped a finger to his hat and headed back to the curb as a second patrol car arrived to pick him up. It made a U-turn, too, and sped off. Halfway down the block its siren came on.

"And I was just thinking to myself how peaceful this town was," Mitch said to Studley.

"You wouldn't know it to hear the sirens at night. The fire engine or the police fly by here at all hours. Peaceful?" Studley smiled ruefully. "It'd wake up the dead."

Moments later, Mitch stood looking down at the white, cold corpse of Tom Cantwell. At first, he wasn't sure it was Tom; his face was waxen, the lips clenched together. Mitch's mouth went dry. He stifled an urge to reach out and touch Tom's hand. Whatever possessed him to want to do that? he wondered. Then he noticed them, the track marks.

"What are those?" Mitch asked Studley, pointing to the thighs.

Studley, who had been standing quietly behind Mitch, stepped forward. "Needle marks, sir."

"Needle marks?"

"We found vials of insulin among his effects," Studley explained. "We've already given them to the sheriff to send back to the deceased's home."

"Oh, I see," Mitch said, relieved.

"If you're through," said Studley, reaching for the sheet to cover the body. "We'll dress the body before sending it north."

Mitch turned away. He hadn't wanted to remember Tom this way. Thank God Abigail wasn't here.

Studley escorted Mitch to an office in the rear of the house. It was decorated in soft, muted colors. A vase of fragrant magnolias, the official state flower, sat on a low table under the window.

Studley asked Mitch to sign several forms that he took from

a tray on his desk, explaining as he did so what each meant.

"Will you be accompanying the body?" the undertaker asked.

"I'll see the coffin on the plane tomorrow," Mitch replied, not bothering to look up as he signed the last of the papers. "I've arranged for it to be picked up at Newark Airport."

"We'll leave for the airport at nine," Studley said, taking back his pen and putting it carefully in a holder on his desk. "By hearse, of course."

Mitch nodded. "I'll be here," he said, rising. He shook Studley's hand, expecting it to be weak, but it was firm and strong.

"Our condolences and sympathies to Mrs. Cantwell," the undertaker said. "Please convey them for us."

As he left the funeral home, Mitch decided to drive to the motel to get a room. He had an uneasy feeling about what the sheriff had said. He had always told his students to follow up anything they sensed amiss. He realized he had been on edge since the plane landed. After all, his experience with the police couple aside, he was in the heart of David Duke country.

THE MAYOR'S PHONE call had surprised him. Mitch had no sooner checked into the Caddo Motel than Everett Bulloch buzzed him. Bulloch had graciously invited him to dinner that night at his home. "It isn't often that we get another chance to have a distinguished journalist out our way," he told Mitch. "You'd oblige us with your company. My wife won't speak to me if you say no." Mitch said he would be honored to attend.

The mayor's home bespoke history. It was a large, rambling house, modeled after the plantation homes that had graced the southern part of the state. A covered veranda ran around the entire first floor. It was deep enough to create shade on the sunniest of summer days. Inside, heavy maple and oak furniture, the patina shiny with age, filled each room. The walls were covered with paintings and portraits and so many photographs, many of them browning, that the home seemed more like a museum than a residence.

Bulloch took Mitch through each room, pointing out ancestors, souvenirs, and trophies, until Mitch's eyes started to blur like they always did after an hour in a museum. "Look at this here row," the mayor said, indicating a series of photographs of men in uniform. "We Bullochs have served in every war since Secesh days. Recognize me?" He pointed to the photo of a thin, clean-shaven, crew-cut young Marine in fatigues leaning on an armored carrier. "I served in 'Nam." Mitch looked from the photo to Bulloch and back again. The mayor was now an anachronism, a robust man who kept his hair cut short and pomaded in a fashion that had been popular during the 1940s. His brown suit was obviously expensive, as was his patterned silk tie and white percale shirt with cuffs, but they were a tad short of fitting perfectly and made Bulloch look—Mitch snobbishly thought—like a country hick politician.

"Over on this wall," said Bulloch, crossing the room, "is Flora May's side, though just about everything got lost in Hurricane Audrey in '57. That's her father, though—Orko Parker—and his wife Mary Lou. Flora May looks just her mother—you'll see." Mitch peered close to the photograph. It had been taken on a warm spring day. Trees in the background were just starting to sprout leaves, and the Parkers were dressed in light, short-sleeved clothing.

"Here, try it yourself," the mayor said, offering Mitch a scabbard sword with a silk cord dangling from its hilt. It was heavier than Mitch imagined. "Be careful," Bulloch added as Mitch tried to draw the weapon.

Bulloch's wife appeared at that point to offer drinks. She set down on a mahogany sideboard a silver tray containing crackers covered with anchovy paste. She was, Mitch thought to himself, what Val would call formidable. Certainly not the frail Southern belle of romantic literature. Instead, she was a sturdy, brown-eyed woman with broad hips who, though not especially tall, made it seem as though she had to look down her nose to see you. It was the tilt of her head that created that illusion, Mitch reasoned. She wasn't given to an easy smile; in fact, Mitch mused, she looked downright mean. Or am I being unfair? he asked himself. I don't even know the woman.

As they sat down for dinner—the mayor at one end of a rather long, mahogany table, his wife at the other, and Mitch seated in the middle on one side—Mitch started to reach for his water glass when Bulloch began, "Lord, we thank you with all our heart for your blessings. We thank you for the bread on the table, for the . . ." Embarrassed, Mitch withdrew his hand and lowered his head. "Give us, Lord, your continuing kindness and . . ." Suddenly, an image of childhood came back to Mitch: seated at table, his own father, a fervid Catholic, intoning a prayer, the words sounding so hypocritical to Mitch coming from a man who was otherwise cold and distant, not the least bit charitable. . . . Maybe that was what had driven Mitch from the Church—the huge gulf between the spoken word and the deed. "We thank you, Lord, and we ask your continual blessings." Bulloch looked up and smiled benignly at Mitch. "Amen." His wife echoed, "Amen."

The dinner was abundant if nothing else. Mitch sat back afterwards as Juju, the Bullochs' stout black maid, cleared away the dishes. Four kinds of vegetables, fresh and preserved, turkey with stuffing, candied yams, hot muffins, and then pecan pie for dessert. Val would have been aghast at the calories he'd ingested.

The mayor was effusive. "Call me Rhett," he said right off. "Short for Everett. That's what everybody else calls me. No standing on formalities here."

His wife, Flora May, hardly said two words during the meal. She sat looking back and forth between her husband and Mitch, brooding almost, Mitch thought. Not outwardly impolite, but not friendly either. Mitch wanted to engage her in conversation, but the mayor talked incessantly—and his wife had seemed so unapproachable.

"I've never experienced Southern hospitality," said Mitch, turning down Bulloch's offer of a cigar. "You people really believe in it, don't you?"

"Yes we do, sir, yes we do. And we mean it, too, Lord knows. That welcome sign you saw outside of town is not just say-so. You got one up in New York but you don't mean it. That city scares me and Lord knows I don't ever intend to visit it ever again."

"I know a lot of people who feel that way—unfortunately. It really isn't that bad, Mayor."

"Rhett, please."

The conversation continued on in this fashion, Bulloch poking fun at New York and Mitch defending it to the point where he finally felt that both he and Bulloch had said everything trite that could be said.

It was Bulloch, however, who changed the conversation. "I'd like to take you around the area tomorrow, Mitch. Show you the parish. Get you up to where the Washburn place used to be if you want to go."

Mitch thanked him. "I've got to go to Shreveport in the morning, and then I was kind of hoping that I could meet James Deal, the parish clerk," he answered. "I was told that he's the keeper of all your records."

"Why? Was there something wrong with the way Cantwell's death certificate was filed?" the mayor asked.

"No, not at all," Mitch said. "It's just that I'm thinking of taking over Tom's—Cantwell's—book and I wanted to check out a few things."

Bulloch looked momentarily chagrined. "Yes, of course. You'll want to see Jimmy. Yes, that's a good idea. Of course." He took a deep puff on his cigar. "Why don't you go right on ahead and see him, and then come by my office after that and I'll give you the grand tour."

"Is Manton very far away?" Mitch asked.

"Manton? What's that got to do with what you're looking for?"

Mitch explained about the blind old lady that Tom Cantwell was supposed to have interviewed.

"You-all going to trust the memory of someone that old?" Obviously, Bulloch wouldn't.

"I'd like to see her and judge for myself," Mitch said. "It sure would make a terrific addition to the book."

Flora May Bulloch was looking hard at her husband. They locked eyes for a moment, then she said, "If you-all will excuse me, Mr. Stevens—Mitch. You gentlemen stay and enjoy yourselves. I have to attend to the kitchen. Juju always needs supervision."

The mayor waited to speak until his wife had left. "She's all tuckered out lately. You'll have to excuse her. It's not like Flora May. She's usually the life of the party—has more energy than a yoke of oxen."

"Is Juju a name down here?" Mitch asked.

"Hell, no. Juju's name is Jezebel, but we've always called her Juju. All the niggers I know have nicknames like that."

Mitch flinched. He wasn't used to hearing blacks called "niggers." Although he didn't say anything, the mayor sensed his displeasure.

"You know somethin' about colored people I don't know, Mitch?"

Mitch didn't want to get into an argument with the man, so he kept silent.

"We don't mamby-pamby down here," the mayor continued. "We call a spade a spade." It was a terrible pun, but Bulloch didn't seem to mind. "I can think to the time all kinds of wimps from up North came down here and stirred things around. What did they call it? Voting rights? Hell, the colored can hardly speak English let alone sign their own names. Letting them vote is like putting a gun in an infant's hand. Did you see what happened when Duke ran for governor? The man would have gotten us out of a financial rut, but, no, your lousy northern press decided he wasn't good enough for us. And the darkies ate it up."

Bulloch drew on the cigar and blew a smoke ring toward the

chandelier overhead. It broke apart into wispy white threads as it touched the hanging beads of glass.

"Let me tell you a story, Mitch. Something that could have happened yesterday it's so common around here." The mayor leaned back. "This nigger—pardon me, colored man—we had doing our gardening around here was curious. I don't mean *curious* curious. I mean peculiar curious. He talked to himself, sang to himself, but all the time minded his own business. Well, one day a salesman came down the road from Shreveport and stopped by his door and sold the nigger—Claudell was his name, but we called him Claw because he had two twisted fingers from getting caught in a mower belt—anyways, this here salesman sold Claw a whole set of Encyclopedia Britannicas. Can you imagine?" Bulloch laughed aloud and put the cigar to his lips. "And do you know what Claw said afterward, you know, when people pointed out to him that he had never gotten beyond the fourth grade and wasn't even up to reading the local weekly? You know what Claw said?

"This'll kill ya," the mayor continued, blowing another smoke ring. He leaned forward conspiratorially. "'Mr. Bulloch,' he says to me, 'Mr. Bulloch, the man promised that if I bought all those books I'd be wise and full of knowing everything about everything. He didn't say anything about having to read them.'"

The mayor, Mitch knew, had told that story a hundred times but there he was, laughing away again at Claw's pathetic ignorance.

"Claw's still paying it off," Bulloch said. "Can you imagine? And they're all like that. No common sense. Little children."

Mitch fidgeted in the cushioned dining chair, increasingly ill at ease. He could feel the heat rise to his face, the result of control fighting rage. He pushed his eyeglasses up on his nose. Reporters were trained not to get involved no matter whom they were interviewing or what they were witnessing; they were observers, not participants. You kept what opinions you had to yourself. Mitch had spent a lifetime on the sidelines, a neutral. He had dealt with neo-Nazis, religious fanatics and political charlatans without ever losing his self-control. But he felt such anger now at Bulloch's blatant racism that he was finding it difficult to stifle an outburst. To calm himself down, he reasoned that an argument would lead nowhere. It certainly wouldn't change this man's ingrained attitudes. And he was a guest in this man's house. The wisest thing to do would be to leave.

"I'd better be going," said Mitch, rising. "It's been a long day for me. I was up at five this morning to catch the flight down here. Would you please thank Mrs. Bulloch for her hospitality. I hope to get a chance to meet her again."

Bulloch escorted Mitch down the hallway to the front door, talking to him as if they were old friends, his arm hanging over Mitch's shoulder. It took an enormous effort on Mitch's part not to pull away. "I do hope you'll grace our portals again before you leave, Mitch. I'm sure Flora May would like to hear all the details about what you've learned. She's a regular bedbug when it comes to local goings-on and the like."

"I meant to ask," said Mitch, pausing beside the open door. "Did Tom Cantwell talk at all about what he was doing?"

"Not a word, really," the mayor answered. "A fine man, a gentleman. He said he was a diabetic."

"I'm surprised he told you," said Mitch.

"Well, what I mean is we didn't know when we asked him to join us for dinner," Bulloch said. "We asked him as soon as we heard he was in town—just like with you. I guess he felt he had to tell us. He said he had to watch his diet. So Flora May went easy on the sweet things." Bulloch rubbed his chin. "He was very close-mouthed about what he was doing. He said he was like most writers and didn't like to discuss things he hadn't put on paper yet. I'm not sure I understand that reasoning."

Mitch thought about Bulloch's remarks as he drove down the driveway of the mayor's home. In a small town like Virgil, gossip was the number one sport. He knew Tom would have wanted to keep a low profile and not be the topic of everybody's conversation if he could avoid it.

FOUR

ITS HEADLIGHTS ON, the hearse drove a moderate 45 miles an hour in the right-hand lane along Interstate 20 to Shreveport. Mitch followed two car lengths behind, his eyes trained on the back of the black vehicle, his mind racing through memories of Tom Cantwell and the time he had spent with the *Brunswick Guardian*. The hearse had triggered the first memory, reminding Mitch of the time Cantwell had gone to bat with the publisher over Mitch's exposé of the outrageous overcharges made by local morticians, who took advantage of a dead person's grieving family to reap huge windfalls. Tom had lost that battle; the story was squelched by the publisher, who didn't want to jeopardize the classified ad dollars brought in by death notices in the paper.

The hearse was turning now into a side road just before the main entrance to the Shreveport Airport. Mitch did, too, seeing the cargo sign that the hearse had momentarily blocked as it turned. He continued to follow it through a gate near a hangar, where a shiny twin-engine jet was sitting. A truck was feeding high octane fuel into the plane's wing through a black hose. A cargo attendant scampered up the ramp leading to the rear loading area in the tail as a small tractorlike vehicle pulled away, towing two empty luggage carts toward a bay in the rear of the terminal.

Mitch pulled up behind the hearse and got out. Wallace Studley and an assistant, both dressed in black, were already walking around the hearse to its back door. Studley opened it, and they both reached in to pull out the simple cherrywood coffin. It was resting on a gurney that unfolded as it came out of the hearse, its wheels touching the tarmac. They rolled it to a portable loading belt that was angled up into the forward cargo hold of the plane.

Mitch watched as the coffin was placed on the belt and slowly swallowed into the belly of the plane.

Studley started to walk toward him, but Mitch pretended he didn't see him. He got into his car, and, without looking back at the hearse or the plane, turned and sped off. He had decided not to wait until the plane took off. He didn't want to talk to anyone. He just wanted to be alone.

JIMMY DEAL HAD his back to the door when Mitch entered the parish clerk's office several hours later. Though he was coatless, Deal was wearing a pin-striped white shirt and a subdued, featureless tie. He was a gaunt man who looked to be in his 60s, but was actually much younger. He had an open, welcoming face, framed by a surprising amount of still-brown hair. His hazel eyes looked alert, despite the heavy lenses of his glasses.

He turned on hearing the door click shut, and Mitch introduced himself, at the same time explaining that he was trying to retrace Tom Cantwell's research steps.

"A gentleman, Mr. Cantwell," Deal said. "He spent an entire day with me going over old Police Jury minutes and land transactions."

"Police Jury?"

"That's what our local governing body is called, Mr. Stevens."

"Call me Mitch, please."

"That's what you might say is our local legislature. We have records going back to the 1840s, which is kinda lucky considering the fact that the first courthouse burned down about a hundred years ago."

"Do you remember anything at all about what he found that might make it easier for me to retrace his steps?"

"Not specifically," Deal answered, pursing his lips in thought. "He was after knowing all there was to know about the Washburns, and everything he found he photocopied on our machine. I'd have done it for him, but I got involved in a hassle about a tax assessment, so I never got a good look at the precise pages he was copying. Must have been a lot, though, 'cause he left me 10 dollars to pay for all the paper he used."

Mitch debated with himself whether he should take the time to study some of the old ledgers. "Maybe I could take a look at one of the books, if you don't mind, just to see how much there might be involved."

"You bet." Deal went into an adjoining room. Mitch could hear him opening a creaky metal door. The parish clerk came back lugging a large, dusty ledger. Written in a white block on its cover was "Minutes of Meetings of Police Jury, Volume A, 1856–1860."

"Mr. Cantwell sneezed every time I brought him out one of these oldies." Which is what Mitch did as Deal placed the ledger on an empty typing table in front of him. "Here, take a seat and make yourself at home. Just holler if you need help."

"Thanks." Mitch sat and turned back the heavy cover of the record book. The entries were in hand, of course. They included records of every deed and land transfer in the parish. The ink had faded to a pale brown, but whoever had kept the log had done so in a neat, legible hand. "This is easy to follow," Mitch commented.

"Huh?" said Deal, looking up from an almost identical ledger he was writing in.

"The handwriting is so clear," Mitch explained. "I saw some of the photostats of the census records that Cantwell found in the National Archives, and they looked like they had been written by semi-literates. Sometimes Washburn was spelled Wishborn, sometimes Washben, even Wishbone. It was a mess."

Deal smiled. "My great-great-grandfather kept that book you got there. We've been parish clerks from the beginning. It's gotten into our genes."

Mitch went back to studying the entries, turning over page after page. When he was finished, Deal brought him the next volume, then another. By then, Mitch was just flipping the pages, stopping only if he spotted the Washburn name. It was tedious work but oddly enough, he was enjoying it. On the drive back from Shreveport, Mitch had agonized about Tom, picturing him in a strange town, dying so suddenly, alone, not even being able to say good-bye to Abigail. Mitch had spent a sleepless night, feeling torn by guilt and what his uncompromising father would have called duty. But this morning, in this room, going through the material that Tom had touched, he felt strangely comforted.

Mitch finally sat back and rubbed his eyes. The old wall clock on the far wall read 10:45. Mitch had been studying the ledgers for nearly two hours. "It's too much to try to do in one sitting, Mr. Deal. I'll have to come back."

"Suit yourself," Deal answered.

"Cantwell was supposed to have sent everything he copied to his home, but his wife didn't receive anything like this material."

Deal looked at him quizzically. "Don't know what to tell you about that."

"Is there a Federal Express office in town, or anything like that at all?"

"No. You'd have to go to Shreveport for that kind of thing."

"So what do you folks do to send things?"

"Why the post office, of course," said Deal, looking a bit stunned. "Right down Main Street. It suits fine."

"So Cantwell would have used it?" Mitch said, but didn't expect Deal to answer. "Maybe I should drop by there and ask about it. Who should I ask for?"

"Try Mr. Bulloch."

"The mayor?"

"No," Deal said. "The mayor's cousin—Billy Bob Bulloch. The mayor used to be the postmaster, but that was before he got into timbering and then got himself elected mayor. He's got some government service in his blood, too. Leastways, we all expect him to run for state office in the next election."

"Really?" Mitch wondered whether the mayor's views on blacks were widely shared. "I take it he has a lot of local support if he got elected mayor."

Deal studied Mitch. "Yes and no. He gets plenty of votes from the people associated with the logging, and we got a lot of others who spout off like him about other things, but we've also got a lot of folks who don't cotton to him."

Mitch took it that Deal didn't. "Want to amplify on that statement, Mr. Deal?" he asked.

"Rhett Bulloch doesn't scare me one damn," said Deal, putting down his pen and walking over to a map on the far wall. "See this here?" he said, pointing to what looked like the entire northern section of the map, which was tinted red. "That is all forest now. Once weren't. Used to be farms there. Forest took over, and the government then came along and helped seed it, too. Bulloch controls the rights. That's made him wealthy, and now he has it in his head to make a name for himself all over the state."

"He's quite a man, your mayor, I gather."

"Well, the Bullochs have been roundabout for a long time now," the parish clerk said. "They're an ambitious lot, by and large."

"Tell me about them, Mr. Deal. I'd appreciate having some feel for the community. Have Bullochs always been mayors?"

Deal thought a moment. "One was a governor once, back in the 1880s, and Everett's father was a state senator for a time.

But mayor? Oh, I guess one was—near time of the war." He pronounced it "Wahr."

"The war? World War II?"

"The War Between the States. That's what we mean when we say 'war' down here. He resigned, though, to join the state militia. He'd come back from the war but the political situation, you might say, had changed. People here were in the worst way."

Deal paused. Mitch waited for him to continue. When he didn't, he said, "Go on, Mr. Deal, I'd like to know all there is to know about Virgil. It would help immensely. You've got yourself an eager audience."

Deal grinned. "You know something? You're just like that Cantwell fellow." And he proceeded to tell how once the territory had been opened by the French, Scotch-Irish settlers had poured into the area. They had migrated from the north, following the foothills of the Appalachians around the curve into Alabama and Mississippi, and eventually into Louisiana. Many families kept on going, heading into what became Texas. Those who stayed in Northwest Louisiana chased the Caddo Indians into Arkansas and beyond, then set about clearing the land and growing cotton.

As Deal continued, Mitch would interrupt every so often with a question, until finally the parish clerk said, "Hold on, I've got work to do. Look here. I've got some booklets our historical association put out. Let me see what I can find."

Deal went into the adjoining room. When he returned he had two magazines as well as several other items in his hand. "Here," he said, proffering them. "I gave some to Mr. Cantwell, too."

The magazines contained articles by several local residents: "Old Virgil, as My Parents Remembered It," "Songs Our Darkies Sang," "Thanksgiving Day in 1934," "The Historic Landmarks of Bulloch Parish." The last was by Flora May Bulloch.

"The mayor's wife," Mitch noted, pointing at the byline.

Deal sniffed. "She's worse than he is. I can't abide that woman."

He stopped abruptly, having said more than he wanted to say. "I'm getting out of turn. Sorry."

Mitch was interested but could see that it wouldn't do any good to try to press the parish clerk further. Deal had decided to keep his opinions to himself for the time being.

Mitch turned his attention to the other items Deal had handed him. The first was a short note, the size of a bank deposit slip. It was dated October 10, 1865 and bore the signature of one John Burchwell. "That's an amnesty oath," Deal explained. "You had to sign one after the war or you couldn't vote or hold office. I have barrels full of them."

Underneath it was a Confederate dollar. "Worthless, of course," said Deal. "I have lots of them, too, wouldn't you know."

The next paper was a lengthy legal document dated April 3, 1858. "That's a slave deed."

Mitch read the flowery script:

STATE OF LOUISIANA

PARISH OF BULLOCH

Be it remembered that on this day the Third day of April in the year of our Lord One Thousand Eight Hundred and Fifty Eight Before me Samuel Norris Recorder and official Notary Public duly Commissioned and Sworn in for the Parish of Bulloch & the State of Louisiana Personally Came and Appeared John A Arnal a resident of the Parish of Jackson and State aforesaid, who acknowledge and declare that he has this day for and in consideration of the sum of Six Hundred Dollars to be paid him in the manner herein after named and stipulated by John R Nugent a resident of the Parish of Bulloch and State of Lousiana.—bargained sold transferred and delivered a certain Negro woman Slave for Life named *Sarah* aged about thirty five years old of dark complexion which title the said John A Arnal warrants to be good and valid against all others. . . .

"They were property then," Deal explained. "And worth— most of them leastways—a lot of money. What you got in your hand is proof of sale."

Mitch stared fascinated at the document. He had never seen anything like it before.

"They're yours for the keeping," Deal said. "I figure you'll appreciate their meaning."

Mitch thanked Deal. "Maybe I can use these as illustrations in the book. They're terrific."

"Mr. Cantwell said he was going to frame his," Deal said. "It was a different world then, but things around here haven't changed as much as we like to think."

"Funny, I didn't notice anything like this in the material he sent home to New Jersey," Mitch said. He rose and shook the parish clerk's hand vigorously. "You've been very generous with your time and with these gifts."

"Don't you want to look at the birth and death records?" asked Deal.

"I don't think I have time now. I agreed to meet the mayor, and I want to stop by the post office first."

"Mr. Cantwell was very interested in them," Deal persisted.

"Well, I'll have to come back for them also. Which floor of the courthouse is the mayor's office on?"

"He isn't here, not most days leastwise," Deal said. "He's got himself a place down Main, in the old hotel. 'Course, it isn't a hotel anymore. It's been turned into offices and stores. Our movie house is in its old ballroom."

"Then it's near the post office?"

"Oh, yes, just a spit from it."

MITCH HEADED FOR the American flag hanging from an angled pole over the entrance to a small, single-story brick building near the end of Main Street. The post office, he figured, cor- rectly. There was a blue metal mailbox on the sidewalk outside. Inside was a long, waist-high shelf with mailing forms in slots on it and walls lined with posters, mostly in red, white and blue, advertising new stamp issues and philatelic publications. A black man was sweeping the floor behind the counter, where an unkempt, heavy-set man with a cigarette dangling from his mouth was tossing parcels wrapped in brown into canvas bins.

"Is the postmaster, Billy Bob Bulloch, in?" asked Mitch, feeling a little silly calling anyone by that name.

The man took the cigarette out of his mouth and dropped it on the floor, twisting his foot to kill it. "You're looking at him. What can I do for you-all?"

Mitch asked whether he remembered anyone mailing a package to Brunswick, New Jersey, in the past week or two.

"Get a lot of packages here," Billy Bob explained. "Brunswick, New Jersey? Hey, wait on now, the sheriff mailed off something or other there the other day. Lucas handled it, but he had trouble with the scale—that's how I know. Lucas is out on a break now."

"Do you remember anyone else mailing a package to Brunswick?" Mitch asked. He described Tom Cantwell.

Billy Bob shook his head, at the same time picking a cigarette out of a crumpled package. He stopped to light it. "Doesn't ring a bell," he said, tossing the match onto the floor. Behind him, Mitch noticed for the first time, there was a bold-lettered sign: NO SMOKING.

"Nothing you remember sent up that way at all? It probably would have been registered and maybe even insured."

"Sorry, mister." Billy Bob took a deep drag on the cigarette and exhaled a cloud of smoke at the low ceiling. "I don't recollect any such package. You-all got a registry number or an insurance number? We could trace it with a number."

"No, I don't. Can't you look up your records? It wasn't that long ago."

Billy Bob squinted as a thread of cigarette smoke wafted up

into his eyes. "You-all kidding, mister? This is a post office, not a lost-and-found. We don't have time for that kind of finicking around. Get a number and we'll be able to trace the package in the flash of an eye."

Maybe, Mitch thought, a receipt was with Tom's effects. He'd have to remember to ask Abigail about that. On the other hand, maybe Tom had sent the material another way. "Do people here use United Parcel at all?"

"Not likely to," the postmaster said. "You-all have to go to Manton, and the drop there is only open for an hour or so in the afternoon. It isn't worth the effort. Heck, we do a good enough job with the mail. We even got Express Mail now."

Mitch thanked him and headed for the door.

Billy Bob returned to sorting his parcels. The black porter started sweeping up the cigarette butts he had left behind.

THE MAYOR HAD tossed his cigar out the window before closing it again and turning on the air conditioning, though the weather was closer to mild than warm. He turned the wheel of the big car, adjusting the rearview mirror as he headed down Main Street. "Every time Flora May uses the car she messes up my mirror."

"This is a Chrysler, isn't it?" asked Mitch, who was seated alongside Bulloch.

"Le Baron."

"It's so unusual. I mean all I've seen are Chevy or Ford pickups and wagons. What do you do for servicing?"

"I have to haul over to Manton." The mayor waved as a school bus passed them going in the opposite direction. "I'll take you to the Washburn place first off." He waved again as they passed two men in their mid-40s walking together along the sidewalk. Each had a small dog on a leash. "That's our fag couple. We have them, too."

They were outside of town now, heading north. They sped

past a cluster of ranch houses with small, neat lawns; some were bordered by chain-link fences. A young black girl was watering a row of rosebushes that bordered one of the homes. "Our rising colored middle class," Bulloch said sarcastically. "See what we do for 'em. Give 'em jobs in civil service. They're up and coming!"

About a mile farther down the road, the mayor pointed to a row of broken-down hovels. Black women in tattered drab dresses and aprons stood outside, watching the car pass by, their faces bare of any expression. "Those are shotguns," Bulloch said, pointing to the houses. "One room behind another room behind another room, with a door in the middle of each room. You can open the front door and the one behind it and the back door and shoot a gun right through the house without hitting anything. That's how they got their name."

"They sure look like they could do with a coat of paint," Mitch said.

"Never been painted. My daddy used to tell me that colored people—hey, Mitch," he turned away from the road to look at Mitch, "did you notice I didn't say niggers?" He turned back to the road. "The houses just weather. Some of them were here before I was born."

The mayor pointed to the other side of the road. "See that one there, that's a dog trot. Two shotguns put together side by side with an aisle in the middle. The dogs run up and down the aisle.

"Them's voters we just passed back there," Bulloch went on. "You tell me that they know enough to decide what's right for this community, or this state, or this whole country."

Mitch refused again to be drawn into a debate. When he didn't say anything, the mayor dropped the issue.

The mayor turned off onto a dirt road. Suddenly the sun was gone, blocked out by tall pine trees. Bulloch switched off the air conditioning and opened his window. Mitch did the same. It was cool in the forest and smelled of resin. "This here section is all federal government property. They planted it."

Bulloch had stopped the car by what appeared to be an old graveyard. There were a number of overturned stones arranged in a little square, but the stones were so eroded that Mitch could not make out what they said. Small animals scampered through the thick underbrush. "Would you believe this was cotton country once?" the mayor said. "They grew lots of other things, too—food to feed themselves—but back before the war the money crop was cotton. The farmers had to cart it all the way to the Ouchita or the Red River to get it to market."

Mitch couldn't picture a farm, a plantation, anything man-made in this wilderness. "What do you suppose happened to the Washburn home?" he asked.

"Probably burned down," Bulloch said. "Everything seemed to eventually then. Fire was a real scourge around these parts until lately. I suppose you could come out here with a compass and reckoner and figure out where the house stood, but all you'd find, if you found anything, would probably just be the stones that the flooring stood on."

The mayor started the engine and began maneuvering to turn the car back toward the highway. "That satisfy your curiosity, Mitch?"

"Interesting," Mitch answered. "I wonder if it was like this when the first settlers came. They must have had to clear out a lot of land in order to plant anything."

The car picked up speed as they turned back onto the highway. "Planning to stay much longer?" Bulloch suddenly asked.

The abrupt change of subject surprised Mitch. "Maybe another day or two," he said, wondering at the same time what the mayor was fishing for. "If I decide to continue with Tom Cantwell's book I'll have to return to do this part of the research properly."

"What's keeping you then? Not that we're not happy to have you here."

"I did want to see that old lady in Manton before I left."

The mayor was silent for a moment. "You speak to her yet?"

"No, she doesn't know I'm coming. She doesn't have a phone, or anyway it isn't listed."

"Just going to barge in like?"

"Well, Rhett, she's an old lady. How far away from home is she going to go?"

"Yes, I guess you're right." There was an edge to Bulloch's voice. "Someone that old can't go far, can she? What do you know about her?"

"Only that she had always wanted to write the same book that Cantwell was working on. She was a school teacher all her life and didn't get around to thinking seriously about it until she retired. Unfortunately, she began to lose her sight, and then a hurricane swept through Manton and carried away most of her notes."

"I remember that hurricane," Bulloch said.

"Cantwell told his wife, though, that the old lady had a phenomenal memory."

"When are you planning to see her?"

"First thing tomorrow morning."

The mayor seemed wrapped up in his own thoughts as they drove into Main Street. They shook hands and exchanged goodbyes after Bulloch pulled up beside Mitch's car on a side street just off Main. Mitch started to get into his own car when he noticed for the first time the lettering on a window across the street: THE VIRGIL WHIG. On an impulse he slammed shut the car door and walked across the street to the shop. He didn't recall seeing a local newspaper in the reception area of the Caddo Motel, only the Shreveport daily. Then it struck him: Of course, a town this size can only support a weekly. As he entered the shop he was greeted by a smell that most newspaper people, though not anyone else, found pleasant—the mixture of printing ink and machine oil that meant a press was located on the premises.

"It's too late, the deadline has passed," said a man in an ink-stained apron who was sipping coffee from a plastic cup. His hands were black with ink, and there was a smudge on his cheek, too.

"Is the editor in?"

"The man who owns the paper is." The man's tone of voice was unfriendly.

"What about the editor?" Mitch persisted.

"He owns and runs it. I'll see if he's out back." Cup in hand, he walked through a back door. Before the door closed, Mitch glimpsed a group of tables on top of which sat a row of metal chases filled with type.

Mitch waited patiently for someone to appear, glancing briefly at the framed copies of the newspaper hanging on the wall; one, a brittle, yellowing front page, was dated September 1, 1921, and carried a banner headline over the logo that said, "Virgil's Own Newspaper: Our First Issue." When no one appeared, Mitch called out, "Hello—anyone here?" several times until a man in his late 50s came out of the back door, eyeglasses perched on his head, his hands black with ink.

"Sorry. Lamar told me you were here, but we're just making up," he said. Unlike the printer, his tone was warm, inviting. "You've missed the deadline for classifieds. Sorry."

It must be Wednesday if the classifieds have closed, Mitch mused to himself. Weeklies routinely come out on Thursdays. He introduced himself and explained the reason for his being in Virgil.

"Sure, I met Tom—Cantwell, I mean," Augustus Leon said. "We talked away a whole night."

Mitch asked him if Tom had seemed unduly agitated or in ill health.

Leon frowned, running that over in his mind. "No. No, I know he was excited by what he was finding out for his book, but he's the last person I would have thought had trouble—physical trouble, I mean."

"Well, I guess that's neither here nor there, Mr. Leon. By the way, I'm an old newspaperman like Tom. In fact, whatever little I learned, I learned from him."

"Well, welcome to the world of the weekly, Mr. Stevens. I daresay it's not as exciting as a big city paper."

"Don't knock it," said Mitch. "I started on a weekly. I know what it's like to cover all the news in town, take your own photos, write the headlines, and do your own layout. Hell, I even delivered the papers."

The two men chatted on for a while, exchanging reminiscences, until Leon glanced at his watch. "I gotta be getting back to the pressroom. Listen, I'd like to have you over to dinner, me and my wife."

Mitch thanked him. "I'm planning on leaving tomorrow afternoon, but if I come back to work on the book I'll definitely drop by, and we'll set up something."

Mitch turned to the door. He stopped when Leon said, "Hell, I meant to ask you, did Tom confirm what that lady in Manton told him?"

"What do you mean?" Mitch said. "Did he tell you something about meeting her?"

"Oh, yes. He was all puffed up like an adder when he came back. He said he'd want to check out what she told him, and if it were true he'd have a lot of thinking to do about what to do next with his book."

"What do you think he meant by that?"

"He wouldn't tell me. He only said that if this was New York it would be a perfect story for the *Enquirer*. So I imagine he was thinking scandal."

THE DRIVE TO Manton seemed so tedious. Mitch had risen at dawn, eaten a hurried breakfast at a roadside diner and driven as fast over the speed limit as seemed wise in order to get to Manton as soon as possible. He was sorry now he hadn't driven the night before and stayed at a motel nearby, so that he could visit Martha Tour Gale first thing in the morning. It would have saved two hours of driving today.

Manton was much like Virgil, but lacked the saving grace of having a courthouse or square. Its Main Street had the same kind of shops—a shoe store, a stationers, a barber shop, two beauty parlors, several attorney-cum-realtor offices, a bakery and a pharmacy. But while Virgil exuded a bucolic air, Manton, Mitch observed, was seedy and depressed, as though a thundercloud constantly hovered over it.

Mitch pulled into a gasoline station at the far end of town and asked directions to Martha Tour Gale's house. The car needed fuel but he was too eager to stop for it now.

The street he finally turned into seemed deserted except for a lone black woman leaning on a broom outside a modest white clapboard house. Mitch slowed down and opened the window. "Can you please tell me where Miss Gale lives?"

"Not anymo'," the woman said.

Mitch turned off the car engine. "I'm sorry, I didn't hear you."

"Not anymo'," the woman repeated, annoyed.

"What do you mean?"

"She done live next door."

"Isn't she in?" asked Mitch, wondering what was going on.

"I say, not anymo'—what can't you unnerstan 'bout that?"

Mitch decided not to argue with the woman. He started up the engine and drove the short way to the next house. It, too, was a clapboard house, but it had been painted yellow. He got out and walked up to the front stoop. He rang the doorbell several times. There was no response.

"I tol' you, not anymo'."

Mitch jumped with surprise. The old black woman had followed him up the stoop, her slippers muffling her steps.

"Please," Mitch said, "this is important. Where is Miss Gale?"

"They done took her but an 'our pass," the old woman said. "In a rubba sheet. She dead."

Mitch was stunned. "What happened?" he asked, trying to retain his composure.

"Doc Walla say she fall. She ver' old, more than me. She fall, she done kill herself."

"She's dead? Martha Tour Gale?"

"Hey, boy, you not hear me. Not anymo'. Miz Gale not anymo'."

Mitch stared at the old woman. There was spittle coming out the side of her mouth, and her eyes were red and watery. Every part of her body seemed wrinkled. She turned suddenly and started down the stoop, using the broom to help herself down the steps. "Not anymo', not anymo'," she kept repeating, shaking her head.

FIVE

"GIVE ME A chance to explain, will you, Val?" Mitch was getting exasperated.

"Mitch, I was already getting adjusted to the idea that we wouldn't be together most of the summer. Now you tell me that you're not coming home before I leave for California. I don't like it one bit."

"Val, something's going on here."

"And you've gotten the itch again, is that it?"

"If I leave now I'm afraid I'll miss out on finding out what's going on." Mitch was holding the phone in his left hand. His right was pounding on the pillow of his bed in his room at the Caddo Motel. "Look," he said, "I promise that I'll fly straight out to you from here once I get things under control. I won't even go back to New York first. Straight out to L.A., I promise."

Val hesitated on the other end of the line. "Are you going to get into trouble again, Mitch?" The tone of her voice told him that she was starting to get used to the idea that he would be staying in Virgil and miss her departure for the West Coast.

"Val, honey, I learned that lesson last summer." Mitch had stopped hitting the pillow. "I'm just going to nose around a bit, satisfy a few things nagging at me and then I'll head your way."

He lowered his voice slightly. "I miss you, Val."

"Me too, Mitch. Don't stay too long."

"I'll catch the first flight out when I'm through—or I'll charter one. The mosquitoes down here are big enough to carry passengers."

Val laughed softly. "I love you."

"Me too, Val, me too."

THE RECEPTIONIST OUTSIDE the sheriff's office—Mabel, Mitch had learned her name was—was pushing up the back of her beehive hairdo when he arrived. Mitch wondered whether there was only one beauty parlor in town; most of the women sported the same hairstyle. "Just tell Mabel I expect you, Mr. Stevens," Bochard had told him. "I'm calling from my squad car, but she'll let you into my office till I get back."

Mitch roamed around the sheriff's office, reading the award citations the sheriff had received and studying the photographs—Bochard as a young patrolman, Bochard with his arm holding a handcuffed cowboy, Bochard speaking at a state sheriffs' convention. He returned to the first photograph. The badge Bochard was wearing was a five-pointed star, not like the badge he wore now. Mitch squinted, trying to read what the badge said, when the door opened and the sheriff walked in, his face flushed and grim.

"Damn loggers," he said, throwing his Stetson at the windowsill. "I'm sorry, Mr. Stevens—"

"Mitch."

"I get worked up every time I have to go out to their camp. They're animals." He picked his hat off the sill and hung it on the coat tree in the corner.

"I was looking at your pictures, Sheriff. And your awards. Very impressive. How come the badge in that one over there is five-pointed?"

"I started out in the Texas Rangers," Bochard explained. "That's where I'm from originally—Beaumont. When the

townfolks here have a mind to tease me, they call me Tex. I'd
made a little reputation back home and got lured away here.
They needed someone when old man Tomkins died eight years
ago. If I had seen that loggers' camp the day I came here, I
would've turned right around and gone back home.

"You asked to see me, Mr. Stevens—Mitch," he continued,
sitting down behind the desk. "What can I do for you?"

"A couple of things, Sheriff. Do you mind if I sit?"

"No, of course. Please do. Pardon my manners."

Mitch crossed his legs. "A woman died in Manton yesterday,
an old lady."

"That's way out of my district," said Bochard.

"I realize that," Mitch said, "but I wondered if you could find
out a few things for me about her death. I went down to visit
her and got there too late. She'd already been taken away."

"Dead? Or did she die on the way to the hospital?"

"Dead as far as I know," Mitch said. "I just want to verify
what happened to her."

The sheriff reached for his phone. "What's her name?"

Bochard apparently knew his counterpart in Manton well.
The two chatted, Mitch, of course, hearing only Bochard's side
of the conversation, but they were obviously trading gossip. At
last, the idle prattle over, Bochard asked about Martha Tour
Gale. The question was followed by a series of "Uh-uhs," the
sheriff looking over at Mitch every so often or asking a question, until he finally said into the phone, "Thanks, Orv. I appreciate your telling me." A few more pleasantries were exchanged
before Bochard hung up.

"Miss Gale died in a fall in her home. She was dead when the
police got there."

"Did your friend have anything else to say about her?"

"Well, there was nothing suspicious about it. She was well
into her 90s and had gotten up on a small step stool in her
kitchen to get something from a cupboard. That's where they
found her, in the kitchen."

"Nothing else?" asked Mitch.

"Well, if you want the gory details, she hit her head as she came down. Her skull was crushed in on one side."

"Crushed?"

"She was an old person, Mitch. Their bones get brittle."

"Wasn't her hip broken, too?" Mitch asked. "That's what usually happens when an old person falls."

"No, Orval didn't say anything about a hip being broken."

"And no signs of any disturbance, nothing suspicious—you know, like a break-in?"

Bochard looked at Mitch sharply. "Whoa, what are you getting at, Mitch? A break-in? You don't have to break in around these parts, at least not outside the towns. People leave their doors unlocked, old ladies, too. What did she have worth taking? Do you know?"

Only what she had in her head, Mitch said to himself. "Sheriff, the other day, the day we met and went over to Studley's—"

"Did Wallace have the body sent on yet?" the sheriff interrupted.

"Yes, the body was flown to New Jersey. Mrs. Cantwell decided to have her husband cremated. She's put off a memorial service until after the summer."

"Cremated? Wallace could have done that here," Bochard said. "It would have saved some money in shipping back the body. An urn doesn't weigh much."

Mitch grimaced. He didn't like talking this way about Tom Cantwell. He had tried to persuade Abigail over the phone not to have Tom cremated, but she said she couldn't bear the idea of his being in a cold, dark grave. Only she didn't want "some stranger in Louisiana," as she put it, doing the cremation.

"Sheriff, can we get back to what I was about to ask? The other day you intimated to me that you weren't satisfied with the explanation for Tom's death. Can you tell me why?"

Bochard turned and looked out the window. Mitch wondered what he was thinking.

"It's important to me," Mitch coaxed. "I sense something's wrong but I can't put my finger on it."

The sheriff turned to Mitch. "I did, too, Mitch. But I couldn't put a pinkie on anything."

"What bothered you, Sheriff?"

"It was just odd, didn't add up, the way we found him. The maid discovered him in the morning. She went in to do his room, and there he was in pajamas sprawled across his bed. It looked normal on the surface but there were bits and pieces that . . ." Bochard's voice trailed off momentarily. He stood up, crossed his arms and sat on the window ledge.

"Cantwell had complained to the front desk when he got in the night before. He said his papers were out of order or something. He was upset and told Carter to tell the chambermaid not to touch his things when she was cleaning up."

"That doesn't sound suspicious to me," said Mitch.

"No, it doesn't on the surface," the sheriff said, "but the chambermaid swears she didn't move anything he had on the desk in there. She purposely steers clear of personal items because she doesn't want to be accused of mislaying something or stealing."

Mitch shrugged his shoulders. "Well, that's kind of weak, isn't it? The maid was probably lying. They're always in a rush to get their rooms done."

"Especially at the Caddo Motel," the sheriff agreed, smiling. "The place has a reputation for getting you up and out early."

Mitch nodded. The maid had tapped at his door before eight that morning, while he was shaving. A persistent tapping, one that said, "Hurry up, I've got a lot of rooms to do," even though there were hardly any other persons staying there.

"Anyway," Bochard continued, "I can't explain why, but I never felt comfortable with that explanation."

"It's more than possible," Mitch said. "It's likely."

"The truth is," the sheriff conceded, "that nothing seemed out of the ordinary. We found what you'd expect to find. Cantwell evidently tested his urine for sugar before he went to bed. A typical routine for a diabetic. There was a beaker for a urine specimen and a used reagent paper. It was blue. Doc J. J.—Dr. Dexter—said the blue paper indicated there was sugar in his urine and he needed insulin. Cantwell kept a supply, several doses, in the mini-bar in the room. And, yes sir, there was a syringe by Cantwell's bedside, a needle and an empty vial of insulin and the tiny box it came in in the waste basket. Just as you'd expect.

"So, sure, the maid could have rearranged things while dusting. It's likely. And it's likely that the hairpin I found was from some previous guest and hadn't got picked up in her vacuum cleaner."

"You found a hairpin?"

"A lady's hairpin," Bochard said. "On the carpet, plain as day, right by the desk. At first I thought, well maybe Cantwell had a lady in his room. But the truth is, having met Cantwell, I didn't get that feeling from him."

"His age, you mean?"

"Yes, that, but also the kind of man he was. It didn't hold."

"Tom supposedly died in the middle of the night. What made you sure it was the middle of the night, Sheriff?"

"Doc J. J. He's the official police physician. He answered our call that morning and came over. He took Cantwell's temperature and figured out that his death must have taken place about two or three in the morning."

"And no autopsy was called for? Right?"

"On what basis?" the sheriff asked. "My suspicions were faint ones. After all, what else could have happened? No money was missing, as far as we could tell. Cantwell had cash in his wallet and traveler's checks as well. His wife hasn't complained that anything is missing. It was all there."

"What about his papers?" Mitch asked. "Maybe something was stolen?"

"How could we know that?" asked the sheriff. "We didn't know what papers he had in the room; I mean, there was no way of telling if any were missing. And he'd been doing historical research. What could he have had of any real value?"

"But you're not satisfied, are you, Sheriff?"

Bochard rose and stood behind his chair, gripping it with both hands. "No, I'm not, Mitch," he said softly. "And if you can think of any reason for me to look into this further, I'll do it."

The sheriff's phone rang. Moving over to his desk, he picked it up. "Yes, Mabel?" A pause. "Damn!" He slammed the receiver down. "I have to get out to the logging camp," he said to Mitch. "They're at it again."

A FARMER IN a checkered shirt and visored cap with "Deere" emblazoned on its peak was at the counter in the parish clerk's office, leaning over a map with Jimmy Deal. "The bottom 10, Jimmy, where I got the fence."

"I see what you mean, Ed, but you didn't register it and you got to make it legal."

"It's my own land. Since when can anyone hunt on it without my permission? Damn it all." The farmer pushed off from the counter. "Okay, give me the forms. It'll cost me, won't it?"

Deal went behind the desk and reached into a folder. "Five dollars a year. The state gets it, not us. Here, you can bring it back any time."

Mitch watched the little scene, waiting for the farmer to leave. "Good day, Mr. Deal. Have you got a minute?"

"Uh-oh, the last minute I had stretched into an hour with you." But Deal hadn't said no. "Go ahead, young man, what can I do for you today?"

Mitch asked to see the birth and death records that Tom Cantwell had been interested in. "I always thought churches kept the records back then," he said loud enough for Deal, who had gone into the adjoining room, to hear.

"They did," an echo of a reply came back. "Marriages, too." Deal returned with one of his by now familiar ledger books.

"This here is the one Mr. Cantwell was keen on."

"May I?" Mitch asked, sitting down at an empty desk along the side wall of the office.

Deal didn't raise an objection, so Mitch opened the ledger and started to study it. He remembered seeing a note Tom had written to himself that said that the family Bible gave one birth date for Thomas Clay Washburn, but that the "official record" showed another date, one day later. "A midnight child?" Tom had written.

"Lots of Washburn names back in the 1830s and '40s," Mitch observed, not knowing whether Deal, who was immersed in one of his ledgers, had heard him. "Bullochs, too. I wonder they didn't intermarry before now."

"They did." Deal had heard. "Lots of cousins got hooked together in time."

Mitch kept turning the pages. The handwriting seemed to change in the mid-1860s. He commented on it to Deal, who explained, "That's when great-grandfather Lucius died. A woman in the parish kept the log going until my granddad Lucius Junior came back from the war and took up the job."

Still leafing through the pages, Mitch was amused by the names parents had chosen for their newborn infants. There were fashionable trends, of course: a lot of Theodores around the time of Teddy Roosevelt, several Hueys when Huey Long was the kingpin in the state, and many Johns during John F. Kennedy's administration.

"Is this the mayor—Everett Blaine Bulloch? That's quite a handle."

"They called him Ebb when he was a kid," Deal said. "That riled him, so he came up himself with his nickname, Rhett. He said it sounded more like a real Southern name."

Mitch was flipping the pages backwards. "Look. Here's Martha Tour Gale. She was old—what, 95, no 96." A thought struck Mitch. "I haven't noticed many black births here. Weren't black births and deaths registered also?"

75

"Depended," said Deal. "Of course, we never had as many here as downstate. There were farms hereabouts, not plantations. Some used slaves for the work, but the ratio to the white population was never really large. Before the war the census counted every black person and gave them a name. The tax assessors, too. But afterwards, well it depended on whether the parents took the trouble to report a newborn. We had no hospital or clinic for them folks then; we still don't hereabouts. They give birth at home, and sometimes we learn about it and sometimes we don't."

"Doesn't it show in school records when they sign up for kindergarten?"

"Lots of them don't go to school, and we may not even know they're alive and should be in school. They're on a backwoods farm somewhere, doing their chores, isolated. Every so often one gets into trouble or has an accident and everybody wonders where the deuce he came from."

"So to be black is to be invisible in a way," Mitch said.

Deal looked up sharply. "We're over that business," he said, irritated. "But it's still up to the parents to report things. You know, they die, too, and don't tell us about that either."

"How would I find out more about the Washburns?" Mitch asked, deciding to change the subject but too late to mollify Deal.

"Ask them!"

SIX

$\mathbf{M}$ITCH POKED HIS fork at the piece of steak and raised it to his lips. He eyed the condiments sitting on a dish on the table: catsup, three different steak sauces, Tabasco sauce and a clear liquid in a cruet that he had sniffed but failed to identify. He debated whether to try one of these. The steak was overcooked and tasteless. Which, he thought, accounted for the profusion of sauces that sat on every table in the dining room of the Caddo Motel.

Mitch was the only customer, which didn't surprise him either. There was a crude, hand-painted banner pinned onto the wall behind the counter in the office of the motel—WELCOME PARISH XIAN CHURCH AUXILIARY—but the conventioneers weren't due to show up for two days. He was seated at a table for four—there were no smaller tables—and had spread a copy of the *Virgil Whig* to his left. It ran only 16 pages, half of which were taken up with advertisements for the town's two supermarkets ("Spring Lamb Sale" said one, "Bar-b-que Time A'Comin'" said the other) as well as for the local shoe shop ("Summer is Sneaker Time"), the gas station ("Tune-Up Special"), and the pharmacy ("Get Ready for the Summer Now"). The book store—in anticipation undoubtedly of the upcoming convention—advertised "Bibles, metal and wooden crosses, hymnals, and books of spiritual Christian uplifting."

There didn't seem to be anything that had happened in Virgil in the past week that Augustus Leon hadn't made note of in the news columns—the mayor's approval, finally, for a new road grader; the recreation department's summer schedule of activities at Rebel Park; a neighborhood garage sale to benefit the Rescue Squad; the wedding of the daughter of the school athletic director to a Baton Rouge mechanic; and, of course, spread across two pages inside, stories and score charts about every league softball game played at Rebel Park. There was a page of classifieds, and another listing all the Sunday church services and the announcements of betrothals and marriages, each one of which was accompanied by a photograph of the prospective or actual bride. An announcements page recorded every activity of every organization, including tea parties, and everyone who had attended or spoken. ("Get as many names into the paper as possible," Mitch remembered the editor of the weekly he once had worked on saying. "Everyone will take the paper just to see his name. They'll all clip it out and put it in a scrapbook, no matter what, even if they've been caught in a traffic violation.") Augustus Leon was trained in the same school. Every call that had come into the sheriff's office or the volunteer fire department was recorded. ("A brush fire was put out at 4:32 P.M. Tuesday at Clyde Smith's farm off the Juniper bypass. . . .")

And, of course, obituaries. ("Mrs. Ettie Lee Dunsmore died at Virgil Nursing Home Monday after a long illness. She was a resident of Virgil and 68 years old. . . .") Mitch searched the page for some mention of Tom Cantwell. After all, it couldn't be every day that someone died at the Caddo Motel.

Mitch hunted through all the pages but couldn't find any story whatsoever about Tom. That was surprising. Why not? Could his death have appeared in the previous edition? Mitch mentally counted back, trying to figure out when Tom's death had occurred in relation to the weekly's publication day. No, it should be in the current edition. Mitch leafed through the paper again, his eyes moving up and down the pages until he finally spotted the story below the fold, in the first column, near the gutter, on page nine:

T. CANTWELL, VISITOR, DIES AT CADDO MOTEL

The sheriff's office reports that a visitor to Virgil, Thomas Cantwell, was found dead Wednesday morning in his room at the Caddo Motel.

Mr. Cantwell was believed to be about 70 years old. According to motel records, his home was in Brunswick, N.J.

Sheriff Willard Bochard said that Mr. Cantwell was discovered by the motel's chambermaid about 8 A.M. Dr. J. J. Dexter was immediately summoned and pronounced Mr. Cantwell dead. He said he had died of heart failure.

Mr. Cantwell was in Virgil to work on research for a book about the town's most notable hero of the War Between the States, Thomas Clay Washburn. He had arrived 10 days earlier.

The sheriff said that efforts were being made to reach Mr. Cantwell's family in New Jersey. In the meantime, the deceased's body is being held at Studley's Funeral Home.

It wasn't much of a story, and didn't add any information to what he already knew, but Mitch carefully ripped the item from the paper and put the clipping in his wallet. Still hungry, he checked his change pocket to see if he had enough coins to buy something from the vending machine in the hallway next to the ice machine. Maybe I ought to take Augustus Leon up on his invitation to dinner, he said to himself, pushing the plate in front of him away. He had to wait until the waitress—Olivia Carter, the motel owner's wife—reappeared in order to get his check, so he glanced again at the *Virgil Whig*. The headline on a brief story caught his eye, making him grin at the double meaning: "Baby Safety Week Stresses Parents." Below the headline was Flora May Bulloch's name. There was to be a meeting of the Rebel Daughters of America at her home the next night to discuss the town's annual celebration of Dixie Day. "All are welcome," the story read. "Refreshments will be served."

Mitch decided he would attend, speculating whether he would be welcome. Olivia appeared, ambling lazily toward him. "There's a phone call for you, Mr. Stevens. You can take it in the office." She saw Mitch's unfinished steak. "Want me to keep that heated for you?"

IT WAS THE mayor. "Thought I'd catch you there," he said. "I've been tied up with a union meeting at my place all day but I'm heading out to the logging camp soon and thought you might want to see it. There's a parcel out there that used to be Washburn land, and maybe their old house was on it."

Mitch accepted. He could phone Leon after he got back. As he drove up the driveway to Bulloch's house, the mayor came out of the doorway. He waved at Mitch, who parked his car on the verge of the gravel road and went to meet him. They shook hands, and Bulloch invited him into his car.

"Damn it all," the mayor said, adjusting the rearview mirror.

"Why don't you get your wife her own car?" Mitch asked bemusedly.

"She has her own, but it's laid up being worked on," Bulloch said, starting the engine. "We're going to be driving the same route we took before, only we take a later cutoff. So sit back and enjoy the scenery. Want a cigar?"

Bulloch drove without speaking, making Mitch feel uneasy. He tried to start a conversation—"I see that your wife is going to host a meeting tomorrow night of the Rebel Daughters that

I thought I might attend. Would she mind, do you think?"—that had drawn a mumbled affirmative but nothing further. So Mitch turned his attention to the countryside. They passed the few well-tended homes of Virgil's "up and coming" blacks and then, farther on, the ramshackle houses of poorer blacks that lined both sides of the road. With time to observe carefully, Mitch saw details he had missed on their earlier car ride. What looked like rags hung from clotheslines. The children as well as the women were barefoot. What few men he saw were either very old and bent over or crippled. The yards they stood in were hard and dusty, their homes a patchwork of amateurish repairs, with shutters to stave off the heat of day hung askew. Passing swiftly by the shacks, Mitch sensed a look of monotony, and wondered whether the lives of the people who lived inside them were monotonous also.

They had turned off and were driving into the forest, but the dirt road was firm and newly surfaced with gravel where potholes had occurred. It was a wide road, too, wide enough to permit huge flatbeds with long pine logs to pass through without any difficulty. Bulloch had lowered his window now that they were again in the cool shade. Mitch could hear the whine of a saw in the distance. It grew louder as they swung around a curve in the road and into the camp, which consisted of a group of wooden cabins set off from a sawmill. A large, partly open building was surrounded by shavings. Smoke curled from the metal chimney of one of the cabins, the kitchen apparently. The whine was jarring. Mitch noticed that some of the roughly clad workers were wearing earphones to protect their ears from the noise. Some also wore white masks to guard against inhaling sawdust.

"I'll just be a minute. I just have to talk to Ernie," the mayor said, leaving the car and walking over to a stocky, ruddy-faced man in coveralls and a red and white checkered wool shirt. Mitch recognized him as the driver of the pickup truck that had been parked in front of the roadhouse on the way into Virgil.

Bulloch returned after a minute or so and squeezed back into the driver's seat. "We do some milling ourselves, as you can see, but a lot of what we cut gets shipped out to yards all over the Southwest. I'll take you up to where we're timbering now. It's right by that Washburn parcel I told you about."

The road they took ran uphill. They passed a field of stumps, the sun finally finding a place to shine. Bulloch stopped the car in a narrow pass-by when he saw a rig coming down the road ahead of them. Trussed to its flatbed was a stack of logs, held in place by huge chains. The rig grunted by slowly, Bulloch waving a hello at the driver who raised a hand in return.

A few yards farther along they passed a plateaulike area, the mayor pointing at it, saying, "That's it. Why don't you get out. I can't park here. The road's too narrow. I'll catch up with you."

Mitch slammed the door behind him and walked into the copse. He could hear a different sort of whine now, chainsaws, and, nearby, the noise of a tree collapsing onto the floor of the forest. Mitch stumbled into small holes and slipped on the forest carpet as he made his way toward the center of the area. He looked around for some indication of a house—stone supports, the remains of a chimney. Suddenly he felt a rush of air and looked up. A huge pine was coming down at him, seeming to fall so sluggishly that Mitch briefly sensed he was watching a slow-motion movie. He cried out, "Oh, my God," and ran to the side, falling to the ground as the tree hit the earth and hid him underneath its branches.

Mitch struggled to get out of the tree's clutches. His face had been scratched. He felt his cheeks, then looked at his fingers to see if they had touched blood. If he was bleeding, it was slight. I'd better get back to the road, he told himself and looked about. He had lost his sense of direction. Where was the road? He went over in his mind where he had been standing and from what angle the tree had come, then started walking gingerly through the woods, searching the trees above him suspiciously.

A short way ahead was a small, cleared space. Logs had been dragged to it and laid one above the other in a pyramid. Mitch didn't recall seeing them before. He must have headed the wrong way. He turned back into the forest again.

Suddenly there was another rush of air. Without even looking up, Mitch ran straight ahead, almost falling again as his knees buckled under him when his right foot tripped over a boulder. He could feel his heart racing, and panic seized him. The tree fell well off to his right, a heavy crunch and then silence. But Mitch kept running, half stumbling, until he was out of breath.

He slumped to the ground, his back against a tree, gasping, trying to slow down his heart by taking deep breaths.

"Stevens—Ho, Stevens!"

The shout came from the left. Mitch wanted to answer it, but his throat had constricted. He slowly rose, holding onto the tree for support. If he couldn't shout back, maybe at least he'd be spotted if he stood up. He leaned back against the tree, still gasping, when Bulloch appeared from behind a pine not 30 yards away.

"Stevens! Hey, where did you go to?"

Mitch watched the mayor approach. The worker named Ernie was behind him. "Jesus, boy, you scared us for a minute there. We couldn't find you."

Mitch swallowed, clearing his throat. "I got lost."

"You don't want to do that here," the mayor said, looking back at Ernie, who was chewing on a plug of tobacco. "That can be dangerous."

"I thought," said Mitch, struggling to keep his voice under control, "that when you cut down a tree you were supposed to yell 'Timber!' or something. I almost got killed—twice."

"You're supposed to," Bulloch said, taking out two cigars from his coat and passing one to Ernie. "But if a man's working a clump on his own he won't bother to. Who's to hear him?" Bulloch started to walk away, expecting Mitch to trail after him. "You got to be cautious around timbering land. That was a close call you had."

No sorrys, no regrets, no sympathy for what Mitch had experienced. The mayor was a cold fish, Mitch realized. A heartless, cold fish.

Mitch pushed himself off the tree. "Is this the way back?" he asked.

"Follow me," Bulloch said, walking off. "Find anything?"

SEVEN

"THAT'S THE TROUBLE I found with working on a weekly," Mitch said. He wiped his lips with a napkin, smiled at Lyda Leon and added, "That was the best blueberry pie I ever ate." Lyda glowed. Obviously, Mitch thought wryly, the trick in this town is to get invited to private homes for dinner.

"I don't get your gist," Augustus Leon said. "I like being a part of the community. I know everybody in this town, I think. Maybe not on a first-name basis, but everybody. I'm sort of their chronicler. They depend on me to guard the history of the town, to keep the daily record of their lives straight, just like they expect Jimmy Deal to keep the official records straight."

Mitch turned slightly in his chair so he could cross his legs. Lyda Leon had the pie plate in her hand and was about to hand it to him, but he said, "No, no thanks, Lyda. I don't think there's any space left in me."

"Did you ever hear of the *Hillville Courier*?" Mitch continued. "It won a number of awards back in the 50s, so you might have. I worked on it when I first got into newspapering—after it won the awards. That was someone else's doing. We covered everything imaginable, two of us, Pete Johnsen and myself. Did everything just like you do. And I meant it when I said I delivered the papers, too. We'd stuff up my old Volkswagen with the bundles and I'd drop them off at the delivery boys' homes. And if one of the boys was ill, we'd get his route book from his mother and do the rounds ourselves. In the middle of the night, usually.

"Hillville was a small town in Connecticut, but it was much like Virgil in a way, far from any big city. People were more concerned with local issues than with much else. Good people, helpful to each other. They cared about Hillville. I sort of fell in with the community spirit."

Lyda had gotten up and was taking away the empty dessert dishes. She tried to minimize the clatter so as not to disturb Mitch and her husband. Mitch handed her his plate and fork before continuing.

"The fall I was there we had a bang-up football team at the high school. It was in the running for the state championship. I'll never forget when the big game that would decide it came around. I was on the sidelines with a Rollei, taking pictures. It was the last quarter, near the end of the game, and Hillville was behind by three points. And it was third down and they were way upfield. I knew they'd give it to Mike Audrey, their star running back, so I trotted down to the 10-yard line, near the end zone, all by myself and waited. I set the Rollei to shoot for about 15 feet, figuring I'd catch Mike coming down the field with the ball."

There was a crash of silverware in the kitchen. "Sorry," said Lyda. "Please go on. I'm listening."

"Damn if they didn't give the ball to Mike, and he came running like hell down the field, followed by a bunch of defensive backs chasing him. I was perfectly positioned for a picture of the winning touchdown. Only I got so excited, I started yelling with the crowd, 'Come on, Mike, come on!'

"Mike scored all right, but I forgot to take the picture. I had to settle for a shot that showed him from behind. That's the one we ran in the paper. I was so embarrassed. I couldn't believe what I had done—lost my objectivity. I learned a big lesson that day."

"You didn't stay in that town, did you?" Leon said. "You moved on, didn't you?" Mitch nodded that he had indeed moved on to another paper. "It's a different ball game when you plan to spend your entire life in the same place on the same newspaper," Leon said. "You can't help but get involved. It's expected, maybe more so in a rural community like Virgil."

Mitch shrugged. "You're probably right. I've never been in one place or on one newspaper for any great length of time. I took the classic route—to a daily after the weekly, then to a paper that had a Sunday edition, too, and then to a major metropolitan one. I always moved to a bigger paper, until I wound up in New York. But," Mitch smiled ruefully, "that paper folded on me."

"There's something else, too, about a weekly," Augustus began, then paused. "I don't know how to say it—I think it's going to come out wrong—but I feel a responsibility to protect this town. I see—we all read about—all the things going on around us, whether it's in the state, or the country or the world, and I say to myself, I don't want this to happen to Virgil, I don't want the crime and the drugs and the nastiness or anything at all that's bad."

"You want the status quo."

"Yes and no," Augustus said. "I want things to stay as they are. I want people in town to get along with each other as they do now, but I also want to see progress."

"What kind of progress, Augustus?"

"More jobs for the blacks—better jobs—and someone to see to it that they get an education, that the kids go to school and take advantage of the opportunities their parents never had."

"Augustus," said Mitch, hunching forward in his chair and clasping his hands together, "I haven't seen any opportunity for blacks in Virgil. Correct me if I'm wrong, I could be blind to it, but the blacks I've seen are all doing menial jobs if they're doing anything. The only black I've met in a position of any authority is a state trooper, and he is originally from up North.

"No, that's not fair," Mitch corrected himself. "The mayor pointed out some homes on the way to his lumbering camp and said they were owned by middle-class blacks—blacks in civil service, he said."

"He means they work for the town or the parish, in jobs they could only have dreamed about before the civil rights movement," Augustus said. "We've got black teachers in our schools now, too, and a black lawyer and a black doctor.

"It takes time, Mitch, you know that." Augustus fussed with his cuffs and rolled up his sleeves. It made him look more like the country editor he was. "Your attitude—pardon me for saying so—is what we expect of Northerners. Kind of typical."

"Yes, I suppose so," Mitch said. "I'm still trying to get a handle on things down here. What I've seen actually has been contradictory. I see the progress—just the fact that that state trooper is black must represent enormous progress—but I've also seen those shacks by the road going out to the forest, the Confederate flag in a drinking tavern, and you people celebrate something called Dixie Day."

"That's just a reason for a local to-do, Mitch. Shreveport's got the annual state fair, and we wanted to have our own celebration. We just call it that, sort of in memory of the fact that the area was spared from invasion in the war despite the two Red River campaigns the North launched."

"That sounds," Mitch conceded, "like something New Yorkers used to celebrate just to have something to celebrate of their own. Evacuation Day. It commemorated the day the last British troops left the city after the Revolutionary War was over. It's not observed anymore, hasn't been for pretty near a hundred years."

"Well, that's really what Dixie Day is all about. A long time ago the town picked out a day toward the end of May—a Sunday—and called it Dixie Day. I suppose they could have named it something else, like Virgil Day, but that doesn't have the same ring to it, does it?"

"How come the Rebel Daughters run it if it's a town project?"

"Someone has to, and it gives the Rebel Daughters something to do," he smiled.

"In a way, what you're saying only confuses me more, Augustus. I've heard the way your mayor talks. What is the truth?"

"It's both things I guess, Mitch, and I, for one, would like to see fellows like the mayor get their comeuppance. I can't stand the way they go on any more than I gather you can. Jeez, all the progress we've made seems to go up in smoke whenever one of his type opens his mouth."

"Then how does he get elected?" Mitch asked. "Who votes for him? They must know his views. He makes no secret of them."

"I believe, I really do believe," Augustus replied, "that most people, they see it as just talk, sort of expected like, and just that—traditional Southern polemics, part and parcel of being a Southerner—something you acknowledge but don't really believe in."

"Do you really believe that? Do you really believe it's all talk?"

"A lot of it."

"Not genuine talk, not the kind of talk that frustrates the progress you want to see?"

Lyda suddenly came back from the kitchen. "Let's move back to the living room," she said.

The men got up and headed into the room next to the dining area. The Leon house was not spacious, but it had a warm, lived-in quality that was appealing. Lyda, who taught the second grade at Virgil Elementary School, had framed a number of colorful watercolors that her students had painted. One was of the statue of the soldier in the town square. The youngster had taken the liberty of adding a Confederate flag; it flew from the soldier's musket.

"Some folks still seem to take the Civil War seriously."

"Some people, not me," Leon said.

"I was planning on going to that meeting of the Rebel Daughters at the mayor's house tomorrow night." Mitch checked his watch. "I should be getting back to the motel. I have a big day tomorrow."

"Those Rebel ladies are something else," Lyda said, settling herself on the couch. "They have their noses stuck up in the air all the time. A bunch of snobs. And bigots! I don't claim to be a radical or anything, but you'd never believe some of the things they think—and say."

"We've clung to a lot of things," Augustus said. "For a long time, during Reconstruction days, it was something to be ashamed of, being Southern. People finally got their pride back, but it took an ugly turn and certain attitudes persist. The folks who hold them insist that they're right. They'll tell you that they live next to blacks and know blacks better than anybody else. And when someone, like you, comes along from the North, they snicker at what he says and insist that he can't possibly know what it's really like living with and dealing with blacks."

"Listen, I have to be going if I'm going."

The pleasant spell lingered as Mitch said a warm good-bye to the Leons. They were holding hands at the doorway as he left.

DRIVING TO MANTON the next day, Mitch went over in his mind the little he knew about the deaths of Tom Cantwell and Martha Tour Gale. His suspicions, he realized, were just that—suspicions, nothing concrete. But Bochard, at least, shared his doubts about the cause of Tom's death, enough to phone his friend in Manton, Sheriff Orval Tooms. Tooms arranged for Mitch to see the elderly lady's only known relative, a grandniece by the name of Willa Dee Fogge, who lived in Manton also, but at the far side, almost a mile from Martha Tour Gale's home. Mitch couldn't believe that the old lady's death had been mere coincidence. He needed to convince himself that she had died in an accident. That would lay to rest any doubts he had about her death—and might erase his doubts about Tom's also. If he only could find out what she had told Tom. It was hard for Mitch to imagine what could be so earthshaking about a Civil War hero, something so profoundly disturbing that someone would kill to prevent its being broadcast.

To be honest, Mitch thought as he rang the bell at Willa Dee Fogge's home, I may be confusing fact with fiction just because I have nothing to do this summer. That feeling gave way to surprise when the door opened. Willa Dee Fogge was regal, a strikingly handsome woman, who seemed out of place in the seedy, dying town. Her graying hair betrayed her age—mid-50s, Mitch guessed—but it only accented her almost patrician attractiveness.

Mitch must have stood at the front door looking at her for some time, because she finally said, "You're Mr. Stevens aren't you? Please come in."

Mitch followed her down a hallway and into a parlor filled with heavy mahogany furniture. She caught his staring. "I seem to inherit all the hand-me-downs from everybody. All this, this entire house for that matter, was once my uncle's."

She sat in a heavily padded wingchair, Mitch taking a sofa opposite her. He explained the reason for his visit.

"But I can't imagine what my great-aunt knew," Willa Dee Fogge insisted. "She never confided in me, not at all. I hardly even ever saw her. Oh, I'd drop over now and then, especially around the holidays, and we'd exchange presents, but we spoke only perfunctorily if at that.

"I wish I could be of help, Mr. Stevens, but Aunt Martha never said a thing about any Civil War spy, or anybody else for that matter. She may have been almost totally blind, but she had a grand memory. I know she knew all about our family—if I ever cared to know about any of them. But about others? Not a word to me."

"What about her notes, or anything she may have left around, papers or documents?" Mitch asked. "Was there anything unusual?"

"To be perfectly frank," Willa Dee Fogge said, "I haven't even gone out to her house yet. I just haven't had the time. There didn't seem to be any reason to rush. I'll be putting it up for sale, but I can't until her will is probated."

"Then would you mind my looking?"

She studied Mitch.

"I'll leave things just as they were, and if I find anything I'm looking for I'll let you know right away. I won't remove a thing."

"Well . . ."

"It's very important to me, Miss Fogge, and I don't expect to get back to Louisiana until I don't know when. My friend Tom learned something from your aunt that was crucial to the book he was working on. If I'm to continue with his book, complete it for him, I'd like very much to know what that was."

Willa Dee Fogge rose, almost languidly, Mitch thought, and went over to a bureau. She opened the top drawer and drew from it a key ring with two keys on it. "All right, Mr. Stevens, go. Here are the keys. I think the door is locked, but it wouldn't matter. There's nothing of value there. Aunt Martha was a loner, a hermit of sorts who squirreled away information but not possessions. I don't think you'll find anything." She handed the key ring to Mitch. "Please return them before you leave town," she said. "You can drop them in the mail slot in the front door. I don't expect to be home when you get back."

Mitch returned to his car and drove toward Martha Tour Gale's home, wondering as he did about Willa Dee Fogge. There's a story there, too, he said to himself.

The door wasn't locked when Mitch tried it. No one had bothered to latch it. Mitch entered the old woman's home gingerly, though he couldn't explain why he felt the necessity of moving so slowly and quietly. It was dim inside. The few windows were all grimy and covered with stained, off-white shades. A smell of decay akin to old garbage permeated the hallway. A shiver went through Mitch when he stepped inside and the floorboard beneath him creaked. He searched the walls for a light switch. A rose-patterned wallpaper may have once brightened the house, but it was so faded and dirty now that he could barely make out the roses. He looked up. There was a dusty chandelier, with wisps of spiderwebs hanging from it. There had to be a switch for it. As he neared a staircase, he spotted it. The lights, fortunately, were working. So no one had bothered to alert the electric company either. There were two rooms downstairs just off the front door, one a dining room, which was musty and obviously unused; the other must have been the living room or parlor, but had been turned into a large bedroom. Aunt Martha didn't want to climb stairs, it seemed. Mitch did, though, flicking on another switch that lit the landing above.

Each step up the staircase brought another creak. The balustrade was filthy, as though no one had cleaned it for a long time. The second floor contained three rooms. One had been used as a sewing room—an old Singer sat gathering dust on a sewing table—another was given over to bookcases filled to the brim, and the third was a study, with a desk and lamp that looked neglected. Martha Tour Gale had evidently abandoned the second floor years before as she got increasingly old and enfeebled. Mitch went back into the room with the bookcases and started browsing through the titles. Almost all the books were textbooks, history mostly, with a smattering of English classics. None looked like it had been disturbed for many years. There were no books in braille whatsoever. Mitch went through the books methodically, looking for scraps of paper, clippings, anything. The house was so deathly quiet that he jumped, dropping the book he was holding, when he heard what sounded like a whispered hiss. Mitch stood perfectly still, listening, but as hard as he strained, he could hear nothing.

Mitch went back down the stairs, slowly, warily, wondering whether his imagination was playing tricks on him. He walked into the dining room and quietly eased open the swinging door that led to the kitchen. It was deserted. The kitchen was large, with a long table pushed up against a wall and a door leading to a bathroom near the back door. While the rest of the house seemed dusty and unlived in, this room was warm and inviting. There was a bowl of fruit set out on the kitchen table, the aroma of overripe bananas filling the room. This was obviously where Martha spent most of her waking hours. And this was where she died. There, on the worn linoleum floor, turned over, was the stool she had stood on—and fallen from. Mitch wondered if anyone had touched it or if this was exactly the way the police had found it.

Mitch sidestepped the stool and searched the cabinets under the sink: detergent, soap, scouring pads. Nothing unusual. He tried the drawers: silverware, ladles, a pie knife. Nothing there. He didn't even know what he was looking for. Crumbs and the detritus of other foods covered the work area. A few strands of long white hair, too, lay curled amidst the clutter. A sideboard was filled with canned goods, all within easy reach—soups mostly, but canned vegetables, too, all in the smallest size tins you could buy, the single-person variety. I wonder how she could read the labels and tell one from another, Mitch thought, or didn't it matter to her what she ate?

Mitch looked around. There was a small radio set perched on the windowsill; it was plugged into an outlet near the table. A blind person's entertainment center. Two chairs for the table, both padded. And, again, the step stool, the two-rung kind. On an impulse Mitch turned it right side up and stepped on it. He could reach the cabinets above the sink easily. He opened one. Nothing. He tried another. Nothing. The third finally. Nothing. The cabinets were completely empty. Too high up for an elderly woman to want to store anything in, at least if she were wise enough to guard against an accidental fall. And if that was so, what the devil was Martha Tour Gale doing climbing up on that step stool—if indeed she had climbed onto it? Obviously, no one had troubled to look for what the old lady was after. If they had . . .

Mitch's heart began to race. This was no accident. Martha Tour Gale's death was deliberate. Made to look like an accident, but deliberate. And then the door into the kitchen swung open slowly.

Mitch jumped, startled.

Pushing through the door was the old black woman from next door, the one he had met the other day.

"Wat you doin' har?"

"Oh, my God, you scared me," said Mitch, trying to take in big gulps of air to settle himself down.

"Wat you doin', boy?"

"It's all right. I have Miss Gale's grandniece's consent to be here. She gave me the keys."

"Keys? Don't need keys here. Wat you up to?"

"I'm just looking for some information, something about Miss Gale's death," Mitch explained. "I'll be going now."

He started out of the kitchen, the old black woman turning with him as he walked by her, when he stopped abruptly. "You knew her well, didn't you?"

The old woman cocked her head. "Know her? We be sisters. We be sisters all de time since she moved here."

"Oh, I see. You were close. That's nice." Mitch was purposely talking slowly to her, patronizing her, he realized. "Was she a careful woman—I mean, because of her blindness, was she careful about the way she took care of herself?"

"She bettera than me, always bettera. Why you ast?"

"Nothing really. I just found it hard to believe that she had such an accident, that she fell off the step stool."

"Wha step stoo'?"

"There, over there, on the floor. Her step stool."

"Miz Gal no step stoo'. Wha for? She almo' blin'. She neva have no step stoo'. Le' me see it."

The black woman walked over to the step stool and bent over

to look at it, holding her right hand on her hip as she did so. "Nah, tha ain't Miz Gal's. I knowed ever'thin' she have. I do her shoppin', her washin', her cleanin' up. We neva have no step stoo'."

Mitch picked it up. It was an ordinary metal stool, nothing special about it—except that it wasn't Martha Tour Gale's step stool. He returned it to the way he had found it when he first entered the kitchen.

"Thank you," he said to the old woman.

Mitch didn't bother to lock the door as he left. The old woman followed him, her broom in hand, mumbling to herself.

"MITCH, I WON'T hear of it." Val's voice was almost shrill. "You've got nothing substantial to go by, nothing."

Mitch, who had expected his wife's reaction, was half-listening. He glanced at his watch. It was seven o'clock in Los Angeles. Maybe he should have waited until after she had eaten dinner to phone her.

"Mitch, are you listening to me? Say something."

"Aw, come on, Val. You get nervous if I cross the street, for Chrissake. I wish you'd stop treating me like a kid."

"Hold it, hold the phone a minute, I just want to get something," Val said. A slight hum filled the phone line until she spoke again several seconds later. "Here it is, in the paper just this morning, a story on accidents in the home. Mitch, are you there?"

"Yes I am, Val. Go ahead," he said resignedly.

"Okay, let me read to you from it. Wait, I'll just have to find— here it is. Okay, quote: 'Last year 6,300 people died in falls at home, half of all home-related deaths, and 4,900 of the victims were 65 or older. Falls account for two-thirds of deaths at home among people aged 75 or older.'

"Now don't tell me, Mitchell Stevens, that your old lady was murdered, that the accident was a phony. Sixty-three hundred deaths a year, forty-nine hundred of them people 65 or older! Do you realize how many a day that is?"

"Val, Val, Val. Have I ever been wrong about things like this?"

"Oh, Mitch, I don't want to argue this endlessly. You don't know for certain that anything unusual happened. For all you know, a neighbor lent her that stool. Maybe she thought she had left something in the cabinet and was feeling around, trying to find it. You have nothing solid to go on."

"How come that friendly neighbor hasn't shown up, asking for his stool back, or simply taken it? The door's open."

"I'm just worried that you'll get into some sort of trouble, that something will happen."

Thank God, Mitch thought to himself, I didn't tell her about that accident in the forest. Or was it an accident? Val's nervousness is starting to get to me.

"Tell you what," he finally said. "I'd like to give Tom's book a try, I really would." Mitch was astonished by his own words. Without realizing it, he had made up his mind, and the more he justified it to Val, the surer he became. Of course, he was not being entirely truthful. After all, why frighten her needlessly. "It's an interesting story. But there's a lot of work to do. I've got to read all of Tom's notes carefully, make sure he covered all the bases. I don't mind at all, though. It'll keep me busy during the summer, while you're away. And maybe it'll keep Jack Reed off my back, too, just to know that I'm working on a book project."

"I thought you promised to fly to California to be with me?" Val sounded hurt.

"I will, I promise, I haven't forgotten, honest to God I haven't," Mitch said, trying to soothe her. "But first I'll fly back to New York, go over things, make sure everything is all right with Abigail—I really should do that now that I've been here."

There was a sigh from Val's end of the line. "You're going to do it anyway, aren't you, Mitch?"

"Not without your okay."

"Okay," she said grudgingly.

"I love you, Val—very much."

"Well, at least you remember my name," she said.

"I only need a day or two more and I'll head home, honey. Really, the time will go quickly till I see you again."

"It had better, or I'm filing for divorce. It's easy to do out here."

"Okay, fair enough, and if worse comes to worse and you do, I get Ken and you get the dog."

"What dog? We don't have a dog."

NEARLY A DOZEN cars sat on the shoulder of the Bullochs' driveway as Mitch drove up to the house. Slowing down almost to a crawl, he searched for an empty space to park where he wouldn't block another car. He had to drive all the way around the sweeping curve until he found a spot.

Lights blazing throughout the ground floor of the mayor's home made it easy for Mitch to walk to the house without stumbling. The door was slightly ajar. He pushed it open, looked in and, not seeing anyone in the hallway, entered. Off to the right, where he knew the living room was, he could hear a babble of voices. He made his way toward it. As he walked into the room, the voices died down, all eyes on the new arrival. Mitch almost blushed with embarrassment.

"Mr. Stevens—Mitch—so glad you-all could come." With more friendliness than he imagined her capable of, Flora May Bulloch swept toward him from the center of the room. "Welcome to our meeting." She took his hand—a familiarity that also surprised Mitch—and led him into the room. "I want you-all to say hello to some wonderful people. I've been telling them all about you."

Pleasantries and handshakes were exchanged as Flora May escorted Mitch among her guests. Most of them were women, and most of them were Flora May's age or older. But there were several men, too, all wearing suits and ties and appearing stiff and uncomfortable. That is, all but one, the man—about 45,

Mitch gauged—whose hand he was shaking now. "And this is Dr. J. J., Mitch—J. J. Dexter—our very special general practitioner."

"Doctor," Mitch said, gripping Dexter's hand. The doctor, thought Mitch, sizing him up, was what Val would call debonair. Smartly dressed but not ostentatious: Dark pin-striped suit, white shirt, thin-striped conservative tie, hair just a tad longer than the other men wore theirs. And two searching blue eyes, which, Mitch suddenly perceived, were sizing him up, too.

"Flora May has some very nice things to say about you, Mr. Stevens," Dexter said, holding onto Mitch's hand just a bit longer than was necessary.

Nice things to say about me? Mitch wondered. After the other night I didn't think she could talk at all.

"J. J. supports all our efforts even though he's not from around these parts," Flora May was saying. She beamed at the doctor, touching his arm with her hand. "He's more a Virgilite than most folks in town. Aren't you, J. J.?"

Dexter ignored her comment. "I'm curious," he said to Mitch. "What brings you to a meeting of the Rebel Daughters?"

"J. J., that almost sounds unfriendly," Flora May said. "Everyone is welcome when we're planning Dixie Day, you know that."

"Well," said Mitch, making a point of looking straight and hard at Dexter's eyes, "I thought when I saw the notice in the paper that it might be interesting to get to meet some other people in Virgil. Who knows? I'm doing research on a book, and you never can tell when someone might have something interesting lying around her attic that would be of help. Besides," he said, smiling toward the mayor's wife, "it said refreshments would be served."

Flora May giggled. She was behaving, Mitch thought, just like an adolescent girl. This wasn't the same woman I sat down to dinner with. "The refreshments come afterwards," she said, "after we get parched from all our chattering. Come on, you two, I've got to get this meeting going or we'll be at it all night."

Purposely avoiding Dexter, Mitch took a seat on a settee next to the pharmacist's wife, to whom he had been introduced earlier. Her hair had been washed in a blue rinse and carefully combed and lacquered. Her nails were, to Mitch's taste, overly long, painted a red that matched her lipstick. She smelled of perfume—not a cheap one, Mitch knew, but a case of using too much of a good thing.

While everybody sat, Flora May stood, clipboard in hand, reciting a list of participants for the Dixie Day parade. "The trouble this year is that our float just can't be used. It got so soaked last year that all the decorations liked to die. So that's number one on our agenda tonight, what to do about it."

As she continued, Mitch studied the people sitting around the living room, decent-looking people really, he acknowledged, gathered together to keep up a town tradition, to see that the celebration was done properly, and to ensure that it would be something everyone would be proud of, a celebration that the children would remember and continue, too. One of the men raised his hand to interrupt Flora May. "The school's got a new flatbed truck for toting around benches for the football games. Maybe we can get to borrow it and dress it up some." That remark started a debate on the merits of asking anything of the school principal, who was at loggerheads with the school board over a sex education course he wanted to introduce in the grammar school.

Across the room from Mitch, Dexter sat alone, his legs crossed, hand to his chin. Watching, Mitch saw that the doctor's eyes followed Flora May Bulloch continously, never wavering, though to tell from his face, what she was saying bored him. For goodness sake, Mitch said to himself, he's got a crush on her. And she? Maybe that's the reason for all that giggling. Hell, if it's that obvious to me—and Val says I'm oblivious unless I'm hit over the head—then how come no one else seems to have noticed? Or have they, and it's an accepted relationship? I wonder if the mayor has picked up the vibes. Where is he, by the way?

No sooner had Mitch speculated on Everett Bulloch's where-abouts than the mayor strode into the room, brandishing a cigar in one hand and waving a hello with the other, looking a bit harried. "Please, please, go on folks. I'm sorry I'm so late but Tad Walter refused to repair the road paver unless I—" The mayor stopped mid-sentence when he spotted Mitch. "Well, well, you really did come." He walked up to Mitch and extended his hand, saying over his shoulder, "Go on, Flora May, I'll get out of the way by the piano." He locked eyes with Mitch, then smiled and moved away.

The refreshments arrived an hour later, after Flora May signalled the end of the meeting with a "Well, that should do it, kind people, unless it rains again. I want to thank you-all for coming, and we'll all be proud, I'm sure, that this year's parade will be remembered forever. Now, don't go away. Juju has some special treats for you."

Mitch chose a piece of chocolate cake and a glass of punch rather than something stiffer. Standing around, making small talk with two aged twin spinsters, he saw out of the corner of his eye that Bulloch and Dexter were talking to each other by the ornate fireplace. Not conspiratorial, but not friendly either. There was a stiffness about the way they carried themselves. I wouldn't be surprised, Mitch thought, if the mayor didn't suspect something was going on between his wife and the doctor.

"I hope we didn't bore you." Flora May's interruption sent the spinsters scurrying away. "Dixie Day is an important holiday for us Southerners."

"Not at all," Mitch replied, looking around for a place to put his cake plate down.

"Here, let me take that," she said.

Mitch handed her his plate. "You said the doctor wasn't from Virgil. You aren't either, are you?"

"No, I'm not. I'm from New Orleans," the mayor's wife said. She watched Juju put a dish of cookies on the coffee table, then turned back to Mitch. "Rhett and I met when we were at LSU in Baton Rouge. I'm a delta girl."

"New Orleans is a bustling city."

"You mean, how do I stand it here in dear old Virgil?" Dexter was walking out of the living room, heading for the coat rack. Flora May's eyes were following him. "I get by, I do. There are lots of things to keep me interested here."

Funny, Mitch thought. Dear old Dr. J. J. didn't bother to thank his hostess before leaving.

"Will we be seeing more of you-all?" Flora May asked.

"I don't know," Mitch said. "I'm flying back to New York to-morrow. I have a lot of catching up to do on the book research. But I wouldn't be surprised if I had to return here."

Flora May forced a smile. "I'm delighted you-all are even considering coming back. Rhett will be, too, I'm sure. We don't get many visitors here. Do plan on seeing us again."

At dinner she had been polite but cold and uncommunicative. Tonight she had been not only friendly but warm. What a turnabout. I wonder why, Mitch thought as he made his way to his car. I wonder why.

EIGHT

$\mathbf{M}$ITCH RANGED THROUGH the apartment, turning on a light in each room and opening the windows in an attempt to bring life into the empty home. Without Val's presence, the apartment felt deserted. Every sound seemed to echo in the vacuum. Even with the windows open, the noises from the street below—a car horn, the blare of a ghetto box, the scream of a passing fire engine—seemed remote. Val had left a note taped to the front hall mirror—a terse note, mostly instructions for Mitch to pass on to their housekeeper, who came in two days a week to clean the apartment, and then a curt "Take care of yourself. Love, V." No "I'll miss you," or the funny little face with an arrow through it that she would ordinarily draw at the end of a message to him. Her anger seemed palpably present in the room.

He stood now, arms crossed, eyeing the cartons piled atop one another in the foyer. Where to start? They contained all the notes, photocopies, photostats, documents, and books that Tom Cantwell had amassed for the book on Thomas Clay Washburn. Mitch had carted them up from the Cantwell's home in Brunswick, using a hand truck borrowed from the superintendent to get them from his car into the apartment. He and Abigail had labeled each box to make it easy for him to locate the material.

I can always catch up on the general Civil War stuff, Mitch thought. I'll save that for last. What I should go after is the biographical material on Washburn himself, delve into that, try to figure out what led Tom to Martha Tour Gale. I'll never be able to convince anyone that her death, and maybe Tom's, too, were not natural, unless I can come up with a motive, something they shared, some bit of information that she passed on to Tom.

Mitch hefted a carton labeled "Washburn" and lugged it into his study. He placed it on the floor and opened it, transferring the papers inside to his desk. By the time the box was empty, he had two tall piles stacked on the desk. He walked around to his chair, sat, heaved a sigh, reached for the top paper of the left-hand pile, and began to read.

The Washburns were of Scotch-Irish descent—part of that same band of pioneers that Jimmy Deal had spoken of. They had originally settled in the Carolinas in the latter part of the eighteenth century. Then, as the family multiplied and became too large to support on its land, several of the sons migrated southward, one eventually settling in Georgia, two others moving farther westward until they reached the northern section of Louisiana. The Washburns of Virgil were the descendants of one of these first Washburns, Dr. Hamish Washburn. Photocopies of the Bulloch Parish land records showed that he, or his wife, had acquired several different parcels of land in the 1840s, not all of them contiguous, near his initial plot. One was purchased from the family of a veteran of the War of 1812 who had been awarded the property as a bonus for his service. Other records showed that every once in a while Hamish Washburn sold off a piece, too. In the margin of one such sale, in 1849, Tom had written, "To pay taxes? See parish tax roll for 1848."

Mitch took another handful of documents from the first pile. The first was a photostat of the inside cover page of the family Bible. Different hands, different pens, and different inks had recorded the births, marriages, and deaths of Hamish

Washburn's family, dating from his marriage in 1835. Several of his children had died in infancy, not an unusual occurence then. Thomas Clay Washburn, his oldest surviving son, had been born in 1837. Tom's scrawl appeared again farther down the page with arrows pointing to two of the doctor's daughters: they had been married to the same man. Tom had left a series of question marks beside their names. Mitch studied the names— Suzanna and Caroline Washburn—and the dates next to each. Suzanna had two children by her marriage to Hyder Harrington before dying in 1859; her sister Caroline then married Harrington in 1860 and bore three children by him. "Aha," Mitch said aloud. A not unfamiliar happenstance: the younger sister—Caroline was two years the junior—probably took over the care of Suzanna's two children when Suzanna died, and the inevitable took place. Harrington either fell in love with her or decided to make a convenient situation permanent.

The next photocopy was stamped on its back with the seal of the National Archives in Washington, D.C., and bore, written in pencil, the file in which it had been found—the citation that would be necessary for a footnote: RG 94, AGO, Military Academy application (RG—Record Group, AGO—Adjutant General's Office). The document was a copy of Hamish Washburn's petition to have his son, Thomas Clay Washburn, attend West Point. It was addressed to "Mr. Franklin Pierce, President of the United States" and endorsed on the back by Representative Roland Jones, who had written: "The within applicant is a permanent resident of the Parish of Bulloch in the 5th Cong Dist of Louisiana & I hereby recommend him for the appointment of cadet."

Mitch turned on the desk lamp as dusk began to darken the study, glancing as he did so at the photograph of Thomas Clay Washburn against it. Sifting through the records, reading them, and trying to figure out Tom's marginal remarks had taken the good part of four hours, and Mitch hadn't even tackled the second stack of documents. He pushed back his eyeglasses and rubbed his eyes. The material was interesting but only provided the details for what he already knew in general. Nothing out of the ordinary so far.

Mitch rose from his chair, stretched, and sighed again. "Break time," he said aloud and started to move around his desk to go to the kitchen when his hand bumped into the second stack of documents, and most of them fell to the floor. "Damn it all." Mitch crouched down and started to pick up the papers when one of them caught his eye. It was a photostat from the National Archives of the census taken in Bulloch Parish in 1840. He recalled seeing it the day he had visited Abigail Cantwell after hearing of Tom's death. He had spoken to Jimmy Deal about it in Virgil, commenting on the way the Washburn name had been misspelled. Studying it now, Mitch realized that the census taker had also listed the slaves the Washburns owned— 23, most of them adults who helped to farm the arable part of the sizeable (for upstate Louisiana) 3,000 acres that Hamish Washburn owned. The names of the slaves and their ages were given also: Price, 48; Prince, 47; Mary, 39; Samuel, 32; Beulah, 29; Moses, 27; Lisalee, 19; Hannah, 3; Eliza, 2; Benjamin, 1; and so forth. First names only. Slaves were not accorded family names. Mitch hadn't noticed it before; there was a circle around Benjamin's name and a line under Eliza's name. Tom's pen must have been running out of ink because the lines could only be seen when the light hit them in a certain way. Now why, of all the names on the census, had Tom chosen to pick out the names of two youngsters, Benjamin and Eliza?

Mitch rose with the census record in his hand. He opened a side drawer in his desk and pulled out an empty file folder. He put the census record in the folder, then labeled it "Benjamin/ Eliza." It was the first unusual thing he had come across. He would have to check out what Tom meant by his marks.

The next afternoon when Mitch had almost completed going through the second stack of records, he found a clue. In a four-page monograph privately published in 1914, "The Washburn Family Over the Years," written by Caroline Harrington when she must have been well into her 70s, Mitch read that a slave named Benjamin accompanied Thomas Clay Washburn, his childhood playmate, when the young officer went off to New Orleans to enlist in the Louisiana Infantry in May, 1861, shortly after the firing on Fort Sumter. The slave must have been the same Benjamin that the census of 1840 had listed, Mitch reasoned. The Benjamin who was one year old in 1840 would have been 22 or 23 by the time of the war. And in the early 1920s, when he was in his 80s, Martha Tour Gale must have interviewed him. But Benjamin who? Had he taken the name of his former owner, as so many former slaves did? Benjamin Washburn?

Mitch brought another carton into his study and unloaded it on his desk, again creating two stacks of documents but this time, just to break the monotony of routine, starting with the right stack rather than the left. The box was also labeled "Washburn" and contained additional material related to the family, including an old map of Bulloch Parish on which the various Washburn parcels were drawn. The map was undated, but from what Mitch now understood of the family's history, it must have been drawn up shortly before the Civil War, when the Washburn holdings were quite extensive. During and after the war, Hamish Washburn had been forced to slowly sell off portions of his property to meet expenses. In fact, a series of accounts that was underneath the map bore that out. Cotton had been the main money crop of the Washburn holdings, but with Thomas Clay and his younger brothers—Jeffrey and William Nestor—off to war, there were too few men to keep the farm fully working. Anyway, though never occupied by federal troops, Bulloch Parish had become virtually cut off from its usual commercial arteries by Union blockades. What cotton the farmers grew could not be shipped. Sales slips bore this out; the number of bales they sold fell precipitously after 1861.

Even before the war, Hamish Washburn, Mitch discovered on a page from a ledger dated 1859, had been forced to sell some property because of a loan he could not meet. "Storm" was written in what Mitch had come to recognize as Hamish's hand along with the notation: "Repaid Truman Moore—in lieu of $1250—ten acres bottomland, north field, and one slave worth $500." But which slave, Mitch wondered.

Mitch rummaged through the file folders on the couch until he found the one marked "Census." There were now three photostats in the folder, copies of the census records for 1840, 1850 and 1860. Mitch cross-checked the names of the slaves credited to Hamish. Only two failed to show up after 1840: a John, aged 62 in 1840, did not appear in 1850. Dead? Probably, Mitch thought. And Eliza. She had been only two years old in 1840, twelve, of course, in 1850—there was her name—but there was no mention of her in the 1860 census. She would have been 22 then, a year younger when and if she were the slave Hamish Washburn had given to Moore as partial payment on his debt. What a way to do business, Mitch said to himself. But why, he reminded himself, did Tom make a point of picking out her name if she had left the Washburns? And what could have happened to her after 1859? Was there a reason to track her down?

Mitch stared at the photograph of Thomas Clay Washburn propped up against his desk lamp, trying to imagine a connection between a Confederate officer and Tom Cantwell's death. He leaned back in his chair, his hands cupped behind his head, his eyes closed. Where do I go next? Tom had exhausted the possibilities at the National Archives. At West Point, too, to judge by everything Mitch saw while packing the carton containing Washburn's record at the academy. The young lieutenant's career after school had been typical and without incident—postings at forts in the West—until, having served his tour, he resigned from the army and returned to Louisiana to help his father with the farm. The family might be able to supply more information about Washburn, letters and such, but Mitch hadn't found any mention of them at all, nothing beyond the photograph he was looking at now. That was strange.

Tom had traced the family, had found a descendant. The photograph was proof of that. Tom would surely have kept a name and address, but so far Mitch had found no reference.

Looking at these old documents, Mitch understood the excitement that Tom must have experienced in researching the various phases of Thomas Clay Washburn's life and background. Piecing together the data fascinated him, too. Was it some sort of psychic connection for Tom—their names being the same, Tom and Thomas? That was farfetched, Mitch realized, and irrelevant.

Tom . . . Abigail. Mitch realized he had promised to let Abigail know whether he would do the book after going through all the research. On the phone with Val, he had committed himself, or so he thought. But now, he was nagged by doubts. Mitch was not sure he had the patience to bury himself in countless files and records, looking for an unknown key that might be eternally elusive. He had to decide whether he was willing to put the time and energy into the book, even if the answer to Tom's death would always be tantalizingly out of reach.

Even as he was pondering his decision, Mitch knew he was not ready to let go yet. He would phone Abigail, leave himself an out, but at least see how she was doing. When he left her in Brunswick last week, she had seemed terribly drawn and worn out.

"Are you all right, Abigail?"

"Why, yes, Mitch, I'm doing fine."

"I was worried after the other day," Mitch said. "You seemed all—I don't know—drawn out."

"Oh, that passed, really it did," she said. "I'm not as young as you are, you know. Now you tell me what you're up to."

Mitch hesitated. "Well," he began, "to be honest, I'm at an impasse."

"Won't you do the book, Mitch?" Disappointment crept into her voice. "Isn't it possible?"

"I'm not sure yet. I've hit a roadblock."

"What do you mean?"

"I need to trace Washburn's descendants, and I can't find hide nor hair of them in Tom's papers. Tom traced the Washburn family downstate and got hold of that photograph from them. But I can't find any reference to them in the records I took from you—no address or phone number. Could I have missed something?"

"No, no, I don't think so." Abigail paused. "Hold on now. I got a package of Tom's effects in the mail from that sheriff. I haven't had the stamina to open it yet. It's mostly clothing and toilet articles, he told me—oh, yes, and some papers. Hold on. I'll get it and see if anything is there. I imagine Tom would have carried the name and address on him if he was going back to Louisiana—you know, just in case he had to contact them for any reason."

Mitch waited patiently for Abigail to return to the phone, doodling on the pad of paper he had ready to copy down the information.

"Mitch, you there?"

"Yes, go ahead, Abigail. Did you find anything?"

"Oh, Mitch, I don't enjoy doing this."

"I'm sorry, Abigail. If you'd like, I'll call back some other time." In truth, Mitch hoped she wouldn't take him up on the offer.

"No, it'll be all right. Now or later, I'll have to do it some time. Just bear with me while I open the package."

Mitch could hear her unwrapping the bundle. After a while, she came back on the phone. "No, Mitch, nothing that I can find—no address book or anything like that."

"How about a post office registration receipt, or an insurance one? I can't get the post office in Virgil to do anything about looking for a package of materials Tom might have sent on to you unless I have a number to give them."

"There's nothing like that at all, Mitch. I'm going through the items now and I don't see anything like that."

"Call out to me what you find, Abigail. It might be of help."

"If you insist, Mitch, but I'm not enjoying this." There was a pause on the other end of the phone. "Well, here goes. Three wash-and-wear shirts, three pairs of underwear and socks, two ties, several hankies, his shaving kit—you want me to tell you everything that's in it?"

"No, just see that everything that ought to be in it is there."

"All right, I'll open it and check." There was another pause. "It looks like it's all here, Mitch, his shaving cream and cologne, the syringes and insulin he carried—you know he had diabetes?"

"Yes," said Mitch, grimacing as he remembered the needle marks on Tom's body. "Anything missing?"

"No, not that I can tell."

"What about the papers? What are they?"

"They're in a folder. Wait a minute." Mitch's eyes searched the ceiling as he waited for Abigail to continue. "Just some hand-written notes and a few photostats of maps."

"What do the notes say?"

"They're from a book on Louisiana history. It looks to me like quotations about what the countryside looked like in the nineteenth century."

"And the photostats?"

"War maps—battle maps, I think—and one of New Orleans."

"New Orleans? I wonder why New Orleans? Is there any indication in the margin or on the map, any note attached to that map?"

"No, Mitch, it's just a map of the city as far as I can make out. It's dated 1860."

Mitch shrugged. Often, when doing research on a newspaper story, he had picked up bits and pieces of information and made copies of anything he came across, just on the off-chance that it might be of use later on. Tom must have been conducting the same sweep, knowing that he probably would not be returning to Louisiana again.

"Oh, here's that clipping," Abigail said suddenly. "It was caught in the bottom of the folder." She hesitated. "That's funny," she added.

"What is it?"

"Well, Tom got the idea of how to trace the fellow's family from a story in the *Times*, a story that ran several years ago and he'd clipped. He was always clipping stories about history and slipping them into the books on his shelves. The story that gave him the clue is here, but you'd think he would have kept it together with the name and address of the family."

"Do you mind reading it to me, Abigail? Maybe I'll be able to retrace what Tom did."

"Of course. Here goes. Got a pencil?"

"Shoot."

"It's from the Thursday, July 29, 1982 edition. I'll read it slowly, and you stop me if you need something repeated."

REBEL DAUGHTERS RECALL CONFEDERACY

BATON ROUGE, LA, July 28 (AP)—As a child, she shook the bushes to chase out squirrels so that her father could shoot them. That's one of the few childhood memories Lillian Robberson has of her father, Josh Taylor Steele, because he died when she was very young.

But Mrs. Robberson has a special sense of history when she thinks about him, because he fought in the American Civil War. And she says her mother, Minnie Doscia Steele, still talks about life with the Louisianian who rode off to fight Yankees one warm May morning in 1862.

Mrs. Robberson is 83 years old and her mother, at 103, is one of only three surviving widows of Confederate soldiers in Louisiana still receiving monthly pensions from the state. The others are Kate Nelms, 83, and Bessie Winstead, 94.

"I was just a child when he died in 1914, so I barely

remember him," Mrs. Robberson says. "I do remember that gray hair of his."

Her mother was 15 years old when she married the 60-year-old Mr. Steele in 1903. It was his second marriage, coming several years after his first wife was buried on his farm.

Unlike Mrs. Robberson, Nell Green said that she grew up with her Civil War father, James J. Nelms.

"My father died in 1942 at the age of 93, but he lived to see my oldest child born," the 66-year-old Mrs. Green said. She explained that her mother was only 18 and her father 68 when they were married.

Records at the state Department of Archives and History show that Mr. Steele was assigned to Company G of the First Louisiana Infantry and was paid $88 for serving from November 1862 until June 30, 1863.

Robert Walters, historian with the department, said records show that in 1970 Louisiana had 450 widows of Civil War soldiers but by 1977 the number had fallen to eight.

Widows of Confederate soldiers receive $140 a month from the state.

Abigail's voice was a little hoarse by the time she finished reading the story. "Got it all, Mitch?"

"I think so."

"What do you suppose it meant to Tom? Do you think that one of those women is related to the Washburns?"

"I don't know, I really don't," Mitch said, "but it does give me a lead to find out where: the Louisiana Department of Archives and History. Personally, I'd bet that that's where Tom went next. If they keep records on widows of Confederate soldiers, it's quite possible they would have something on a Washburn descendant."

Abigail coughed lightly. "Whew, I have to get a drink, Mitch. I'll put the clipping into the mail for you just so you have all the names correct."

"Thanks, Abigail. I appreciate it. I think I know what to do now."

TWO TELEPHONE CALLS to Baton Rouge later, Mitch sat back, satisfied that he was on the right track, yet, at the same time, deeply troubled. Robert Walters at the Louisiana Department of Archives and History had been cooperative and helpful—a pleasing surprise considering that Mitch was a stranger on the phone and a Yankee at that, thought Mitch, though, true enough, Mitch had pulled a bit of rank and identified himself as a professor.

Yes, Walters had remembered being contacted by Mr. Cantwell, through the mail at first, then by phone in response to his answering letter. Yes, there was a descendant of the Washburn family in Louisiana, in Carmineville, but the last name was not Washburn. If Mitch could call back in 15 minutes, he'd have all the files out and could tell him everything there was to know, everything he had told Mr. Cantwell. Martha Tour Gale? Yes, that name was familiar also, very much so. Miss Gale, recalled Walters, had also written him, oh, several years or so ago, a barely legible letter explaining that she had lost her notes on Thomas Clay Washburn and could he please send her photocopies of the file. The letter was in the Washburn file. He had told Mr. Cantwell about her because it seemed so unusual to have two people inquiring after the same family for the same reason. Had he done the wrong thing? Was that unethical? Walters hadn't thought about it from that point of view before, only just now. He had been trying to help out both people. And now, believe it or not, here was a third person trying to trace the same family.

"I'm sorry to say, Mr. Walters, but both Mr. Cantwell and Miss Gale are dead," Mitch said. "They died within days of each other a short time ago. That's why I'm calling you. They did meet and speak, and I've been trying to find out what Miss

Gale told Mr. Cantwell so I can finish his book for him."

"Within days of each other?" Walters was astonished. "I've never in all my born days heard of anything so curious."

"That's one of the reasons I want to find out what they both knew. But can I ask a favor of you, Mr. Walters?"

"Well, I guess so. It depends. Nothing illegal—I'm a state employee."

"No, no, nothing illegal. But I'd appreciate if you didn't tell anyone about my inquiries."

"May I ask why, Professor Stevens?"

"Let me put it this way, Mr. Walters. I haven't an explanation why yet, but I don't think those two deaths were coincidental."

"Oh, my!" was all Walters could muster in response.

"Mr. Walters? Can I have your word on that?"

"Oh, my, oh, my."

"What is it, Mr. Walters?"

"I just remembered. What you said reminded me. My assistant got an inquiry about the Washburn file, too, while I was at an archival convention two weeks ago."

"From whom? Did he get a name?"

"She. My assistant's a woman, a young graduate student. She told me about it because I'd asked her to draw out the file for me to copy for Mr. Cantwell."

"Can you ask her whom she spoke to?"

"It's too late. She's in Europe, on a fellowship. And I can't remember whether she said it was a man or a woman. One thing, though, come to think of it. Whoever it was, my assistant said that he—or she—seemed more interested in what Mr. Cantwell had learned from us than anything else. They never asked for a set of records—I mean copies like Mr. Cantwell got. That seemed peculiar, leastways odd enough that Lana told me about it when I got back. What's going on here, Professor Stevens? Can you tell me what's going on?"

MITCH THREW THE covers off and turned over, punching the pillow back into shape as he did so. His eyes were closed, but he felt wide awake. He couldn't get comfortable. He kicked out his foot, turned over again, repositioned the pillow. He sensed he was on to something, was eager to return to Louisiana, was so excited that he couldn't calm down and sleep. He finally opened his eyes and reached toward the sideboard for the remote control tuner for the television set. He pushed the on button and winced as the set started to glow with light. He pressed the forward button, going from one channel to another, not knowing what kind of program he wanted to watch—an old movie, a talk show, MTV. He kept on switching stations. A Laurel and Hardy one-reeler looked appealing. The two comedians were dressed in overalls and trying to raise a ladder against the side of a house. Hardy was having trouble getting up the ladder, and Laurel was pushing him from behind. The silent film was accompanied by a jaunty piano score.

What was that noise? Mitch cocked his head. It sounded like the front door closing. Hardy was on top of the ladder now, balanced unsteadily against the side of the building. A pretty young girl passed by, causing Laurel to take his hands off the ladder to tip his hat and wave discreetly at her. The ladder started to sway, Hardy flailing his arms, losing his balance, and starting to fall.

There, he heard it again. A noise. In the apartment. And off in the distance, down the long hallway where his office was beside the front door, a light had been turned on. Now the light went off. Mitch quickly got out of the bed, his feet finding his slippers in the dark. He stepped to the door, then stopped abruptly. Someone was coming down the hall. His heart began to race.

"Mitch?" A whisper. "Mitch?"

Mitch took a deep breath. "Val? Is that you?"

"Mitch, are you awake? I was afraid I'd wake you."

Mitch reached out and hugged his wife. His heart was still pounding. "You gave me a scare."

"I heard some music from the bedroom, but I wasn't sure you were still up."

"I'm not complaining, dear, but what the hell are you doing home?"

The two moved into the bedroom. "The director came down with a virus or flu or something," Val explained as Mitch turned on the lamp on a bedside table. "We're about to do a critical scene and he refuses to let his a.d. handle it for him. So we got a couple of days off, and I didn't know what to do, except I miss you so much that, what the hell, I figured the expense of flying home was worth it."

Mitch sat on the bed watching Val undress. "I'm glad you did. I've so much to tell you." She had slithered out of her dress and was trying to unhook her bra. Mitch suddenly felt his throat go dry. "Here, let me do it." Val came around the bed and stood with her back to him. He stood up and undid the hook and reached around her to hold her breasts. Val leaned her head back toward him. He kissed her shoulder. "I don't think we've ever made love during a Laurel and Hardy movie," he said. "Let's try," she said, "but don't laugh . . . promise." Mitch snickered and kissed her shoulder again and inhaled the odor of her body. Of all the senses, for Mitch, the sense of smell was the most provocative. She turned to him and smiled. "Oh, my, Mr. Stevens, I can see that long trip was definitely worth it." On the television set, Hardy bent over to pick up a piece of wood and Laurel accidently swatted him from behind with a long board.

"I HAVE TO go back to Louisiana first, Val, I really do." She looked around his study, dismayed at the mess he had made. All the research cartons were now opened, the rows of file folders sitting against the back of the sofa-bed filled with their contents. The entire room seemed about to burst. It had taken Mitch almost a week to read and sort out the material, and now, with the name of Washburn's descendant in hand, thanks to the archivist from Baton Rouge, Mitch was eager to follow Tom's lead. "I'm on to something, Val. I just spoke to Abigail and told her that I will definitely do the book if my trip down there is a success. I'd hate to disappoint her. I figure maybe a week more down there, to touch base with the Washburn descendant and to drop into Virgil again."

Mitch had been doing all the talking because Val was strangely silent. "Mitch, you're full of it, and you know it. One minute you're doing the book, the next you're not sure. There's more at play here than just finishing Tom's book. I can sense it. Mitch, be honest. You know I can't stand it when you try to protect me."

Mitch looked at Val and felt ashamed. They had always been honest with one another. "Forgive me, Val, but I'm damn sure Tom was murdered, and I can't let that go. I just can't. Please understand."

Val turned away for a moment. When she finally spoke, her voice was cool. "And what about the July Fourth weekend, Mitch?" she finally said. "You remember your promise to me about that? Your family"—she was being sarcastic now—"was going to get together that weekend just to see whether we're all still alive."

"I haven't forgotten, honey. I spoke to Ken already, and he said he thought he could arrange to get away and meet us out your way on the Coast. We'll be able to have time together for sure."

"For sure?" Val sounded skeptical.

"For certain."

"You're not putting me on, Mitchell Stevens?"

"Honest, Val, love."

There was a tense silence. Then Val came over, kissed him gently, and said, "Mitch, be careful."

MAYBE, MITCH THOUGHT later as he was packing for his flight back to Louisiana, maybe it was another of those coincidences that Tom, Martha Tour Gale, and some third person had inquired about the Washburn family. Coincidences happen enough in real life. You read *War and Peace*, for instance, and you think how impossible it is for lives to crisscross each other like that years later, but they can. Mitch recalled the time his son Ken brought home a friend from grade school. The boy's name was Ken, too. It turned out he was the grandson of the childhood playmate of Val's father when he lived in England, before he came to the United States. That their two grandsons bore the same name and were classmates had amazed Mitch and Val, and now when coincidences occurred they were often not surprised. So maybe this was just another coincidence. A meaningless happenstance. Someone else, perhaps a graduate history student like Walter's assistant, had been looking for a theme for a master's thesis, for a Confederate hero.

I hope that's the case, Mitch said to himself, but the truth is, I don't think so.

NINE

T HE PLANE WAS descending slowly, banking gently over Lake Pontchartrain. Glints of sunlight made Mitch's eyes blink before the plane finally straightened out for the landing. Mitch gazed out the window by his seat as the tops of houses and trees began to loom closer, the plane and the ground coming together in a sudden rush. The wheels touched the tarmac, sending a slight shudder through the aircraft, the engines immediately beginning to screech as the craft braked. New Orleans Airport.

The rental car sat in the parking lot behind the terminal. Mitch got in. He studied the dashboard, trying to sort out the headlight switch from the windshield wiper lever. The digital clock read an hour later but he couldn't figure out how to reset it. Starting up, Mitch set the mileage indicator to zero. Carmineville, the rental agent had told him, was about thirty miles to the west. He wouldn't have to drive into New Orleans proper at all.

The land was low-lying, surrounded, it seemed to Mitch, by brackish water on all sides. The Mississippi delta. The vegetation was lush, the air heavy. This was the Louisiana most people thought of. The Pelican State. Creole and Cajun. Bayou country. A sharp contrast to Virgil upstate.

Carmineville was actually 32 miles from the airport, a neat, unpretentious community. Mitch had said he'd arrive about noon and was annoyed with himself when he saw that the clock said a quarter to one, until he remembered that it was an hour off. The directions he'd been given were simple: a right turn off Oleander at Cypress Boulevard, three houses down on the left, a white clapboard. The street—boulevard was a misnomer—consisted of modest homes. Middle class, a working man's neighborhood. Carports instead of garages. Mitch pulled in at the third house. There was no sidewalk, but a cement path led up to the front door.

Marguerite LaSable was a plain-looking but not unattractive woman, wearing, Mitch surmised, her best dress. Her hair was coiffed, her smile inviting. Fiftyish, he guessed. Her greeting was warm and gracious. Mitch was shown into the parlor where a tray with cups and a cake—a traditional French-Acadian cake he later learned was called a *gâteau de sirop*—rested on a coffee table. The furniture was covered in chintz, and the curtains were made of the same material. An upright piano sat against one wall, a fringed shawl draped over its top. The few paintings on the walls were reproductions and lacked vitality, but the overall effect was one of coziness and comfort.

"I'm the last of the line," Mrs. LaSable was saying as she poured Mitch a second cup of chicory-laced coffee. "On the father's side. A Washburn, but a dying breed. Herbert and I have no children." She said the last matter-of-factly, with no regrets, accustomed it seemed to reciting that bit of data and putting the anguish, if there was any, behind her. "My mother kept all the family heirlooms and I inherited them."

The old album Tom Cantwell had viewed lay on the sofa next to Mitch. Mitch had already been through it, seen the old, blurred photo of Hiram Washburn, undoubtedly a copy of a copy that made it difficult to distinguish his features clearly. But the photos of his sons and daughters were sharp. All had been posed stiffly by the photographer, probably a roaming one with his own dark-room in a covered wagon. There were portraits of Jeffrey and William Nestor—neither men had returned from the Civil War—Hyder Harrington, sitting alone with his elbow on a round side table, and portrait shots of his two wives, Suzanna and Caroline. The Washburn sisters almost looked like twins. Perhaps Harrington had seen the resemblance, too, when he married the second after the first died. There was Hamish's wife also, an undistinguished woman with sad eyes. Mitch wondered if her photograph had been taken after the war. Family legend, he had already learned from studying the notes Tom Cantwell had amassed, said that she always answered the door when someone called, hoping it would be either Jeffrey or William Nestor, both of whom had served with Bob Wheat's Louisiana Tigers. There had been no word about either of them after the Spotsylvania Campaign in Virginia in May of 1864. It was one of the series of bloody battles that Grant initiated as he tried to envelop Lee and move on to Richmond.

Mitch opened the album and took out the photograph of Thomas Clay Washburn that lay loosely between two pages. It was affixed to a cardboard mounting. "And no one really knew who this was?"

Marguerite LaSable shook her head. "Isn't that amazing? We all knew about Thomas Clay Washburn, of course. He was the family hero, but we never put two and two together. The picture was like that in the album when my mother passed it along to me. We all thought it was some relation who had once paid a visit up North and had had his picture taken there."

Thank God you kept it and didn't throw it away, Mitch thought. He turned it over in his hand. On the back was imprinted the name of the studio, "Clarke's Union Photographic Gallery, 643 Broadway corner of Bleecker Street, N.Y." Among the documents Tom Cantwell had photocopied at the National Archives was the pass permitting a photographer and assistant to enter Fort Hamilton to take Washburn's photograph three days before he was hanged. The pass identified them as being from Clarke's studio. Already aware of Thomas Clay Washburn's description from newspaper accounts, Tom had made the connection without hesitation or doubt.

"He had a copy of it made by a camera store here in Carmineville," Mrs. LaSable was saying. "I mean, we had it made for him and mailed it to him. Both sides, so that you can read the studio's name. He paid for them."

"Yes, I've seen them. I have a copy in my attaché case now," Mitch said. "He purposely had both sides taken to verify the identification if anyone questioned it. Was there anything else you recall speaking about with Mr. Cantwell?"

"He asked a lot of questions," Mrs. LaSable said, "but I'm afraid that I didn't know any of the answers."

"Like what? Do you remember any of them?"

"Well, let's see now," she said, pouting her lips. "He ran over the family tree with me to check whether there were any other Washburn descendants that I knew of or had heard about. He asked whether I had any other kind of family papers or memoirs. I gave him—had made for him—copies of what I had, letters and such, and a little kind of booklet that Caroline Washburn had written in her old age. I enjoyed doing it. He was such a nice man, a real gentleman." Mrs. LaSable smiled. "Oh, yes, he was interested in knowing what happened to the Washburn slaves. He asked about one, no two. He asked about them by name, but I'd never heard of them. He said one of them was mentioned in Caroline's book, but I hadn't paid any mind to that."

"His name was Benjamin," Mitch said. "Does that ring any bell?"

"No."

"How about the name Eliza?"

"No. Nothing. I don't see how the family would have kept up with the coloreds after the war. They all left the farm, what there was left of it, and scattered all over. Except for one, an old seamstress. My mother told me she was given the old house to live in when the family finally abandoned the place. To live in until she died, not deeded or anything. I thought Caroline said something about her in her book."

"She did. But that was someone else by the name of Hannah who was in her 70s or more by then."

"Well, that's all I know, Mr. Stevens, all I was able to tell Mr. Cantwell about."

"I appreciate your sharing it all with me also," Mitch said. He handed the album to Mrs. LaSable. "I wish I had photos of my family going back over a hundred years. One generation is about all I can muster."

"Southerners have always taken their heritage seriously," Mrs. LaSable said.

IT LOOKED LIKE another dead end. The irony of it struck him: He had talked to a Washburn descendant, just as Tom had done. For Tom, identifying Thomas Clay Washburn's photograph must have been an exhilarating moment. For Mitch, it appeared to be precipitously close to the end of the line. Seated behind the wheel of the car, Mitch reached over to his attaché case and took out the copy of the photograph that he carried with him. He studied it until his eyes began to lose focus. Look, Mitch, he reasoned with himself, you're here in Louisiana. Use the opportunity to tie up at least one loose end, that business about the female slave whose name Tom had marked—Eliza. Maybe, just maybe, there was something on file in Virgil about the guy who took her. What was his name? True something or other. Truman. Truman Moore. That's it. Tom must have had a reason for singling her out.

"Next stop, Virgil," Mitch said aloud, starting up the car. He decided to drive the more than two hundred miles to Virgil rather than bother with returning the car, waiting for a plane to Shreveport, and then renting another car to get to Virgil. But no sooner was he on the highway than he regretted his decision. It was going to be a long and not very pleasant drive. Dispirited, going through the motions, Mitch drove by rote, feeling, among other things, guilty about having spent the time, energy and money to return to Louisiana when Val was still in New York, waiting for her callback. He could have stayed at home and still be with her. He hoped she understood.

East of Baton Rouge, Mitch stopped for a hamburger and coffee at a diner and bought a bar of pecan candy to have for a snack later in the afternoon. He picked up Interstate 55 and headed north until the junction with Interstate 20, passing over the Mississippi at Vicksburg before reaching Monroe and heading into Bulloch Parish. If he had stayed on Interstate 20, instead of turning off for Virgil, he would have eventually reached Shreveport.

It was nearly dusk when Mitch reached Virgil, driving across the town line from the eastern side this time, where the Caddo Motel stood. Although he was tired, he decided on a whim to drive into the center of town before checking into the motel. As he reached the square, there was still enough light to make out the writing on the long white banner that hung above Main Street from lampposts on either side of the street:

DIXIE DAY—This Sunday, Noon, Reb Park—DIXIE DAY
Come One, Come All
Parade, Picnic, Fireworks in Evening
Citizen-of-the-Year Award

What's today, Friday? The parish clerk's office was open Saturday mornings. He would try to check on Truman Moore then, see Jimmy Deal about him. Then maybe get a chance while he was here to talk to J. J. Dexter about Tom's death, ask whether there was anything unusual from a medical standpoint. Might as well ask. It couldn't hurt. And might as well stay into Sunday and take in the celebration. Hell, he'd have a problem getting a plane out of Shreveport over the weekend anyway.

Mitch circled the town square and headed back toward the Caddo Motel. Damn, he thought, as the vacancy sign blinked at him from the distance, I should have stopped to eat supper somewhere along the highway. He didn't relish the idea of eating again at the Caddo.

LEAVING THE MOTEL the next morning, Mitch saw the cleaning woman coming down the cement walk that girded it outside. She was pushing a cart laden with towels, sheets and rolls of toilet paper. A woman in her mid-40s, she wore a nondescript kerchief over her hair, a common housedress and apron, and a dirty pair of sneakers.

Mitch hailed her. "Do you have a moment, ma'am?"

The woman wore a bored expression as she waited for Mitch to continue.

Mitch explained that he was a friend of Tom Cantwell's and asked whether she was the chambermaid on duty the morning that Tom had been found dead in his motel room.

"It was me who discovered him," she acknowledged.

"And did anything catch your attention, anything out of the ordinary?"

The woman pursed her lips. "Nope," she said finally.

"Nothing?" She shook her head. "Can you describe the room when you entered it?"

"Just like any other room in this here motel, mister. Messy like it always is in the morning. Some people are just pigs."

Mitch winced. "My friend wasn't like that at all. That's why I'm asking."

"Well, he was."

"And the papers that were there, what happened to them?"

"Sheriff got them—them and the clothes and such." She looked at him warily. "I didn't take a thing."

"No, of course not," Mitch said quickly. "I didn't mean to suggest that."

"Look, you got more questions, you speak to Mr. Carter. I just work here." She threw her body at the cart to get it rolling and started off. She mumbled so softly that Mitch wasn't certain what she said.

Mitch checked his watch. It was almost nine o'clock. The punctilious Jimmy Deal would be at the parish clerk's office by the time he got downtown. Mitch got into his car and drove off.

JIMMY DEAL DIDN'T seem either happy or unhappy to see Mitch. He didn't even register surprise. He was assuming a stance of bureaucratic neutrality.

Deal was already at work. There were two ledgers open side by side on his desk. He looked up from them and said, "Mr. Stevens. What can I do for you?"

Mitch explained about the debt Hamish Washburn had owed Truman Moore and how he had paid it off. "Would you have a record of that, and anything at all about Moore?"

"Moore?" Deal scratched his chin. He took pride in remembering all the property owners in the parish, but Moore was obviously a name he hadn't encountered, or didn't recall. So instead of turning over the record of 1859 land transactions to Mitch, he began to pore through it himself, poking at the columns on each page with a finger. "Moore, Moore, Moore." He turned a page, traced down it with his finger, then turned another page, following the same routine. Mitch stood watching by his shoulder, but too far away to make out the entries.

"Aha," Deal said finally. He pointed at the entry. Mitch bent down to study it. "Washburn transferred the acreage to Truman Moore on September 6, 1859. 'Storm' you said was written on the note?" Mitch nodded. "We had a hurricane come through here late that summer. It's in our local history almanac."

"Anything about a slave transfer?"

"No, there wouldn't be," Deal explained. "Just a piece of paper, like that slave deed I gave you. That's all Moore would need to prove ownership, as long as it was notarized."

Deal scratched his chin again. "Funny, I keep track of most things, but the name Moore still doesn't ring a bell. Let me check the next year's ledger. I have a feeling Mr. Moore didn't ever settle in Virgil at all."

Deal searched the 1860 records without success. Looking annoyed now, he got out the next year's ledger and had only begun to peruse it when he called out triumphantly, "Here it is! Just after the first of the year, Moore sold those very same acres to Elroy Stamper—that must be Floyd Stamper's relation. He has a farm out that way, about two hundred acres. Elroy Stamper was probably hoping to expand his cotton crop."

"Anything else about Moore?" Mitch asked. "Was he a local resident?"

"No, according to this, it gives his address as New Orleans."

"New Orleans? That far away? That sounds unusual."

Deal shook his head. "Moore must have been a cotton merchant down there. He probably loaned Washburn money against his next crop, and when the hurricane ruined it Moore called in the debt. That sort of thing happened all the time."

So the slave—Eliza?—would have gone to New Orleans to work for him. "Moore's a pretty common name down there, isn't it?" Mitch asked Deal.

"Not that common then," Deal said. "You find French names mostly in New Orleans. You might be able to trace him, especially if he was a merchant. They had lots of dealings that had to be recorded." Deal began closing the ledger. "Anything else on your mind, Mr. Stevens?"

A YOUNG WOMAN sat at the desk in the reception area of J. J. Dexter's medical office, which occupied the ground floor of a two-story home off Main Street. She couldn't have been more than 19, a pretty girl despite the overdone makeup. She was trying to put an earring back on after putting down the phone. For someone who has to answer the phone frequently, she must have to spend half her time putting the damn thing back on, Mitch thought.

There was an elderly couple sitting in a corner of the waiting room, reading magazines. Otherwise, the office was empty. Mitch asked the receptionist if he could see Dr. Dexter and, in response to her question, no, he did not have an appointment, but he was from out of town and would appreciate a minute of the doctor's time.

"Tell him Mitchell Stevens. I met him at the mayor's home several weeks ago. I'm from New York."

The girl's eyes flickered when he said New York. That impressed her. She took up the phone and buzzed an extension without bothering to take off her earring. She spoke into it, listened to the reply and said to Mitch, "He'll be free in two minutes. He's just bandaging a leg."

Mitch thanked her and sat down across from the elderly couple. The woman looked up at him and then went back to *Reader's Digest*. The man was reading *People*. Within a few minutes a young man came limping out of the doctor's office. The receptionist beckoned to Mitch. "Okay now," she said. That got the elderly couple's attention. They stared at Mitch with open hostility. For a minute he thought one of them was going to raise an objection but instead they both resumed reading.

J. J. Dexter was seated behind his desk, closing a folder and putting it aside as Mitch entered. "There goes our drummer," he said, gesturing with his head toward the door. "He broke his leg sliding into first base yesterday. I've convinced him to get his father to put the drum on the back of a pickup and follow the band."

The Dixie Day parade, the reason for our first meeting that night at the Rebel Daughters get-together. Dexter, Mitch appreciated, was picking up on it.

"I wasn't certain you'd remember me," Mitch said.

"Of course I do," Dexter said, waving Mitch into the seat facing him. "A new face in town makes quite a stir. Tell me, surely you haven't come all the way back from New York to consult me on some ailment, have you?"

"No, not that I wouldn't mind," Mitch said, causing Dexter to smile. "No, actually I'm just tying up some loose ends on the research I'm doing, and I thought I'd drop by and satisfy myself about something."

"And what's that, Mitch?"

"I'm really asking for Tom Cantwell's wife—Abigail Cantwell." Mitch thought a white lie would be less provocative. "She asked me to ask you whether you noticed anything unusual the night that Tom Cantwell died. Anything at all."

"Did she have anything in mind?" said Dexter. "I mean, does she suspect that something else was troubling him, some illness I don't know about?"

"It isn't that, Doctor. I think she's just trying to reconcile in her mind the fact that she wasn't there when it happened and maybe could have prevented it from happening—unless it was something totally unforeseen."

"Well, Mitch, you just reassure her that, one, it was perfectly understandable what happened considering Cantwell's age and medical history, and, two, that she couldn't have done anything to help him had she been here."

"And you found nothing strange at all?"

"Strange? What do you mean?"

"Nothing out of the ordinary?"

"No, I just said so. There was nothing strange or unusual about Cantwell's death."

"How come you knew his medical history?"

"Hey, Mitch, what's going on here? I *know* about his medical history because I learned about it afterward. I was told about it by the sheriff after he spoke to Mrs. Cantwell."

"But you didn't know about it at the time you were called to the Caddo Motel, so why did you decide not to have an autopsy done?"

Dexter rose, straightening his vest as he did so and buttoning the long white physician's coat he wore over it. "I'm also the parish medical examiner. I would have conducted the autopsy. I didn't see any need to. I didn't think I would find anything more than what was certainly an untimely but medically logical death.

"And that does it, Mr. Stevens. I'm not going to go through this again. Mrs. Cantwell—and you—will have to be satisfied with the facts as they are. Please, I've got patients waiting outside."

Mitch took the cue and rose to leave. He decided to take a gamble. "I didn't mean to upset you, Doc," he said.

"What the hell do you mean now?" Dexter was getting red in the face. "I'm not upset. What the goddamn hell are you after?"

Mitch was heading out of the door. He turned briefly and said, "See you tomorrow at the parade."

Now why, Mitch thought as he walked in the sparkling sunshine toward Main Street, is J. J. Dexter so uptight about Tom's death?

As Mitch headed for his car, the sounds of the local high school band rehearsing filtered faintly across the square from off in the distance. It was a tune he had heard once before, many, many years ago, but he couldn't quite place it.

TEN

THE BAND CAME into sight out of the trees behind left field, the strains of "The Bonnie Blue Flag" reaching ahead of it. A chorus of shouts went up from the spectators gathered in the bleachers astride the first- and third-base lines of the ball field. "Here they come! Here they come!" children called to one another. Rebel war yells erupted from a group of teenagers who had chosen to stand behind the fence in back of home plate.

Preceding the band were two Boy Scouts in uniform, one carrying the American flag, the other the Confederate battle flag. Immediately behind them strode the mayor, dressed, despite the noon-hour heat, in a suit and vest, a broad red, white and blue ribbon slashed diagonally across his chest. He was followed by the twenty-odd members of the Rebel Daughters of the Confederacy, each of the women dressed in a long, antebellum white dress with a red sash. The mayor's wife was in the first row of the women, keeping perfect stride in time to the music. The band itself, however, seemed to straggle along, its members more worried about keeping in tune than keeping in step, much to the consternation of their leader, a high school teacher, dressed, as they all were, in blue trousers, a white shirt and a blue Confederate campaign hat. Bringing up the rear was the bass drummer; he had apparently abjured his father's pickup truck and was being pulled along in a cart by a hefty youngster, his leg propped up beside his drum, which he was beating thunderously.

As the flag bearers reached a small wooden platform draped in bunting that was positioned on the pitcher's mound, they came to a halt and, marking time, waited for the rest of the marchers to catch up and get into position. The band spread out by second base, bringing "The Bonnie Blue Flag" to an unwieldy conclusion. The trumpeters, clarinetists, trombonists and tuba player fussed with their music and then, at the cue given by their leader, struck up "The Star-Spangled Banner."

Mitch was seated in the top row of the stands, crowded in between two families. He rose with the others to stand for the national anthem. As he did so, he saw Augustus Leon step out from the sidelines and point a camera at the color guard. Some of the older spectators were singing along with the band; a few men were standing rigidly at attention and saluting. Mitch shielded his eyes with his right hand and scanned the bleachers, searching for faces he knew. He had passed the sheriff driving into Rebel Park; Bochard had shunted him to a large, almost full parking lot where one of his men pointed him to a narrow space between two cars. Lyda Leon, Mitch saw, was over by third base, with a young child on each hand. Behind her, in the bleachers, Jimmy Deal stood, hand over his heart. Mitch circuited the crowd again but didn't see J. J. Dexter.

The anthem over, everyone sat down, the youngsters next to Mitch pushing and shoving for room, and the mayor stepped up on the platform and engaged in a comic struggle with the microphone stand, pulling it either out too high or pushing it down too low. Finally a young man sprinted up on the platform, whispered something in the mayor's ear and easily got the height just right. A few snickers went through the crowd but were quickly shushed.

"Welcome friends and neighbors to the 95th annual Dixie Day." A round of cheers went up from the teenagers behind home plate. "I want to say hello and welcome also to those of you who have come from all over the parish to join us on our day of celebration." This time the cheers came from a section in the stands in front of Mitch. "But first, the Reverend Father Samuel Lucas of St. James Church in Shreveport will open our festivities with an invocation. Reverend Jackson."

A benign-looking man dressed in black approached the lectern. He stretched his neck above a clerical collar before speaking. "O, Father, which art in Heaven, bless us today and help us to . . ."

His memory was suddenly vivid. The pungent smell in the air made him think of incense. A Sunday morning. His father on his right, his mother on his left. The droning responses in Latin—this was well before the reforms—praying in a language he didn't understand. How could it be a real prayer if you didn't know what you were saying?

My God. Mitch wondered why here, in this unfamiliar small town, so different from where he had grown up, these memories were rushing in, twice in just a few days. It was a rhetorical question. Prayer was just not a part of his daily experience and hadn't been for 20 years. Here it was a way of life, taken for granted, accepted.

". . . and bring us peace, Father. Amen."

Another cheer went up. Bulloch nodded his thanks to the priest as he returned to the lectern. "Our forefathers," the mayor began, "initiated this celebration in commemoration of our good fortune in being spared the horrors of a terrible war. A war that took the lives of many of our sons and threatened the very livelihood of our forefathers. A war that—though it didn't touch us physically—affected each family in our beloved town." Mitch suddenly became aware of how few blacks were in the audience, and how those who were there were standing off to the side by the right field line. "We were fortunate then and we are fortunate now—fortunate because Virgil has remained an oasis of goodwill and spirit in a difficult period of our nation's history."

Mitch wondered what perspective the black families of Virgil would bring to the mayor's remarks. Mitch recalled reading about how the New Orleans City Council had voted unanimously to outlaw discrimination in the carnival clubs that sponsor the city's Mardi Gras parade. It hadn't taken long for the club leaders to respond and to respond in no uncertain terms. They had called the proposal a "tragic mistake" that would kill the carnival. Mitch could well imagine how Flora May Bulloch and the other Daughters of the Confederacy would feel about black participation in the Dixie Day parade. On the other hand, he smiled ruefully, I wonder just how many black citizens of Virgil have any interest in celebrating anything "Dixie."

"I won't bore you with more speech-making," Bulloch continued to an even louder wave of cheers from the teenagers. "You're here to have a good time. However, each year at this time your mayor has the honor of announcing, and introducing to you, Virgil's Man-of-the-Year, our most outstanding citizen, selected by the sponsoring organization—the Rebel Daughters of the Confederacy—and approved by a committee made up of past winners."

Bulloch took a handkerchief from inside his jacket pocket and wiped his forehead free of perspiration. "This year," he continued, "the person selected is not a man." Catcalls from the teenagers. "It is not even a boy." More catcalls. "For the very first time we are honoring one of the fairer sex, a young woman who has devoted herself to our children, to making them intelligent and worthy fellow citizens. If I may read the proclamation inscribed on the award." The mayor put on a pair of horn-rimmed eyeglasses and picked up a bright bronze plaque. "'To Lyda Baker Leon'"—on hearing her name, the crowd burst into applause, many children in the bleachers screaming with delight—"'For outstanding service to the community of Virgil and to the Virgil Elementary School District, we the citizens hereby proclaim her Man-of-the-Year.'" There was a burst of laughter as Bulloch read the last phrase. He flushed and shot his wife a look of annoyance. "'Woman-of-the-Year,' it should say," he amended, leaning back into the microphone. "Lyda, will you step forward, please."

With the two youngsters in tow, Lyda Leon stepped up to the platform amid a warm round of applause. She was flustered but smiling. The mayor held up his arms for silence. "Lyda," he said, turning to her, "no one deserves this more than you." He handed her the plaque and, amid another round of applause, kissed her lightly on the cheek. He then nudged her toward the microphone.

"I want to say thank you," she said slowly, searching for the words, "and also I want to say that I feel that I am accepting this honor on behalf of all the teachers at Virgil Elementary, men and women alike. All of us care very much for your children—our children. Thank you and bless you."

Lyda's husband Augustus was beaming as he photographed his wife taking the plaque from the mayor, speaking to their fellow townspeople, and descending from the platform with the two youngsters in tow again. As she started back to the stands, he let his camera drop to his chest on its straps and tried to hug her, but the camera got in the way and people who were watching the couple began to laugh good-naturedly.

Bulloch, meanwhile, was speaking again. "There are games today for the children and for adults as well, all supervised by our own chapter of the Rebel Daughters of the Confederacy. We'll have the pool open after one o'clock, and the picnic will commence after these ceremonies. I've been asked by Sheriff Bochard to make one announcement: Please exit by the east gate when you leave so that there's no danger of anyone getting hurt by the picnic grounds.

"And now, I'm going to ask all of you to join the band in our traditional singing of 'Dixie.'" The mayor turned to the band leader. "Mr. Hancock, please. We are ready."

The opening bars were weak, but by the time the refrain began the band had hit its stride. Everyone was singing "I wish

I were in the land of cotton . . ." except the few blacks on the sideline, who had already begun to leave the area, and Mitch. His attention had been arrested by the appearance of J. J. Dexter, who had arrived along the path leading to the picnic grounds. The doctor was carrying a black satchel. Perhaps, Mitch thought, one of the volunteers setting up the picnic had taken ill. Dexter seemed preoccupied. He halted by third base but didn't join in the singing.

". . . Look away, look away, look away, Dixieland."

Rebel shouts from all over the stands broke out as the song came to an end. The band did an about-face and regrouped to march off the field, but even before it began to play a Sousa march, the bleachers were being abandoned. The children on Mitch's right were tugging at their parents' sleeves, pleading with them to go to the games area. Those on his left were shouting at their parents that they were hungry. Below, on the ball field, the white dresses of the Rebel Daughters were lost in a flurry of people jostling each other, but Mitch, still in the stands, waiting for the area around him to clear, saw that the Bullochs were standing together at the pitcher's mound. The mayor was berating his wife. Dexter elbowed his way through the crowd to reach them. The mayor turned on him, too. The noise of the crowd drowned out what he was saying, but it was obvious that he was angry. Dexter was defending himself now, his mouth working acrimoniously. The argument ended abruptly when Bulloch's attention was diverted by a man in coveralls and a lumberman's jacket tapping him on the shoulder from behind. It was Ernie, the mayor's foreman. As the two men huddled together, Flora May and Dexter walked away, their heads close together, talking.

Mitch started to step from one row down to another when he saw Augustus Leon waving at him from ground level. "Hold it," the publisher said, raising his camera to his eye. "Give us a smile." Mitch couldn't help smiling at the idea of being front-page news in the *Virgil Whig*. When he looked up again, Ernie was gone and Bulloch was talking to someone else—a familiar face, someone, Mitch racked his brain, that he should know. Someone associated with dirt. No, not dirt. Ink, printer's ink. Lamar. Augustus Leon's assistant at the newspaper. Mitch wondered what he and the mayor had in common. Leon was calling to him now, "Join us for the picnic, Mitch. Lyda's here somewhere. I just have to take some photos of the goings-on and I can catch up with you. In about half an hour."

Mitch acknowledged that he would by nodding and continued to make his way down off the bleachers. Jimmy Deal was walking ahead of him, on his arm an elderly woman whose white hair was tied in a bun in back. His mother or his wife? Mitch wondered. He almost tripped over a toddler who had decided to sit down on the grass and play with his shoelaces. A young couple burst by him, hand in hand, running toward the town swimming pool.

Without thinking where he was going, Mitch allowed the flow of the crowd to carry him to a grassy, treeless meadow surrounding a small pond. On one side, pairs of children were stumbling about in a three-legged race. Others, in singles, were pushing wheelbarrows. On the other side of the pond, a group of grown-ups were huddled around a huge galvanized tub. Curious, Mitch walked over to them.

"Here you go, Mitch." It was the mayor. "Try your hand at this."

The tub was filled almost to the top with water. Bobbing on its surface was a big red apple. An apple ducking.

"The idea is to get your teeth into it and pull it out," Bulloch explained. "No hands allowed.

"Here you go," he went on, beckoning to J. J. Dexter, who was standing on the outer edge, his black satchel on the ground at his side. "Try it with the doc."

Mitch eyed Dexter, who stared back at him unflinchingly. There was no love lost between them, Mitch understood. The doctor took off his coat jacket and draped it over his satchel. He kneeled down on his side of the tub. Following his example, Mitch knelt on his side.

"Hands behind your back, gentlemen," the mayor said. "Get ready. Get set. Go!"

Dexter lunged toward the apple, twisting his head slightly so he could get a grip on it with his teeth. The apple bounced away, toward Mitch, who tried the same maneuver. The apple swerved back to Dexter, water sloshing over the sides of the tub as both men sank their heads into the water. The apple was in the middle now. Mitch and Dexter butted heads, pressing against each other, trying to force the other away from it. The doctor, it seemed to Mitch, was thrusting hard, determinedly. He was making it more of a contest than a game. Dexter suddenly gripped the sides of the tub with his hands, and, bucking his head against Mitch's, pushed Mitch's head deep into the water.

"Hey, no fair," Mitch gasped, pulling himself from the tub, his face all wet and water dripping down onto his shirt.

Dexter was sitting back on his haunches, in his teeth the apple, in his eyes a look of triumph.

Bulloch was grinning. "Don't give up so easy, Mitch. It's just a game."

Dexter was wiping his face with a large red bandanna that someone had handed to him. He put on his jacket, picked up his satchel and walked away without saying anything, the satchel in one hand, the apple in the other.

The mayor tried to persuade Mitch to stay for another game, but Mitch explained that he had promised to meet the Leons at the picnic area. "I've got to go that way myself," Bulloch said. "I'll show you the way. You can come back later and get into another game if you want."

By the time Mitch reached the picnic area, families had already staked out seats on the redwood tables scattered about the grove, and the lines by the food tables were long.

"I'm so glad you came." Mitch turned. It was Flora May Bulloch.

A blue ribbon pinned on her left breast said, "Committee Chairman." "I heard you were back in Virgil," she said, smiling, more composed than Mitch expected after witnessing the little scene on the ball field. "Have we become that important to you?"

"Get along, Flora May," her husband interrupted, his tone firm. "Juju's having a problem with the iced tea. Sorry," he said, turning back to Mitch, "but this isn't the time for her to chatter." The mayor took Mitch by the arm. "Have you tried any of our delicacies yet? Our women can really cook."

Mitch let Bulloch escort him to one of the buffet tables. "Here," he said, going around to the back of it, where three volunteers were busy spooning portions of potato salad, cole slaw, okra salad and snap beans with roux from large white plastic buckets onto serving platters. "I've got certain prerogatives being mayor. What'll you have?"

Mitch was embarrassed at the idea of being served before anyone else in the line that had formed at the end of the table. "I'll wait," he said. "I had a late breakfast. But many thanks, Mayor. I appreciate your hospitality."

Ernie approached the mayor, whispering something in his ear. Seeing that he was distracted, Mitch moved off, circling the picnic area, looking for the Leons.

"Here we are, Mitch." Lyda waved from a table under a tree near the edge of the grounds. The two children she had been holding hands with were seated with her. "I've saved places for you and Augustus," she said as Mitch swung his legs over the bench seat. "And this is Sheri and Julian, two of my brightest pupils. Their father is a policeman and on duty today, and their mother is over there, helping out with the serving."

Mitch offered his congratulations to her. He picked up the bronze plaque from the top of the table and admired it. "Nice going. It's a wonderful honor."

"We're hungry," Sheri, the older of the two children, butted in.

"We're just waiting on Mr. Leon," Lyda said, trying to mollify the youngster. "We'll all eat as soon as he comes."

"Who comes?" said Leon, sitting down next to Mitch and hoisting his camera onto the table. "Lord, what a day. I always dread Dixie Day. Everyone in town expects me to take their picture and publish it. Even my wife." He leaned over and kissed her. "And I thought our dear mayor would drop his pants when he read that Lyda was named 'Man' this year. Would you believe it?"

"I think Bulloch was mad at his wife over that one," Mitch remarked. "I saw him having words with her afterwards."

"Naw, that was something else," said Leon, rewinding the film in his camera. "I only got a smattering of what he was saying as I went by, but it was something else entirely. In fact, I thought I heard him say your name, but I wouldn't swear to it."

Mitch wanted to ask Augustus whether he was sure he had heard his name mentioned, but Julian whined, "I want to eat. I'm hungry."

"I think we'd better," Lyda said to the two men, "or I'm going to have two cannibals on my hands."

They all got up and walked over to one of the buffet tables and got in line, Leon greeting people on the way as he and Mitch approached the long serving tables. Ahead of them, Lyda tried to keep the two children in some semblance of order. They were next in line when J. J. Dexter broke in. "Do you mind? I'm in a rush. I just want to grab a po' boy." The couple behind Mitch, engrossed in conversation, edged back slightly without even looking at the doctor. Mitch had already picked up a plate and was moving along the table, looking at the platters, trying to decide what to take. Dexter moved in next to him. Behind him came Ernie, who elbowed his way by the couple who were still talking intensely.

"Try the crab salad, Mitch," Flora May said. She was standing at the back of the table, a pitcher in each hand. "And those yams over there are especially good, the black-eyed peas, too.

Here let me help you-all." She put down the pitchers and took up a serving spoon.

"Can you pass me one of those loaves of bread there?" Dexter asked.

Mitch reached over with his left hand, his right still holding his plate, trying to keep it level as Flora May served him. He had to wait until Julian in front of him had taken and returned several slices of bread before he could pick one up for himself. He passed a small loaf to Dexter, who began fixing himself a po' boy smeared with mayonnaise and hot mustard and filled with lettuce and slices of ham, cheese, tomatoes and onions. Mitch watched in fascination as Dexter poured a red, undoubtedly spicy, sauce over the concoction. A Creole version of the hero. When he looked down at his own plate, Mitch saw that it was virtually heaped with food. "I'm not sure I can eat all this," he said to Flora May, "though it looks tempting."

"You-all try your best," she said, picking up the pitchers again.

Dexter brushed by with a "Thank you, gentlemen" and left. Next in line, Ernie followed Mitch to the end of the table where the drinks were. Mitch took a cup filled with lemonade and headed back to the picnic table, where the others were already getting settled.

Augustus Leon tore a piece from the slab of bread on his plate and dipped it into thick brown gravy. He brought it to his mouth, looking at Mitch. "Eat hearty," he said.

MITCH TOSSED AND turned in the bed. He had already been up twice with diarrhea. His stomach churned, and when the first bursts of pain came it reminded him, oddly, of the fireworks display at the end of Dixie Day. He was having his own celebration, he mused at first, until the nausea became unbearable and his head seemed to roar.

Mitch groaned. He was sweating profusely. He clutched his hands to his stomach. Sharp pangs of pain shot through him constantly now. He could barely move. "Oh, my God," he gasped. His throat felt like it was on fire. Mitch tried to reach for the switch of the lamp on the night table, but he couldn't pull himself up enough to make it. He took hold of the telephone cord and pulled the instrument toward the bed. It fell heavily on the blanket, knocking the receiver off the hook. He held it close to his ear on the pillow, hoping that someone in the front office of the motel would hear it ringing. He waited a full minute until a gruff voice said, "Yes, what is it? What's going on?" Hollings Carter, the motel owner, wasn't at all pleased to be awakened in the middle of the night.

"A doctor, I need a doctor. Now, please. My stomach—the pain, it's killing me. Get me a doctor. Quickly."

Mitch tossed his head to the other side of the bed in time to throw up on the floor instead of the bedding. The bitter aftertaste lingered in his mouth. He was moaning constantly now, the pain making him bend into a fetal position. He had never experienced such pain before. Time seemed to pass so slowly. I must be dying, he said to himself. Val? Where's Val? Oh, my God. I don't want to die in this place.

There was a knock on the door. Mitch, retching bile, could not answer it. The knock was repeated. When there was no answer again, there was the faint rustle of keys and the door opened. Hollings Carter stood aside and a figure next to him stepped out of the light in the hallway and into the dark room. The door closed.

"Mr. Stevens?" The overhead light turned on, blinding Mitch for a moment. When his eyes cleared he saw a black man standing over him. The man felt his forehead, then took his wrist and pressed two fingers against the vein. "I'm Moses Pemberton, Mr. Stevens. *Doctor* Moses Pemberton. You calm down now. I'm here to help you."

The doctor appeared reserved, stiffly formal almost to the point of aloofness, but Mitch was in too much pain to care. He closed his eyes as the doctor ministered to him, feeling him all over, pressing in against his abdomen, asking Mitch where it hurt. When he stopped, Mitch opened his eyes to see Pemberton move quickly into the bathroom. The doctor returned with a long rubber tube and gently began to insert it into Mitch's mouth, coaxing him to swallow it. Mitch gagged several times but got it down. Squeezing a bulb at the other end, the doctor began to pump out the contents of Mitch's stomach, emptying them into a styrofoam ice bucket that had been on the dresser.

Mitch felt wretched. His entire insides seemed inflamed. He heard the tingle of glass and the water running. Pemberton approached, stirring a glass with a wooden throat swab. "Here," he said, lifting Mitch's head and tilting the glass to his mouth. "This will settle things for a while."

Mitch drank the chalky mixture, stifling the desire to retch again. He lay back on the pillow and looked up at the doctor, who was preparing a syringe, drawing into it a colorless liquid from a vial he had taken from his satchel. "Many thanks." His voice sounded like a rattle. "I appreciate your coming, Dr. Pemberton." Mitch weakly extended his hand to shake Pemberton's. The gesture seemed to take the doctor by surprise. He paused a fraction of a second, then switched the syringe to his left hand and closed his right hand around Mitch's, his reserve disappearing in a broad smile.

"Mr. Stevens, we've got to get some fluid back inside you. Turn over, please." The doctor pulled down the back of Mitch's pajamas, rubbed an area on his buttock with an alcohol-soaked swab, and gently plunged the needle of the syringe into the skin. "This will help some. Can you ask Carter for a cup of weak tea?"

Mitch wondered why the doctor didn't call the motel front desk himself, but before he could ask him the reason, Pemberton had put the receiver into his hand and was pushing the button on the instrument on and off continuously.

"Yes, what is it?" Carter's gruffness was even more pronounced.

"The doctor says I need some tea—weak tea. Can you get it for me, please?"

"The kitchen's closed," Carter said. "We don't open it till seven."

"I know that, but I'd appreciate it if I could just get some hot water and a teabag—"

Pemberton took the phone from Mitch's hand. "Look, Carter, Mr. Stevens is dehydrating. He needs liquids, and he needs them fast."

There was a sullen mumbling on the other end. Pemberton hung up and replaced the phone on the night table. Taking a thermometer from his medical bag, he shook it back and forth several times, then checked the reading. "Open up," he said, poking the thermometer against Mitch's lips. Mitch opened his mouth and let the doctor insert the thermometer under his tongue. Pemberton strode across the room and stooped down beside the mini-bar. Mitch wondered what the doctor was doing, as Pemberton searched the contents of the little refrigerator, then rose and groped about in his right-hand pocket, came out with a fistful of coins, and began to sort and count them. "You have any change?" he asked. Unable to talk because of the thin glass instrument in his mouth, Mitch pointed toward the dresser. The doctor went over to it, found the coins Mitch had tossed there while undressing the night before, and picked up several quarters. "I'll be right back," he said.

Pemberton returned shortly with a can of ginger ale in his hand from the hall vending machine. He opened it and gave it to Mitch. "Here," he said, removing the thermometer from Mitch's mouth, "this is better than nothing until the tea comes along."

Mitch watched the doctor studying the thermometer as he sipped the soda. It felt cold on his stomach, too sweet, the fizz gurgling inside him. "Go on, drink some more," the doctor urged. "We've got to get fluid back into you."

Pemberton sat down on the edge of the bed. "I won't be able to stay long," he said, wrapping the sleeve of a blood-pressure instrument around Mitch's upper arm. "I'm not supposed to be here," he continued, pumping the sleeve up with air. "This is J. J. Dexter's side of town. Carter tried to reach him but couldn't."

"You have the town divided up? What an odd way to practice."

Pemberton wrinkled his brow as he read the gauge. "No, not divided," he said. He started to unwrap the sleeve. "Carter doesn't like to have a black doctor making calls here. I was sort of a last-ditch emergency. He said he didn't want another Northerner dying on him."

"Am I dying? I sure feel like I am."

"No you're not, but I can imagine it seemed that way. What the devil did you eat today?"

Mitch recited the different dishes he had had at the Dixie Day picnic.

"The crab salad probably had mayonnaise in it. That spoils easily in hot weather," the doctor said. "It could be botulism, or even salmonella—either comes from spoiled food, and can be deadly." He shook his head. "On the other hand," he added, "if that was the case, we'd have had an epidemic of food poisoning today and I'd have heard about that. I'll check with the sheriff's office, but I think you're the only one who's reported being sick."

"What else could it have been, Doctor?"

"I can't say. Your temperature is normal." He felt Mitch's forehead. "Perfectly normal. Whatever it was, with the diarrhea, your vomiting and the lavage, you seem to be cleaned out pretty well."

Pemberton started to turn away, then paused. "Did you notice anything funny in what you ate? Anything unusual? Your blood pressure is low. Is that normal for you?" Mitch shook his head. "Did you eat anything with garlic? There's a faint odor I detected when I examined you."

Mitch shook his head again. "The food was very spicy, but I couldn't tell you what the spices were. I took those sort of tastes to be normal. I'm not used to that kind of cooking. Maybe that's the answer."

The doctor looked dubious. "You rest now, sleep late. Then, when you're all rested up, come by my office. I'll be in all afternoon. I'd like to check on you before you go galavanting off some place.

"You know," he continued, "you should really have gone to a hospital with something like this. The rescue squad should have been called out. Shreveport's got a fine infirmary—if you had made it in time."

"You make it sound alarming," Mitch said.

"It might have been," Pemberton admitted. "Look, I wouldn't mind coming back to see you here but Carter won't have it."

"I don't mind, Doctor, I really don't. I appreciate your coming out in the middle of the night. I'll drop by your office."

"I best sneak off before the sun comes up," Pemberton said in a mock conspiratorial tone. "You keep well, you hear."

THE DOCTOR'S OFFICE was on a back street in the eastern end of town, a black neighborhood. A rundown general store with old advertising posters in its windows was on the opposite corner. Two old black men sat on a wooden crate by its entranceway, talking and nodding. A young girl, her hair tied with rubberbands, came running out of the store, an ice-cream cone in her hand.

Mitch left his car by the store and crossed the street. He walked gingerly, uncertain of his balance, still feeling woozy. A mother carrying an infant was leaving the office as he reached the top of the small flight of steps. He held the torn screen door open for her, then walked into the waiting room. A number of women and children and one old man sat on rickety chairs around the room, chatting softly with each other. There was no receptionist, so Mitch took a seat in the far corner. The others stared at him. Mitch smiled wanly at them. "Dr. Pemberton in?"

"He here," the old man said. "Patien' in with him now."

Mitch smiled again wanly. There was the sound of a hearty laugh from inside the closed room next to the waiting room, and the door opened. A young woman came out, her face lit up, and behind her Pemberton was saying, "Just do like you're doing, Ruby. Twins need a lot of nourishment."

The doctor, Mitch suddenly realized, could not have been more than 35 years old. He was a dark, muscular man, with a broad nose and close-cropped hair. In another setting and in different clothes, Mitch reflected, he would have expected Pemberton to be a construction laborer or handyman—and that, Mitch knew, was stereotyping, and he was annoyed with himself for thinking that way.

Seeing Mitch in the corner, the doctor waved him into his office. "You folks won't mind, will you," he said to his other patients. "This is an emergency."

The others looked resentful but said nothing. Mitch followed the doctor back into his office, closing the door behind him. "I didn't want any special consideration," he said.

"They sit there all day, if I let them," Pemberton said. "They like to gossip and this is one of their favorite cracker barrels. Don't worry about it. The important thing is how you are doing."

"I made it here, just," Mitch said.

The doctor tore off a long sheet of white paper and put it over a gurney by one wall. "Take off your shirt and stretch out over here so I can examine you," he said. "Been drinking a lot, I hope."

Pemberton probed and pinched, feeling Mitch all over. "Are you from Virgil, Doc?" Mitch asked, looking up at him.

"No, I'm from downstate, but after I got through with my residency I looked for a practice where the black people didn't have any doctor or any medical service that was handy." He stood back from the gurney. "You can get dressed now, Mr. Stevens."

Mitch began buttoning up his shirt. "Is Virgil everything you expected, Doc?"

Pemberton shrugged. "Virgil. Bulloch Parish. I don't think anything in Louisiana is what I ever expect, though I should have learned by now.

"Look," he went on, "my father was a waiter at a hotel in New Orleans all his life, 40 and some years. He never did anything else, never could. All the captains and the maître d' were white. But he made decent money with the tips and put aside enough to get me into college where I picked up some scholarships. He always said to me—and I rankled when he did—'I owe my good fortune to Major Kenwell.' That was the owner of the hotel. Hell, he owed nothing to any white man. I decided that if I could get through medical school I would treat only black people; I would use all that money that my father thought Kenwell was responsible for his having and giving to me to help blacks.

"So when I got out on my own," Pemberton added, slipping off his stethoscope, "I had the choice of going to a mixed neighborhood in Atlanta or practicing in a totally black one. It was an easy choice. You are the first white person I've ever treated in Virgil."

"Maybe I'll start a trend," said Mitch, smiling lightly.

"Don't bet on it. Anyway, I have enough to keep me busy here, and I'm happy. I'm doing what I want to do."

"I won't take up more of your time," Mitch said, standing shakily. "Will you take a check?"

"Forty-five dollars will do fine, thirty for the—"

"You don't have to break it down, Doc. I'll always be grateful that you came and took care of me the way you did. Should I be doing or taking anything special here on out?"

"You look all right, but you best go easy the next few days. Don't push it. And keep on taking in a lot of liquids. Drink a swimming pool if you can. I'm going to give you a prescription, too, that you ought to take for the next seven days to settle down your insides. It's got belladonna, but only a weak dose."

"So what do you think it was?" Mitch asked.

"Well, it wasn't the food," Pemberton said. "I checked first thing this morning with the sheriff. You're the only one who reported getting ill after the picnic. There wasn't one complaint."

"Want to make a guess then what happened?"

Pemberton studied Mitch a moment. "Some of your symptoms—the diarrhea, stomach cramps and vomiting—are typical of salmonella." He hesitated. "But if I had to say so," he said finally, "I'd swear you had ingested some kind of poison. Arsenic most likely, according to your other symptoms—the low blood pressure, the aroma of garlic I detected on your breath. Arsenic is used in all sorts of insecticides, weed killers, ant killers, even paint. But that's a wild guess, and I really shouldn't even suggest it. I just don't know for certain. And I didn't think to take a sample of what came out of your stomach."

"But you're saying you think I might have eaten something poisonous, that I was poisoned. Isn't that the bottom line?"

"In a word, yes."

MITCH SAT UNMOVING behind the wheel of the car, his eyes squinting because of the glare of the sun. Poisoned? The thought sent a shiver down his back. What the hell is going on here? I've gotten into something over my head. I'm just a journalist, not some goddamned detective. I didn't take on this book to get myself killed. Screw Tom Cantwell—no, I don't mean that. But he's dead and I'm imagining that everything surrounding his death is part of a conspiracy. I'd be crazy to keep at this thing.

A rubber ball bounced off the hood of the car. A small black boy ran into the street chasing it, not looking whether or not a car might be coming. That's me, Mitch said to himself. I'm not looking where I'm going, just blundering ahead.

He turned the key in the ignition. I'm going home.

ELEVEN

MITCH TOSSED THE magazine aside. His fingers drummed restlessly on the arm of the chair. Ever since he returned from Louisiana four days earlier, he couldn't seem to keep still. Val was gone, back to California to continue the movie she was working on, and nothing could hold his interest for very long. He bolted out of the chair and picked up the television schedule from the top of the set in the living room. A horror movie, a sitcom, two game shows, a Yankee game—he hated the Yankees. Mitch flipped the schedule back on the top of the set and walked down the hall into the kitchen. He poked around the cabinets, looking for something to snack on, found a box of pitted prunes, then decided his stomach wasn't up to the fruit and shoved the box back between the cereal and the rice.

He wandered aimlessly around the apartment until he reached his study. A new edition of the *Columbia Journalism Review* sat on his desk where he had left it that morning while opening the mail. He picked it up, flipped through its pages and dropped into his desk chair, turning to the inside back cover where the magazine routinely ran "The Lower case," a compendium of bloopers and *double entendres*. The page was always good for a chuckle. "Hemorrhoid Victim Turns to Ice" ran the headline attributed to a Wisconsin newspaper. Another, from a North Carolina newspaper, read, "Boating While Impaired Wins House Approval." Mitch couldn't help smiling. No newspaper was immune from such blunders; it came with turning out a totally new product every 24 hours.

Mitch leafed back through the magazine. An article on how the government had managed the press during the Gulf war looked interesting. He had begun to get engrossed in it when the phone rang. The sound startled him. "Shit," he said, dropping the magazine on his desk as he reached for the phone. It was his son. Ken didn't even wait to exchange greetings. As soon as Mitch answered, he rattled away almost incoherently.

"Slow down, Ken, you're not making sense." Mitch carried the phone over to the sofa-bed in the study, so distracted that he nearly knocked over the lamp on the end table when he tugged at the coiled line.

"But being a schlepp is, is . . ." Ken groped for the words. "Dad, I don't see the point of it. I'm not doing anything at all that makes sense for my career." Ken was a budding composer, studying music at a conservatory in New England. With Mitch's help, Ken had been able to get a summer job at the Mont Vert Music Festival in Vermont. It seemed like an opportunity for the young man to expand his contacts in the musical field. But Ken wasn't prepared for the kind of jobs that being a front-office assistant called for. "I drive Rukovsky into town for shopping, I pick up and sort the mail, I help set up the stage, I usher at the performances, I—"

"What did you expect, Ken?" asked Mitch, a note of impatience in his tone as he felt a twinge in his stomach. "You knew you weren't going to be asked to compose or perform. They never fooled you about that."

"I hate it, Dad, and I called just to let you know that I'm coming home."

"Now hold it, Ken, you can't quit like that," Mitch almost shouted. His stomach, still queasy, was making rumbling noises.

The past four days he had spent around the house, regaining his strength, living on mashed potatoes and liquids, and pacing back and forth endlessly, had left him on edge. The truth was, he was dimly aware, that he was upset with himself about giving up on the research and investigation in Louisiana. The decision gnawed at him.

"You'd be crazy to leave Mont Vert, for Chrissake, Ken. Those people up there are the very people you'll want someday to play your pieces. Practically speaking, you'll only leave a sour taste in their mouths if you leave. A damn sour taste."

"It's a waste of time, Dad," Ken pleaded. "Nobody knows I exist. The master musicians like Rukovsky can't even remember my name."

"So who the hell are you that—" Mitch caught himself. His stomach rumbled. He tried to soothe it by rubbing it gently.

"I don't think you give a damn about my feelings, Dad. I mean I'm the one up here going bananas. You don't understand what's going on at all. I don't even know why I've bothered calling you. I'll just get in a bus and come home."

"Look, you do your job right and you'll be noticed," Mitch said, realizing that he had to control himself. "You'll be appreciated. You'll be remembered. If you screw up, you'll be remembered, too, in the worst way. Ken, you have a wonderful chance to make contacts, to be able to say you were at Mont Vert. It'll look great on your resumé, and if you ever approach someone for a commission or a job who's been part of Mont Vert, he'll treat you—I promise—like a member of the club.

"Something else, too. Maybe even more important." Mitch stood and walked over to the window, careful now that the cord didn't snag on the lamp. "Do it for yourself, Ken. Stay." He searched for the words. "Look, when you start something you should finish it. When you take on any job or assignment or what-have-you, it's a commitment, and if you get in the habit of breaking commitments you're going to do yourself a disservice, and over the long run you'll regret it and it'll be too late. You finish what you start. It's as simple as that."

"I knew I shouldn't have phoned home," Ken said, his tone wavering. "I should have just quit and come home."

"No, son, you're doing the right thing. You're talking it out. Listen, you got me at a bad time. I didn't mean to knock you. Really. You've got my sympathy, Ken. We all pay our dues at some time or another. Do you remember my telling you how I was a copy boy one summer on the *Times*, and all I could remember about all those hotshot reporters was whether one was a chicken sandwich on white or a coffee without sugar? Talk about schlepping—I used to get so dirty changing the ribbons on the teletype machines that my fingers were purple for days. But I soaked up the atmosphere, heard the talk, got to know what it felt like being in a newsroom and trying to meet a deadline. That all helped in the long run.

"I'm sorry," Mitch continued, almost contritely. "I'm sounding preachy, and I don't mean to. But you're smart enough to know what I'm driving at, Ken. You finish what you start."

Ken had calmed down, too. "Okay, I get your point, Dad. I'm sorry I acted up about this."

"No sweat, Ken. I'm glad you phoned. It's a kind of compliment that you'd discuss this with one of your parents. Are we still on for the Fourth of July?"

"Yes, I got the four days, but I had to give up my days off for a month after that."

"Okay, we'll be in touch. I'll be speaking to your mother and try to work out where precisely we'll meet. Stay well in the meantime, Ken."

"Thanks, Dad."

"I love you, Ken. I miss you a lot."

"Me, too, Dad. I love you."

Mitch turned from the window and sat on the edge of the sill, the phone resting in his lap. I hope that settles that, he said to himself. His stomach rumbled again, reminding him of Louisiana. In a flash he was back in the Caddo Motel, writhing in the bed, full of pain. He fought off the image, trying to distract himself. His hand shook slightly as he picked up the receiver and dialed the office of Jack Reed. I've got to get back to normal, he told himself.

THE CHAIRMAN OF the communications department ate voraciously. Dabs of tomato sauce marked the edges of his mouth. Mitch, on the other hand, was eating his plain spaghetti warily. Hungry, but protective of his fragile stomach, he was now sorry that he'd agreed to lunch with Reed even though he had initiated the date.

Reed was sopping up the sauce on his plate with a slab of Italian bread. "Every time I miss breakfast I make a pig of myself at lunch," he said. "So," he continued, wiping his lips with a napkin and looking up briefly as the waiter approached the next table, "that was your first trip south?"

"Well, yes, in a manner of speaking," said Mitch, twirling the strands of spaghetti on his fork before lifting it to his mouth. He really hadn't wanted to talk about Louisiana, but Reed had expressed a natural interest in his trip there, and Mitch finally had stopped offering only cursory responses to his questions. "I'd worked in Washington, you know. I've covered stories in the Carolinas and a space shot in Florida, but I'd never really been in the South outside of a couple of big cities like Atlanta and Miami, not in the real South."

Reed missed catching the waiter's eye. He turned back to Mitch. "Funny the picture you paint of what you saw. It was totally different in the 60s."

"Were you there then, Jack?" Reed nodded. "On a newspaper? I didn't know you had worked on a paper."

"No, not on a paper. I took part in one of those marches in Alabama. Martin Luther King, Abernathy, Jesse Jackson. We just walked down the middle of an avenue and all hell broke loose. You could smell the rage. It scared the shit out of me. I really thought I might never see my family again. Thank God there were so many of us. I have to confess that I tried to stay in the middle of the marchers." Reed motioned to the waiter, who was resetting a nearby table. "They used everything on us—hoses, prods, dogs, billy clubs if we got out of line." Reed paused to ask the waiter for a cup of coffee. He raised his eyebrows to Mitch, mutely asking whether he wanted coffee also, but Mitch shook his head at the offer.

"It's only been a quarter of a century, Jack. I guess it's too soon to expect that things would change completely. I never felt totally comfortable down there. Their values—the whites, I mean—are not mine. But maybe I'm being unfair. Not everybody is a David Duke. I'm starting to learn that. But I don't know, I always feel wary, out of sync, down there. The situation with Tom's death didn't help matters. It put me off."

Reed put two spoonfuls of sugar into his coffee and stirred leisurely. "You know what I find hard to believe?" Mitch shrugged. "That you've decided to drop the project."

Mitch put down his fork and searched Reed's face. He was in no mood for a lecture. He was still annoyed with himself. He knew in a sense what Reed was going to say. He'd been saying it to himself, one part of him not wanting to hear it, another part knowing that it was still an unresolved quandary for him. He pushed his eyeglasses back on his nose.

"It's so unlike you, Mitch. I've always thought of you as tenacious. Like at school. You never let your students give up. You push them to ask all the questions, get all the facts. I don't know, I don't mean to pry really, but I couldn't help but wonder why you were giving up on the book so soon and . . ."

The book. Was Reed sending another one of his messages?

"And forget what I said about the faculty situation, Mitch. That's not the point at all. I'm almost sorry I ever intimated it was a problem. I'm talking now as a friend—about commitment . . ."

Mitch started thinking. Jack's right, of course. It's exactly what I was saying to Ken. What you start you finish. If I started something, I should finish it. And it's more than the book now. There are a lot of unanswered questions. I never tolerated unanswered questions before. I shouldn't give up now—more than ever, not now. If someone took the trouble to try to get rid of me, then I must be on the right track.

". . . anyway, it's probably none of my business, so I'll just keep my big mouth shut."

"No, Jack, you're right," Mitch said. He sat back in his chair. He took a deep breath, then blew it out. "You're absolutely right. I ask that of my students—of my own son as well. I have to practice what I preach or it's all just hot air. I appreciate your candor."

"You haven't told Cantwell's wife anything yet, have you?"

"No, I was too ill to feel like getting into a conversation and letting her down."

"Does Val know how you feel—felt?"

"No, I had enough to do to keep her from getting all worked up about my illness."

"So do it. You have no embarrassing retractions to make. Just do what you were going to do."

"Fine," said Mitch as the waiter took away his plate. "Only I'm not sure, to be honest, what to do next. I mean I figure I can trace a white merchant in New Orleans. I can certainly try to do that, but I'm after the records of some blacks, too, and they didn't have much of a written history."

Reed put down his coffee cup. "No, not much, but sometimes there's something available. I did some sightseeing before the march. A number of plantations kept detailed records, so if you know a name and the age of a person you can trace a slave. Look what Alex Hailey did in *Roots*. There are documents—not many—but it's not completely a lost cause."

Mitch's face lit up. "Jack Reed, you've just done more for me than all the medicine in China."

"Tea in China. The expression is 'tea in China.'"

"Have another coffee, Jack. It's on me."

"IT'S ABOUT WHAT you'd expect, Mitch. If the weather's good, we shoot outdoors. If it isn't, we do the studio shots. The film will take time, but we'll get there. Just as long as they don't cut me out of too many scenes when the editing's done."

"Did you get to see Jo at all?" he asked. Jo had been Val's best friend in college. She lived in Los Angeles now, selling her sculptures and doing some interior design assignments.

"Not yet. We're supposed to get together this weekend if the shoot doesn't have to go into overtime to make up any scenes. And what about you, Mitch? What are you up to?"

"I wanted to talk to you about that, Val. I think I have to get back to Louisiana again." Mitch spoke quickly, not wanting to give Val an opportunity to argue with him. "I need to do this, honey. I almost gave up on it. But I can't let it go, Val. I need to satisfy myself. I'll only regret it if I don't. Like that time we didn't go see your mother in the hospital, and then she died suddenly." Val would understand that; she had never gotten over the feeling of guilt about it. "I don't want *not* to do this."

"I know what you mean, Mitch," said Val, the tone of her voice a mixture of resignation and support. "And I know you. If you've got something like this stuck in your craw, it's better to get it out—better for all of us. You go ahead and do what you think is best. But more important to me is how you're feeling. What's with your stomach?"

"Much, much better, Val. Just what you'd expect after a case of food poisoning." Lie number one. He hadn't told Val that it had been more than a "simple" case of food poisoning, and he didn't want to make an issue of it now. "The doctor says I'm fine, and he sees no reason why I can't get back on routine." Lie number two. He hadn't spoken to any doctor, Pemberton or his own, since returning home.

"Are you sure, Mitch? From everything you told me, you had quite a siege."

"Val, if it ever was anything serious, you know I would have asked you to return home." Lie number three. He didn't dare tell her how serious the situation had become.

"I don't know what it is, Mitch, but I still get the feeling that this whole business isn't what it seems on the surface."

"Val, love, sometimes I wonder if you don't have the instincts of a reporter." Truth number one. In fact, half the reporters he had known in his lifetime could have benefitted by a dose of her intuitive sense.

"You'll keep your promise about coming out—you and Ken— to L.A.?"

"On the weekend of the Fourth. We're all set to go."

The two talked a while longer, mostly about their son. Mitch repeated for Val his conversation with Ken. When they were through and he had hung up, Mitch sat at his desk, his head back, eyes glued to the ceiling. He remained like that for several minutes, regretting his lies to Val but rationalizing that he didn't want to cause her needless anxiety. He told himself that deep down she really knew what he was up to no matter what he said.

As he righted himself in his chair, his glance fell once more on the photograph of Thomas Clay Washburn propped against his desk lamp. Was he crazy to endanger his own life because of a man with whom he had no connection whatsoever, a man who had died almost a hundred and thirty years ago?

TWELVE

"Y OUR FIRST TIME in New Orleans?" The cab driver tried to strike up a conversation, but Mitch's mind was elsewhere. Returning to Louisiana had touched off all his anxieties about what had happened only a short week earlier. He kept replaying his movements at the Dixie Day picnic, searching for a clue, forcing himself to visualize the moments at the picnic table: standing in line with Augustus Leon; J. J. Dexter's breaking in, Ernie behind him; Flora May Bulloch serving him; eating later with both Augustus and Lyda. It seemed to him the opportunities abounded for someone to slip something into his food. What had he eaten afterwards? He hadn't considered that at all. In the mid-afternoon he had joined Lyda's two pupils in a double-dipper "Virgil Virgin" (no sprinkles) ice-cream cone purchased from a stand outside the park gates. He had drunk twice from the fountain, taking a particularly long draught after participating in the wheelbarrow race at Lyda's insistence (and losing, slipping in the grass in his city shoes). The rest of the day had been spent in an idle walk through the park. Mitch had felt so stuffed that he'd turned down the Leons' offer to join them for a late coffee and buns after the fireworks. He'd returned to his motel room, munched on a granola bar, read a book, and turned off the lights to go to sleep, attributing the queasiness he had begun to feel to having overindulged at the picnic.

Mitch was at a loss to understand why anyone perceived him as a dangerous enough threat to poison him. He didn't seem to know anything incriminating that could possibly be a motive for murder. Unless it was something he would surely stumble across if he persisted in Tom's research trail. Mitch smiled to himself. The murderer obviously had more confidence in Mitch's detecting abilities than Mitch himself did.

The murderer—Mitch ran over in his mind all the people he had seen at the picnic—the mayor, his henchman Ernie, Leon, Dexter, Flora May, Lyda. They had all had the opportunity. For that matter, so had Lyda's two pupils, if you wanted to carry the possibilities to an absurd extreme. Frankly, all the candidates seemed improbable. As far as Mitch could tell, no one seemed to have a motive. Not the mayor, not Augustus Leon. Dexter was annoyed, even angry, when I questioned him about the handling of Tom's death, but that was hardly a strong enough motive for revenge. Then there is Flora May, whom I know nothing about, certainly nothing that would lead me to think she might have tried to poison me, other than suspecting that she and Dexter have a thing going, which an awful lot of other people suspect also.

And if the motive lies in the research I'm following up, what would two slaves born before the Civil War have to do with anyone in Virgil today, more than a century and a quarter later? That's the wild card. Maybe it's right in front of my nose but I don't see it.

RESTAURANT DE LA TOUR EIFFEL. Mitch looked wistfully at the sign. The restaurant, a new one on the edge of the Garden District on St. Charles Avenue, looked like a giant glass bird cage, its curved metal frame reminiscent of the Eiffel Tower in Paris.

In fact, it had been the restaurant in the Tower—called *Tour Eiffel*—dismantled in 1981 because of engineering problems and sold to the owners of this already well-known New Orleans dining palace.

Mitch promised himself to eat there once his stomach settled back into complete normality. He walked parallel to the meandering Mississippi toward the Vieux Carré and his hotel. He passed white, tall-storied buildings, their lacework wrought iron balconies a throwback to another time, another world. The Cabildo, the Pontalba Buildings, the Presbytère, St. Louis Cathedral, Jackson Square. It was like being in Europe.

Turning into Bourbon Street as twilight turned into night, Mitch was amazed at the contrast between the physical feel of the city and the reality of the street life. Music—but not the jazz the city was famous for—blared from honky-tonk bistros and topless bars, where hucksters stood corralling tourists passing by. A hooker fell in step with him. She was a girl, perhaps no more than 19, dressed in a short, tight leather skirt and halter. "Looking for something, mister?" she whispered. Mitch was at once repelled and aroused. She looked so young but so hardened that Mitch could not help feeling sorry for her. He stepped up his pace as she dropped back into the entranceway to a store. Through the open door of one of the topless bars, he caught a glimpse of a scantily clad go-go dancer gyrating on a mirrored stage. He began to ache. It seemed like weeks since he had last seen—and made love with—Val. He started to be aroused, then caught himself. This was no time for him to be thinking carnal thoughts. He was certainly in no mood to watch a lot of gyrating nude bodies. Trying to distract himself, he decided he'd go back to his hotel and order dinner in his room. He turned off Bourbon Street and began walking faster. He concentrated on what he would have: lamb chops or chicken should agree with his stomach, a baked potato, too, but no salad yet. Maybe for breakfast, though, he'd be up to one of those fluffy *beignets* tomorrow, before heading off to the municipal records department. I hope I can trace Truman Moore here—and that slave Eliza. He crossed his fingers, then reprimanded himself for being superstitious. But no Creole cuisine while I'm here, he said to himself, shifting back to thoughts of food. *That* would be poisonous. He felt relieved as he entered the hotel lobby, saved— he was sure—from doing something he really shouldn't do.

"Truman Moore? King Cotton? Why for goodness' sake, there's no need to look up any records. His home still stands. It's a museum over on Chartres Street, right smack dab in the middle of the French Quarter. They have lots of information about him and his family there."

Was it going to be this easy? Mitch couldn't believe his luck. He thanked the clerk and left the Civic Center, walking back the few short blocks to the Vieux Carré.

The Moore House, the sign outside read. The date, 1855, was directly under the name. Another, smaller sign provided the museum director's name and the hours the home was open: 10 A.M. to 4:30 P.M. (last tour leaves at 3:45 P.M.), closed Sundays. What a dreadful idea, Mitch thought, keeping a museum closed on Sundays, the one day that most people can visit it.

The house was built flush to the sidewalk, without any front lawn or garden. Mitch entered it and asked at the reception desk for the museum director. "Would you please tell her that Professor Mitchell Stevens of Metropolitan University in New York would like to see her," he said, using the academic ploy to get attention.

Ten minutes later, accompanied by Hortense Chevalle, Mitch was getting a personal tour of the home. "And this is the court-yard, Professor Stevens." A round fountain sat in its center, surrounded by pots with geraniums. Through a gate off to one side was an old cypress cistern. Oddly, only the servants' rooms and pantry enjoyed the pleasant view; their shuttered windows looked out onto it.

"If you'll follow me through this door, I'll show you the main rooms of the house." Miss Chevalle walked briskly ahead, pointing out the features of each ornately decorated room, the double parlors, and the indoor water closet, unusually modern for its time. "All of this has been painstakingly restored. We had the expertise of highly qualified architects, archeologists, interior designers . . ."

Mitch was half-listening to her talk, trying to look interested, but biding his time to ask questions. She sounded like she had given the same tour a thousand times, the words becoming trite by rote.

"And here we are, finally, at the servants' quarters, a full circle of the house. Notice how plainly furnished these rooms are. Any questions, Professor Stevens?"

"Yes, I am particularly interested in the servants who worked in homes such as these. So little has been written about them."

"You've come to the right place, Professor. Right here, in these rooms, we have posted the names of the servants who lived in each one. Over here, by the door."

Mitch searched the list, but there was no Eliza on it. "Can we return to the other rooms here, Miss Chevalle? I'd like to check the names there, too."

The name was on the list in the next room. Mitch's heart quickened, but the museum director deflated him, saying, "Eliza's a fairly common name—was, that is, in those days."

"Do you have anything further about the servants?"

"Why, yes, we do," Miss Chevalle said, pleased that Mitch was taking an interest beyond the ordinary tour. Not many people who came through the Moore House even bothered to ask a single question. They admired the furnishings, the women especially, then maybe bought a postcard before boarding their sight-seeing bus and going on to the next tourist stop. "Please step this way to my office. We keep all the records pertaining to the home in a safe in there."

Her office was in a back room, simply furnished, and neat

like herself. "The day books only go back to 1855 when the Moores built the home and moved in, but we have material about them that is much earlier, and much later also, after the war."

"I'd like to start with 1859, if you don't mind," Mitch said. "I'm especially interested in an Eliza that might have come to work in the house that year."

The Moores had kept five servants to run their home—a cook, a butler-valet, a cleaning girl, a seamstress and a laundress—until the first week of February, 1859, when a new slave was added to the staff. Her name was Eliza.

Mitch asked for the record books for the ensuing years. Eliza's name appeared again on February 12, 1862, in a notation beside a doctor's fee of one dollar, the words typically brief and formal: "Eliza—died in childbirth. Boy given name Joshua." Mitch felt suddenly deflated again. Eliza had come to New Orleans to work for the Moores but hadn't even survived the Civil War. She couldn't have been more than 22 or 23. Was that all there was?

Mitch's dismay had registered on Miss Chevalle. "She died just before New Orleans was invested by Union troops," she explained. "Benjamin Butler—we call him The Beast—quartered some of his aides here. Truman Moore and his family fled to Mexico. He wasn't able to resume his residence here until the war was over."

"So that's it," Mitch said resignedly.

"No, Professor Stevens," Miss Chevalle said, taking the day book from his hands and turning back several pages. "You missed an entry. Here, look. Mrs. Moore kept a record of everything, like you would in a diary." She read it out loud: "'Eliza paid visit by brother Benjamin in company of Lt. Thomas Clay Washburn, son of former owner. Stayed three nights as guests of Mr. Moore and myself.'"

So Benjamin was her *brother*. That's interesting. "Both Washburn and his slave stayed here? How strange."

"No, not at all," Miss Chevalle said. "Even before the war people traveled with their servants, and it was considered hospitable to put them up for the night or longer. Mrs. Moore kept track of all her visitors. That was a big event in those days, someone coming to call, bringing with them news about the outside world or about family matters. Word of mouth—people were all couriers then."

Mitch still felt at a loss, though. Despite the revelations about Benjamin and the visit, the trail seemed to peter out.

"Want to see the day books for after the war, when the Moores returned?" It sounded as though Miss Chevalle knew more than she was willing to say, wanting Mitch to find out for himself instead.

Well, why not while he was here? Mitch took the record books from her and began to thumb through the notations for 1865 and 1866 when all of a sudden Benjamin's name caught his eye, only it wasn't just Benjamin anymore: "Benjamin Washburn came, took his nephew Joshua. Mr. Moore furious but could not stop him."

So Benjamin had returned to New Orleans at the end of the war, a free, full-fledged citizen, and claimed his nephew. Just the thought that he had uncovered another lead to follow excited Mitch. Now I've got confirmation of a last name, too, he thought to himself. There's something to go after: another Washburn line to track, but this time a black one. Where would it take him?

"Did you find what you were looking for, Professor?"

"Yes, indeed, I did, Miss Chevalle. Many thanks to you."

"May I suggest another avenue of research to you?"

"I'd be grateful."

"Marriage records. Death records. Birth records."

"Just what I was thinking, Miss Chevalle, just what I was thinking."

THE FLAGS ALONG the Civic Center seemed to wave briskly, the Garden of the Americas was positively glowing with color, the sky behind the statues of Bolivar, Juarez and Morazan a bright blue. Mitch entered the 11-story city hall building with an eagerness he hadn't felt since his days on the old *Tribune*. He had no idea what he would find, but having Benjamin Washburn's name as a lead now was like a shot of adrenalin.

Five minutes later, he was bent over the open pages of a marriage register, poring over it, his finger moving from line to line, name to name, at his elbow a blank yellow legal pad. He found the first significant entry quickly. On April 5, 1866, Benjamin Washburn had married Petulia Hall, 18 years old, of Plaquemine. Therefore, it was safe to assume, Benjamin himself had settled in the New Orleans area instead of returning to Bulloch Parish. Mitch asked for the birth records for 1866 and 1867. He searched them without success. He had the records for the years 1868 to 1878 brought to him, but there was no mention of any Petulia Washburn having had a child. Either Benjamin and his wife had moved away, or they simply hadn't had any children. Surely, if they were capable of having children and if they had remained in New Orleans, they would have had a child by 1878. Mitch decided to double-check how long Benjamin had lived. He was supposedly alive in the 1920s, when Martha Tour Gale had interviewed him. Mitch started with the death register for 1921, moved through it and the registers for 1922, 1923 and 1924 before he found what he was looking for. Benjamin Washburn had died on December 22, 1925, aged 86. That confirmed that.

On a hunch, Mitch asked for the marital records for the years 1880 through 1890, when Joshua would have been old enough to marry. Eliza's son, he figured, would have been brought up either as Joshua Moore or Joshua Washburn. He'd look for both names, though he thought that Benjamin probably would have insisted on Joshua's using the surname he himself had adopted. The list of names Mitch had to go through in the ledgers grew longer. New Orleans, after Reconstruction, had enjoyed a renaissance of commercial activity. The city's growth was mirrored in the burgeoning of its population.

Mitch's eyes began to ache, and he had to restrain himself from racing too quickly through the names. He was afraid he might skip something, as he had at the Moore House. On the other hand, maybe he was on a wild goose chase, maybe no marriage had been registered at all. That possibility loomed larger as Mitch plodded through the listings. Nothing was in the ledger for 1880, nor in the register of marriages for 1881, 1882, 1883, 1884, 1885, and 1886. Mitch began to despair. What if Joshua had moved or died? Mitch took off his glasses and rubbed his eyes, causing a flurry of colored dots to race across his eyelids. He sat for a moment with his eyes closed, resting, then opened them, blinking, and started turning the pages in the 1887 ledger. He went through the marriages registered for the first four months of the year before he spotted what he was looking for: the first names on the record of marriages for May 1, 1887—Joshua Washburn, 25, and Callie Spink, 21. At last!

Mitch heaved a sigh, more of relief than of triumph. He leaned back to stretch his arms and bumped into a clerk who was approaching the table he was working at. "We close in 15 minutes, Professor Stevens," he said. "We have to get these books back into the vault before then."

Mitch asked when the office opened again the next morning. "Nine A.M." Mitch thanked him. He would be back, on the dot.

Mitch walked out of city hall amidst a swarm of municipal employees getting an early start home. Unaware of the jostling crowd, Mitch wondered where his digging was leading him. Was he on the right track at all? Walking the short distance back to the French Quarter and his hotel, Mitch decided to treat himself to a special dinner that evening. Maybe he would even try some gumbo or jambalaya.

MITCH SPENT THE next two days in the records office, the sheets of his yellow legal pad slowly filling up with names and dates.

Having exhausted the marriage records, he turned back to the birth records, then the death registers. New Orleans had slowly but inexorably grown into a city of nearly 600,000 souls. That made for a lot of births, marriages, and deaths. But the pieces were slowly falling into place.

As best as Mitch could put the data together, Joshua Washburn and Callie Spink had four children, one girl and three boys. Two of their sons died in infancy. The third, Matthew, born in 1892, married Dara Smith in 1912. They had two children, Henry, born in 1913, and Willard, born in 1914. There was no further mention of Henry, but Willard married Missy Fuller in 1934. Missy gave birth that same year to a son, Franklin, who died when only 18 years old in 1952. Both Matthew and Dara Washburn had predeceased their young grandchild by one year, dying within six months of one another in 1951. There was no further mention of Willard or Missy Washburn. Were they still alive, or had they moved and died elsewhere?

As for Joshua and Callie Washburn's daughter, Susanna, she was born in 1896 and married in 1915 to a man named Mims. The couple had only one surviving child, born in 1920, a daughter they called Mary Lou. Another daughter, Holly, had died a few days after her birth in 1916. Mary Lou Mims married Orko Parker in 1940. She had only one child, also a daughter, Flora May, born in 1946.

Flora May. When Mitch first saw the name it did not register. It was only after he had written it in his notes that he did a double take. He sat back and studied it. Flora May is not an uncommon name, he told himself. No more than Eliza is, or Mary, or Holly.

Mitch could not find any reference to Flora May Parker in either the marriage or the death registers. It didn't seem likely that she was dead, because she would only be in her late 40s now. She could have moved away, or, of course, she could still be living in New Orleans, a spinster. Willard and Missy Washburn were also unaccounted for, though they would be quite old now if they were alive. On an off-chance, Mitch asked the clerk at the records desk for a phone book. Mitch rifled through the P's first without success; there was no Flora May Parker listed. He turned to the W's, going back and forth until he hit the page with the Washburn listings. He found Willard's name immediately. Excited, Mitch jotted down both the address and phone number and left to find an unoccupied telephone booth in the corridor outside the records department.

The voice that answered was frail and weary. "I can't hear you, speak up," she said. "Speak up. Who's this? Willard isn't home."

Mitch tried to explain the reason for his calling, but Mrs. Washburn kept saying, "Please call later when Willard is home." He wanted to leave the phone number of his hotel room, but she resisted taking it. "Tonight. Willard will be home tonight. Please call when Willard is home."

"Look, mister, we are private people. I don't understand what you want. We are all alone. Please leave us alone."

Willard Washburn's off-putting response to Mitch's call that night only served to stimulate Mitch into devising a way to approach him. Should I just show up at his front door without a by-your-leave and take my chances that he'll talk to me? Mitch wondered. No, that might have just the opposite effect. He might be so hostile to my sudden appearance that I wouldn't be able to persuade him to say a word. Should I try phoning again in the morning? Maybe he would more receptive then. Well, I could, but then again another phone call might also touch off the man's resentment. The trouble with being too aggressive in a situation like this is that it can be counterproductive. What I need is an entree into Willard's home. Someone to introduce me. Someone Washburn trusts.

Mitch smiled to himself and reached for the phone.

"Doctor Pemberton? This is Mitch Stevens calling."

"Well, hello, stranger. How are you? You were supposed to check in with me, you know."

Mitch apologized for not phoning the doctor earlier. "I'm much better, thanks to you. I even got up my courage to try some Creole cooking the other night. I seem to have survived."

"Good, good. Well, if you ever get back to Virgil, I'd like to see you again."

"I promise you I'll come by. But in the meantime, Doc, I'd like to ask a favor."

Pemberton laughed. "A favor of me? What can a young but aging black doctor in Virgil, Louisiana do for you, Mitch?"

Mitch told Pemberton about finding Willard Washburn in New Orleans. "It's really important that I get to talk to him, and I wondered if you knew anyone here that might intercede on my behalf. Willard seems so suspicious. Maybe it's his age, or maybe it's because I'm white, I don't know."

"Look, when I was in school down there I made a number of friends in one of the Baptist churches in that section of the city. Let me try calling a couple of them and see what I can do."

EVERYONE'S HEAD TURNED as Mitch entered the church. It was a spartan building, badly in need of painting. Once a Catholic house of worship, the building had stained-glass windows but little else to recall the grandeur it once displayed. Niches that once held statues of saints were empty. A side chapel that had been devoted to the Virgin Mary was now an alcove used to store folding chairs, a broken piano, and other odds and ends. What had been the font for holy water near the entrance was dry. All that remained of a huge crucifix that had hung behind the altar was an outline in soot. The church was stuffy, too, as though it was only used on Sundays and never aired out. Only the choir stalls were as they had been and now were filled with the bright faces of young black boys and girls robed in red. They were swaying in unison from side to side, clapping their hands in time to a hymn, singing the refrain over and over again, pride and joy on their faces: "Jesus won't wait if you can't wait, Jesus won't wait if you can't wait, Jesus won't wait if you can't wait, until he comes on Judgment Day."

A bell tingled. Mitch felt like everyone was watching him. Bethel Chapter Baptist Church. Two young girls dressed in black skirts and white blouses were going down the center aisle, holding out woven baskets into which people were putting money, mostly dollar bills. Mitch slipped into a pew at the back of the church just as one of the young collectors came up. He groped in his pocket for his money clip, slipped off a five-dollar bill and put it into the basket. The girl's face lit up in a big smile.

On the raised altar, the Reverend Abner Duclois waited patiently until the two girls had finished their duties and retreated to a side aisle. "My sermon today," he began, "is from Luke, chapter 16, verse 10. Those of you with Bibles in hand can follow me in reading from it.

"'The man who can be trusted in little things can be trusted also in great.'

"Now what do you suppose Jesus meant when he said that? What message was he trying to convey to us?"

"Tell us," a voice from the congregation spoke up. "Let's hear it," said another.

The minister continued as though he hadn't heard the interruptions. "Jesus—our Jesus—was saying that the character of a man does not change. If you don't lie—if you never even tell a white lie, a little lie—you won't tell a big lie—."

"That's true!" someone in the audience called out. "Hear the Lord," said another.

"And conversely," Duclois declared, his voice starting to rise suddenly, "a man—or a woman—"

"Or a woman!"

"—who does lie, who in the face of truth, knowingly fabricates, distorts, tells a lie will lie about everything, small things and large things—"

"That's right." Others echoed the respondent. "That's right, that's right."

The minister pointed his finger menacingly, sweeping across the aisles accusingly. "And Jesus knows when you are lying. He knows because you know. He knows because in your heart you're telling him, 'Jesus, Lord Jesus, I'm lying. Look here, I'm lying.' Isn't that so?"

"It's so." "It's true." "I hear you."

"You know when you're lying. You know in your heart. And that way Jesus knows. And you know you are doing wrong. How—how in heaven—are we to have brotherhood, love our neighbors, love our family, love our mother, love our father, love our sons, love our daughters, if we are not good in everything to everybody?"

"Amen, Lord." "He says so!" "Mercy on us!"

"You look around you now. Go ahead, look around you. Look at the person sitting next to you. Look at the person in back of you. Go ahead—now."

The minister waited as the congregants turned their heads this way and that.

"And what do you see? What do you see? Someone you can trust? Someone who doesn't lie? Someone who always tells the truth? Someone, I say, who you can trust? Because we must trust if we are to have faith in Jesus." Duclois paused. "We must," he began again, his voice lowered, "trust if we are to have in faith in Jesus. How easy that is to say. How difficult that is to do." He stopped abruptly, his eyes narrowing. "Who," he boomed out, "can say that about himself? Who, right here and now, can say I am an honest man or an honest woman?"

"Oh, Lord, mercy!" "Help us, Jesus!" "Don't leave us, Lord."

"And I mean honest in everything—in everything, you hear. In the small things, as Luke says, as in the great things. Who? Raise your hand, I want to shake it. I will kiss it."

A stillness gripped the church. At last, Duclois bowed his head. "Give us your hand, Lord. Lead us to honesty. Take us from lies, deceit, dishonesty. Give us faith in ourselves so that we may have faith in you, Lord. Help us, Lord, to know you. Amen."

"Amen," everyone responded.

"And now, let us have a moment of silent prayer." Mitch bowed his head. For the first time in his adult life, in a church, he was moved. Mitch suddenly remembered a conversation from years past with a reporter who had recently started work on the *Trib*. By the time Mitch met him, he had worked on 10 different papers in 10 different towns. In each town he had attended a different church, not just a different church building, but often a different denomination. He told Mitch that when he moved to a new town, he visited all the churches and synagogues in the town and then picked the one where he felt the "spirit." When Mitch asked him how he defined this spirit, his friend couldn't put it into words. It was, Mitch guessed at the time, a lack of hypocrisy. And in this simple church, Mitch felt the spirit.

Mitch waited patiently as the congregants walked up the aisle and out of the church, smiling, shaking hands and greeting each other with "Bless you, brother," "Bless you, sister." As they came by him, they reached for his hand and said, "Bless you, brother." He found himself returning the greeting, and the smile, and suddenly feeling good about himself. It didn't matter, he realized, what color he was. He had felt uncomfortable at first, but that was his own doing. Here, in Bethel Chapter First Baptist, he was welcome. An old lady stopped, leaning over a cane, to shake his hand. "You-all come anytime," she said. "You-all always welcome. Bless you, brother."

"Bless you, sister."

"Reveren' Duclois. My goodness. Welcome." Willard Washburn was a burly man who bore himself tall and erect despite his being in his 70s. His moustache and short, curled hair were white. He squinted through thick-lensed glasses at the minister, not even noticing Mitch behind him. The Washburns lived in a ramshackle, wooden, four-story building—"apartment house" would have been too fine a phrase for it. A rickety outside staircase connected the floors, each of which was circled by a narrow porch. Clotheslines sagging with laundry were strung between posts on every floor. Children ducked under the wet wash, chasing each other.

"Mr. Washburn," Abner Duclois said, "I came without phoning you because I—"

"Please, Reveren', step inside. Let me offer you some hospitality."

"Thank you, kindly, Brother Willard." Duclois entered the darkened apartment. The shutters were closed, and the only light came from a lamp by the far wall of the simply furnished room. Beside it, in an armchair, sat an old woman, in her hands a book. Seeing the minister, she began to rise out of the chair, struggling to get onto her feet.

"Please, Missy, don't bother to get up," Duclois said, but the old woman straightened herself and came over to him.

"Reverend, I'm so delighted to see you."

Duclois stepped forward and took both of her hands in his. Mitch followed him inside, the Washburns noticing him for the first time. Willard immediately took a defensive step backward.

"Who is this, Reveren'? Who have you brought with you?"

"Now Brother Willard, there's nothing to be fretful about. Professor Stevens is a friend of Doctor Moses Pemberton. You remember the doctor, don't you? The young fella who helped the Joves boy."

Washburn nodded but said nothing. He continued to stare at Mitch.

"Professor Stevens has some questions he'd like to ask you— questions about your family. He's writing a book."

Mitch extended his hand. "Mr. Washburn. I'm glad to meet you. I promise I won't take much of your time."

Washburn shook hands tentatively, looking toward the minister but still not saying anything.

"A book on what?" Missy Washburn asked, squinting at Mitch.

Duclois turned to Mitch. "Mrs. Washburn was a teacher in our grammar school for nearly forty years."

"A history book, ma'am," Mitch said. "About a Confederate spy."

"I love history," she said. "I've read every history book they have in the library, I think. I—"

Willard Washburn broke in. "I don't understand, Reveren', how we could know anything about a Confederate spy."

"Brother, there is no need to worry," Duclois said, trying to allay Washburn's fears. "Professor Stevens is a good man, a friend."

Washburn relented. "Come. Sit a spell." He pointed to a sofa. Although it and all of the other furniture in the room was old and worn, the room itself was immaculately clean, everything in place. Washburn switched on the tree lamp that stood beside the sofa. On the cushion was a day-old copy of the *Times-Picayune*, which Washburn carefully folded and put in a wooden magazine rack beside the sofa. He pulled up a plastic-seated aluminum chair from the small dining table in the middle of the room and sat down on it.

Mitch sat on the sofa while the minister took another aluminum chair, arranging it out of Washburn's eyeshot. "Willard was night foreman at the old Esso refinery before it shut down," he said. "Got laid off before Christmas back in the 60s without a word of warning." He turned his head in an arc around the room. "He used to own his own home, but he and Missy couldn't manage once she had to retire."

Mitch nodded that he understood Willard's reluctance to talk to a stranger, and a white one at that. "I'll explain this as briefly as possible, Mr. Washburn," he started. "I am working on a book about Thomas Clay Washburn. He was a Confederate officer from upstate Louisiana. In the course of trying to trace his family, I came across the name of Benjamin Washburn who—"

"I knew him as a boy."

"Yes. He was your, I guess you'd say great-granduncle."

"He was a big, powerful man," Washburn said, laughing softly at something he suddenly remembered. "He worked on the railroad, laying ties. He used to carry me on his shoulders. I thought it was the top of the world."

"Yes. Well, Benjamin brought up his orphaned nephew, Joshua Washburn, the son of his older sister, Eliza."

"Yes, that's correct. Joshua was my grandfather. But how did you find out about Benjamin?"

"That's what I've been spending my time doing—unraveling a bit of your family tree."

Miss Washburn, who had returned to her armchair, waved a finger at her husband. "Grandfather Joshua loved learning more than anything else in the whole world. He's the one who encouraged me to go on to normal school when Willard and I were courting. I did, and I became a teacher."

"Well," said Mitch, "you've answered my first question already. You're the descendant of Joshua Washburn through his son, Matthew."

"Matthew was my father. He was a carpenter—could make anything in the world with his hands. He even built the house that Missy and I lived in. I always felt at home in it, like it had been mine all my life."

"Mr. Washburn, do you know anything about the family, the descendants, of your grandfather Joshua's daughter, Susanna?"

"They were cousins, distant cousins." He hesitated. "We, er, we went separate ways. I'd hear about them every so often or read something about them in the *Picayune*, but we never got together or talked."

"They were always too high and mighty—their noses up in the air," Missy Washburn said. "I never did like them."

"Can you tell me anything at all about that side of your family—what they did, where they lived, who they were?"

"They are white."

"I don't understand," said Mitch, looking quizzically at Washburn. "What do you mean?"

"He means they pass for white," Duclois interjected. "They must be very light-skinned. That used to happen often with people who are descended from slaves. Mulattoes, quadroons. There was a lot of hanky-panky on the plantations and in the homes in the old days."

"Mr. Washburn, do you know a Flora May Parker? She'd be about twelve years younger than your son Franklin."

"Please, don't talk about Franklin." Missy Washburn sounded anguished. She pressed her fingers to her mouth. "Willard, I don't want to talk about Franklin."

Washburn rose stiffly. He went over to the woman, put his hand on her shoulder and bent down to whisper something in her ear. She looked up at him with a thank you in her slight smile.

"Franklin died of anemia," Washburn said, sitting down again on the sofa.

"Sickle-cell anemia," the minister chimed in again. "It's mostly a Negro disease, carried in the blood."

"I know," said Mitch, "but I thought it only struck adults." He turned back to Washburn. "About Flora May Parker, do you know anything about her."

"She's as white as her father Orko Parker was white. He was a bank president out in Houma. I don't even know if Parker knew his wife Mary Lou's grandmother was black."

Mitch's mouth had fallen open in astonishment. Washburn was clearly describing the parents of Flora May Parker, the wife of Mayor Bulloch. Flora May Bulloch's great-grandmother was black! "Let me get this straight, Mr. Washburn. Was Susanna, your father's sister, white then?"

"Enough to pass," Washburn said, "at least that's what my daddy told me. Susanna, Mary Lou, Flora May—they were ashamed of us. I don't think Susanna or Mary Lou told their husbands about where they came from." He shook his head back and forth. "I suppose if I could have passed for white, I would have, too."

"Don't you talk like that," Missy Washburn snapped, angry, her mouth set and firm. "You are a good man—a good black man. You have nothing to be ashamed of."

"Have you ever met her—Flora May?" Mitch asked.

"No."

"Then how do you know she's white?"

Washburn looked over at the minister. "I don't think he understands." He turned back to Mitch. "I got a phone call from her. She sounded white. And I got a letter from her once, too."

"When was this, Mr. Washburn? When did you get the phone call? When did you get the letter?"

"Oh, a few years ago. Not long, not long."

"Did you keep the letter, Mr. Washburn?"

Washburn shook his head No. "What for?"

"Why did she write?"

"She said she was looking for her ancestors. She asked about Franklin. She'd heard about his death and asked what he died of."

Washburn's wife turned again at the mention of her son's name. He went over to her once more and soothed her.

Mitch took an envelope from his inside jacket pocket. He took out of it the photograph of Thomas Clay Washburn. "Have you ever seen this man before?"

Washburn held the photo close to his glasses. "Wait here," he said, handing the photo back to Mitch and entering a door on the side. Mitch could see a bed inside the room covered with a brightly patterned Star of Texas quilt. Washburn was down on all fours, trying to reach something underneath it. He finally pulled out an old suitcase . It was held together with straps, which he began to undo. He searched inside the suitcase, taking out several boxes of various sizes, until he found what he was looking for. Returning to the living room, Washburn handed it to Mitch. It was one of the original prints of the photograph of Thomas Clay Washburn.

"It was passed on to me," the old black man said. "Grandfather Joshua told me. That," he said, pointing to Thomas Clay Washburn with a gnarled finger, "was my great-grandfather. He was white, lily-white." He giggled at his own joke. "Look at these hands," he said, turning his wrinkled hands over so that his pink palms showed. "I'm white."

"Willard!" his wife admonished him.

"That, Mr. Washburn," Mitch said, "is the Confederate spy I am writing about."

"Well, I knew he was in the war—an officer. Joshua told me that he was an officer in the Confederate Army, but he never said anything about his being a spy. I would have remembered that."

"I'm curious, Mr. Washburn," Mitch said. "Didn't you ever wonder about him—who he was, or what he was?"

Willard Washburn studied the back of his hands. "I didn't," he said at last, "see any point to it."

Mitch exchanged glances with the minister. "Is that what you came for?" Duclois asked.

Mitch looked at him blankly, his mind going over the irony of the situation. Flora May Bulloch, née Parker, was the great-great-granddaughter of Thomas Clay Washburn and a slave named Eliza. Flora May, wife of the bigoted racist mayor of Virgil, Louisiana, was the descendant of a slave. He hadn't expected that twist. But what did it mean? How did it fit in with the deaths of Tom Cantwell and Martha Tour Gale?

MITCH WAS GOING over in his mind his conversation with Washburn as he walked into the lobby of his hotel. He wasn't sure he was any closer to solving the mystery of Tom's death or that of Martha Tour Gale. What he had discovered didn't seem like a reason for murder.

Heading for the bank of elevators in the rear of the lobby, Mitch passed the tiny newsstand that was tucked into what might once have been a walk-in coat closet. Instinctively, he stopped and picked up a newspaper. It was a *Times-Picayune*. He handed the newsstand operator a dollar and began looking at the headlines as the man dropped change into his open palm.

Back in his room, Mitch kicked off his shoes and sank into a soft chair. He leafed through the newspaper, skimming from page to page, just reading headlines, when one of them, in the section of the paper devoted to national news, caught his attention. He stopped to read the story. When he was finished, he let the paper drop to his lap and sat for a long time without moving. The key to the deaths of Tom Cantwell and Martha Tour Gale lay in his lap.

THIRTEEN

M<small>ITCH EASED UP</small> on the gas pedal, allowing the car to slow back to the speed limit. Thinking about what he had figured out, working it over in his mind, distracted him—and when it did, the car seemed to take on a life of its own, hurtling him down the road into Virgil from Shreveport, a road that had become all too familiar. He knew the landmarks on the way— Chick's place, where he had stopped that first time, the houses and the barns, the bends in the road. They seemed to appear too suddenly and pass by so quickly, as though some huge magnet was drawing him toward—toward what? Mitch braked lightly. Every time he thought about someone singling him out, trying to poison him, his foot leaned heavily on the gas. He had been more than a random target. He hadn't even told Val he was leaving New Orleans to go back to Virgil; he knew he had to return and didn't want to get talked out of it. The story was far from over, but the answers all lay in the quiet, unassuming little town he was now approaching.

It was mid-afternoon, a time when most of the shopkeepers would be telling their assistants that they were headed over to the diner for their regular midday coffee—"come get me if you need me." Tex Bochard, however, would be waiting for him in the sheriff's office. Mitch had decided that the smartest thing he could do at this juncture would be to share with Bochard everything he knew—and suspected. At least then, if something happened . . .

Mitch drove slowly down Main Street, looking for a place to park near the courthouse. He eased into an empty spot, got out of the car, put a coin in the meter and started to walk away, then turned back abruptly. He went around the car, checking that all the doors were locked.

Bochard greeted him grimly. Mitch had already run over the highlights of what he knew when he telephoned the sheriff from New Orleans. Bochard's face reflected the seriousness of the situation. He motioned Mitch into a seat opposite his desk. "Tell me about it—everything you uncovered—from the top."

Mitch recounted in detail what he had found out in New Orleans, concluding with his conversation with Willard Washburn.

"Flora May's maiden name is Parker," Bochard repeated. He got up and looked out the window. "I don't know what to make of it, Mitch."

"I don't either, Sheriff. I'm no detective, but it seems to me there are several possibilities. I mean, let's assume that both Tom and Martha Tour Gale were murdered and that whoever murdered them also tried to poison me. That's a fair assumption, I think. That narrows things down to maybe three people."

"I can guess who you mean," Bochard said. He turned from the window and sat down again, resting his chin on his clasped hands. "I'd like to hear you name them and your reason."

"The mayor," said Mitch, "the doctor and Flora May."

"Okay—and why?"

Mitch shrugged. "Because they all had the opportunity to slip something into my food that day."

"So did one of the Leons," the sheriff pointed out. "And Ernie."

"If Ernie did it, it was on Bulloch's orders," said Mitch. "As far as the Leons are concerned, call it instinct or what you will, but I feel it isn't them."

Bochard stood up and began fidgeting with the band on his Stetson, which was hanging on the coat tree. "And the motive— what in God's name is the motive?" He crossed his arms and looked down at Mitch. "Look," he said, "I came up with the same names you did only on the basis of what happened at the picnic. But I cannot see the motive. We're whistling in the dark about the three most important people in this town."

"It dawned on me after I left Washburn," said Mitch. He pulled his wallet from his back pocket. "Here," he said, taking a folded newspaper clipping from it and handing it to Bochard, "take a look at this. I happened to pick up a *Picayune* at my hotel. It's what triggered my thinking."

The sheriff took the clipping and unfolded it. "Washburn's attitude reflected it, too," said Mitch, as the sheriff started to read:

KLAN SUPPORTED IN RACISM FIGHT

NEW ORLEANS, June 24 (UPI) — In the stormy aftermath of remarks that were called racist, State Senator Calvin H. Hastings refused today to withdraw his support of the Ku Klux Klan, saying it had every right to exist.

"Why even the ACLU [American Civil Liberties Union] recognizes the right of Klansmen to assemble and express opinions," said the senator, a staunch opponent of school busing.

Hastings's remarks were made in a hastily called press conference here after the state branch of the Klan took a full-page advertisement in a Natchez, Mississippi, paper extolling South Africa's apartheid policy. The advertisement was titled "Purity and Godliness: When and Why Race Counts."

"They're right," Hastings declared. "You and I both

know that. I'm not afraid to say so and neither are they."
Alluding to David Duke's campaign for governor in the fall of 1991, the senator said he would . . .

"What's your point, Mitch?" asked Bochard, as he handed the clipping back without finishing it. "We've had no trouble with the Klan up here."

"Correct me if you think I'm wrong, Sheriff, but you folks do have a race problem here." The sheriff began to protest, but Mitch held up his hand. "I know, you can say the same thing about us New Yorkers. Hear me out on this, though.

"That article got me thinking. If it's made known that Flora May Parker has black ancestors, what effect would that have on Bulloch's political career? You don't have to answer that one, Sheriff, because it's obvious, to me at least, that a man who makes no secret of his racist views would be devastated if it came out that his own wife was black, no matter how far removed."

Mitch paused. "Go on," Bochard said. "I'm not arguing with you."

"The question really comes down to, who knows about Flora May's background? Does the mayor? If he knows, he probably wouldn't want it bandied about. But supposing he doesn't. I can't imagine he would have married her if he had known. Did he learn about it afterwards?" Mitch shrugged his shoulders. "Flora May, of course, knows. Maybe she hasn't told her husband—and maybe she knows that if she told him he would have a fit. On top of that, she must be aware that any publicity surrounding who she's descended from would ruin his political chances. So she could be protecting him without his even knowing it."

"And the doctor?" the sheriff asked. "How does he fit in with this?"

"I think the doctor knows—in fact, I'm certain of it. Flora May found out that Willard Washburn's son died of sickle-cell anemia and she was worried about having it, too, no matter how remote that possibility might be. Dexter either uncovered that during a routine test, or she asked to be tested for it after Willard's son died of it. He knows all right. It could be that he's trying to protect her."

"I'm having trouble buying all this."

"What else can it be, Sheriff?" Mitch insisted. "It's connected to Tom, it's got to be. Tom knew something, found out something that someone else didn't want divulged. And the only thing I've run across that is even remotely sensitive is Flora May's background."

"Well," Bochard sighed, "it's the only motive we've got so it will have to do. It looks like we may have two murders and one attempted one on our hands." Bochard rubbed his hands over his face. "But I gotta be honest with you, Mitch. You may think that we haven't changed all that much in a hundred years, but we have. I know this town, and it's hard for me to believe that anyone here in this day and age would kill to keep that kind of family secret." The sheriff looked out the window. "The truth is," he spoke so quietly Mitch could barely hear him, "I reckon I don't rightly want to believe it."

"Well, Sheriff, if it makes you feel any better, not too long ago, something similar happened up North with a young fellow who belonged to the American Nazi Party. He was way up in the hierarchy, going around preaching anti-Semitic garbage, among other things. By pure accident, a reporter discovered that the fellow was part-Jewish, and it made the front pages of all the New York papers. The next morning, the young man committed suicide—murder of a sort. Don't you see, the depth of passion that controlled that man is torturing our murderer. That kind of sickness ignores everything—morality, law, human decency, even human life."

Mitch stopped abruptly, carried away by his own rhetoric. He shared Bochard's skepticism. It was just as hard for him to imagine such a motive for murder.

"All right, so what do you propose doing, Mitch?" The sheriff finally said after a long, awkward silence. "Even if we knew who, I don't have enough to go on to order an arrest. In fact, we don't have a thing."

"I think we have to flush out whoever it is."

"How?"

Mitch scratched the back of his head. "My wife'll shoot me if she ever finds out about this." He poked his glasses back up his nose. "How would you feel about setting me up?"

"As bait?" The sheriff frowned. "You could get into a whole lot of trouble doing that. I don't know that I could condone your doing it."

"How about if you're holding the other end of the tether?"

"You'll be risking your neck, Mitch," warned Bochard.

"Don't I know it," acknowledged Mitch. "But someone has to pay for two deaths—not to mention the attempt on my life. I won't pretend I'm not scared. If you've got a better idea, we'll do it. Otherwise, I don't see any other way to resolve this."

"Let me run down with you what I believe happened." Mitch leaned forward in the wooden swivel chair in Augustus Leon's office at the *Virgil Whig*.

Leon was sitting with his legs up on his desk, playing with a rubber band and looking somber. Twenty or so galley proofs lay in a row beside his telephone. From off behind him, in the room beyond, the chatter of a linotype machine could be heard. "This better be good, Mitch. You're talking about busting open this town, ruining reputations."

"Let me explain, Augustus, all right? I wouldn't be sitting here if it weren't serious, terribly serious.

"Little things bothered me at first," Mitch continued, taking a deep breath. "Tom's death—I don't know, it didn't sound right. The sheriff had the same feeling, but no proof of any wrongdoing. Even Martha Tour Gale's death could be seen as a coincidence. And the step stool and empty kitchen cabinets—well, you can read that a lot of different ways."

"It's all conjecture, Mitch."

"I know that, Augustus. Let me finish. I think I've figured out what happened, and it started back in 1862 in New Orleans."

"You're kidding." Leon swept his legs from the desk top and sat up. "This goes back to the war?"

Mitch nodded. "If you can accept one or two likelihoods it does. I got to thinking about the facts—the historical facts—after meeting a black man named Willard Washburn in New Orleans. And then I read about that state senator, Hastings, and the Klan's ad in Mississippi backing apartheid in South Africa. You must have heard about it, too. I got to thinking, what if?"

"What if what?"

"Listen, Thomas Clay Washburn went down to New Orleans from here in Virgil to enlist in 1861. He took with him a slave, a childhood companion named Benjamin. In New Orleans, they went to visit Benjamin's sister, Eliza. She had been a slave on the Washburn farm here, but Washburn's father gave her to a guy named Truman Moore to pay off a debt. So Eliza goes to New Orleans to work in Truman Moore's household. Then the war comes along—the Civil War—and passing through New Orleans to join a Confederate regiment, Thomas Washburn stops off to visit Moore, and Benjamin gets a chance to visit with his sister Eliza at Moore's home. Moore knows Washburn, of course, and asks both of them, Thomas Clay Washburn and his slave Benjamin, to stay at the house. They do. It was customary. All this is fact. It can be substantiated.

"Now what if sometime during the few days they were there, Thomas gets Eliza pregnant? He knew her, of course, from the farm. Maybe he had something going with her back then. Who knows? It wouldn't have been unusual. Especially since he'd never married. Her brother Benjamin probably figured out the relationship but couldn't do anything about it."

"You can prove this?" Leon asked.

"Hear me out, Augustus. Let me get back to the facts. Thomas and Benjamin leave the Moore home and go off to war. Roughly nine months later Eliza dies giving birth to a child, who is named Joshua. The Moores—or their servants most likely—take care of the child, but the family has to leave New Orleans when Union troops arrive. Thomas Clay Washburn, meanwhile, gets caught as a spy and hanged before the war ends. When the war does end, the Moores return to New Orleans and, lo and behold, who shows up but Benjamin—only he's no longer a slave. He's Benjamin Washburn now. He's taken the Washburn name. He's free, and he claims Eliza's child as his own family. Maybe Moore tried to put up a legal fight. I doubt that he could have won, particularly given the political climate at the time. Anyway, the child is Benjamin's blood kin.

"So Benjamin rears him as Joshua Washburn. Joshua marries and has two kids himself. One, Matthew, was as dark-skinned as you would imagine. Matthew's son, Willard—whom I talked with just yesterday—is as black as night, a man in his 70s, going blind it seemed, with a wife suffering from severe arthritis." Mitch paused, remembering. "Anyway, it gets a bit confusing at this point, but bear with me. Willard is Joshua's grandson. He and his wife had a son, Franklin, who was Joshua's great-grandson, but Franklin died of sickle-cell anemia. That's an important connection to remember, because Joshua's other child was a girl, Susanna, who must have been quite light-skinned. Enough so that she passed for white, marrying a guy named Mims. They had only one daughter who survived, Mary Lou Mims, Joshua's granddaughter. Mary Lou Mims married Orko Parker just before the Second World War, and just after it—Parker must have been away in the service until then—they had a daughter, Joshua Washburn's great-granddaughter, the great-great-granddaughter of your local Confederate hero, Thomas Clay Washburn, and the slave girl Eliza."

"Flora May Parker." Leon's jaw dropped as he said her name. "That's her maiden name."

"Yes, Flora May. You know, Willard Washburn had one of the photographs of Thomas Clay Washburn tucked away among his family souvenirs. And he had heard from Flora May, too."

"Why? Did she acknowledge the background?"

"No, what I think happened was that Flora May got ill once, God knows with what, had a routine blood test taken, and discovered that she was prone to sickle-cell anemia. She must have been scared. She must have known about the other side of the family, about the line descended from Matthew Washburn. Anyway, she inquired about the family and, of course, found out that Franklin Washburn had died of the disease. Which must have really frightened her."

"Mitch, this is fascinating, but what has this got to do with Tom Cantwell and Martha Tour Gale?"

"Look, Augustus, it didn't strike me until then, but didn't you ever wonder why Bulloch and his wife never had children?"

"That doesn't mean anything, Mitch. Lyda and I don't either."

"Well, I think in the mayor's case it's because his wife chose not to have any. She was afraid a child might turn out to be dark-skinned."

"That's crazy and unlikely."

"Maybe so, Augustus, but it's her perception of what might happen that counts."

"Okay, even if I grant that, Mitch, what has this got to do with those deaths?"

"Don't you see, Augustus? Tom came down here to complete his research, and in tracing the family he stumbled on the story. He learned about Thomas Clay Washburn and Eliza from Martha Tour Gale. She must have gotten it from Benjamin, whom she interviewed in the 1920s. That was the scandal Tom cryptically mentioned to you. He had inadvertently dredged up the whole situation. What would ruin the career of a racist politician quicker than people learning that he is married to a woman who has black blood in her, no matter how distant that might be?"

"So you're saying that both Tom and the Gale woman were murdered to keep them quiet?"

"And someone tried to poison me when I started getting too close. I'm not even convinced, now that I look back on it, that an accident I had in the forest wasn't an attempt on my life also."

"Okay, who then? Who is the killer?"

"One of three people, Augustus, and that's why I'm here."

"You expect me to tell you?"

Mitch smiled. "No, but a story about all this would help."

Leon didn't say anything. He looked down at his hands. The rubber band he'd been playing with was interwined between his fingers. He studied it as though trying to figure out how to unravel it.

"Augustus, I know what I'm asking."

"Do you, Mitch? This is a small town, not some big city metropolis where a thing like this would be forgotten the next day. This'll hurt Virgil. We'd get reporters and TV people from the Shreveport station, maybe even New Orleans. It's a big story for a place like this, Mitch. And it wouldn't die overnight. What good would that do?"

"Augustus, I wouldn't ask you to do anything that I wouldn't do as an editor."

"Why don't you go to Bochard, put it into police hands?"

"I have, Augustus, but all we have are doubts and guesses. We have no hard evidence."

"I can't print conjectures, you know that. I'd be sued for libel."

"I'm not asking that, Augustus. I need to flush out the killer. I'm asking you to run a story about me—a feature about my research work on your local hero. And in the story, you drop in the fact that I uncovered an interesting thing about him—that he was the ancestor, the great-great-grandfather, of the woman who is now the wife of the mayor of Virgil."

"And she's a black woman! That's the next step, isn't it? I mean someone would get to wondering who Washburn's wife was who Flora May Parker was descended from. Holy Jesus, what a bombshell that would be! What the hell do you expect that to accomplish?"

"That the killer will get rattled and confess, or do something foolish that will give the whole thing away. At the least it would ruin that person's reputation. At least some justice would be done, someone would pay for the murders of Tom and Martha Tour Gale."

"And if someone like the mayor is innocent, it would still ruin his reputation."

"Come on, Augustus, he's a damn bigot. He almost deserves to be knocked down. What kind of loss would he be to Virgil or the state?"

Leon winced. "That's a pretty callous way of looking at it, Mitch. I don't know if I'm up to destroying a person just because I disagree with him."

"It's the fallout in a situation like this, Augustus. Someone's going to get hurt, I admit that. But two people have already been murdered. In my book, that justifies what I'm asking."

"The end justifies the means?"

Mitch shrugged. He got up, adjusting his jacket. "So be it, Augustus. I can't force you to run the story. But you've got to live in this town, my friend, and that means you're going to be living right alongside someone who doesn't think twice about murdering people. He—or she—is your neighbor, Augustus, not mine. And who knows where they'll stop? If you can live with that, by all means do so."

Mitch was halfway through the door when Leon called to him. "Hold it. Give me a minute to think this out. Christ, Mitch, we go to press tomorrow, and you want a decision in a split second."

"Take your time, Augustus," said Mitch, sitting back down and picking up a galley from Leon's desk. "I'll proof for you in the meantime."

Lamar, his apron smeared with black ink and wearing a hat fashioned out of paper, suddenly appeared, walking into Leon's office without knocking from the half-open door to the composing room in the back of the shop. "You best come, Augustus," he said, the words coming out in a slow drawl. "The lead pot is overflowing again."

"I'll be right there," Leon said as the printer returned to the composing room.

Mitch gestured with his head toward Lamar's retreating figure. "Could he have heard anything we've been talking about?"

"Lamar?" Leon scowled. "He's not what you might call close-mouthed, but he's never betrayed a confidence of mine." Mitch looked skeptical. "Don't worry, Mitch.

"Look," he continued before Mitch could say anything more, "I know I'm going to come back to the same decision no matter how long I think about it. I can't print such a story, no way. I'm sorry."

Mitch was disappointed but tried not to show it. "I understand." He rose again. "How about doing me a favor, then?"

"Name it."

"At least run one of your little inside items about my returning to Virgil to complete my research on the book about Thomas Clay Washburn. Include that I said that I've fortunately been able to trace *everything* Tom Cantwell had unearthed while here. And say that I'm staying in Virgil only a few days more before returning home."

"I'll do it, Mitch, but you're making yourself a sitting duck if everything you say is God's truth."

FOURTEEN

T EX BOCHARD BRUSHED the crown of his hat with the back of his wrist and hung it on the coat tree. "Are you certain you want to handle it this way, Mitch?" he said, hefting his holstered gun out of the way as he dropped into his armchair.

"Can you suggest another way, Sheriff?"

Bochard frowned. "Damn. If we only had some solid evidence!"

"We're never going to get any, you know that." Mitch cupped his hands in front of his face. "All we have are your shreds— what, a lady's hat pin, a mysterious kitchen stool, and some empty kitchen cabinets?"

Bochard bit his lip. "I just wish . . . Oh, hell, we have to make some move, though I gotta say that the more I think about it, the more I think that that news story about you coming out today in the *Whig* was—if you don't mind my saying so—a piss-poor idea. I'd like to have had some more time to set up a security arrangement."

"I apologize, Sheriff," Mitch said. "I should have alerted you about it first. But we talked about getting the word out some way, and Augustus had his deadline coming up."

Bochard clasped his hands behind his head. "All right," he said, "we'll flush whoever it is out, but I'm going to be on your tail every minute of the way. I want to know where you are and where you're going, even if it's to the bathroom."

"That's okay by me," said Mitch. "I'd just as soon know that you were behind me."

"And I call the shots," Bochard insisted. "I can't afford to let you or anyone get hurt. Here, I'll write down my home phone, too, just in case. But Floyd or whoever's on duty out there always knows where I am."

The sheriff reached for a pad and pencil. As he did, the room suddenly darkened. Outside, the sky was blotted out by a low, heavy, black cloud that was racing northeast.

"Mitch?" Bochard leaned forward, speading his hands, palms down, on the desk. "This is serious. It's not a game we're playing. If our feelings are correct, there's someone out there who's not above pushing another obstacle out of the way."

A splatter of heavy raindrops hit the windows. The drenching rain made it impossible to see anything outside. Everything was a blur.

By the time Mitch drove into the parking lot of the Caddo Motel, the rain was torrential. He managed to race into the lobby without getting soaked. As he walked toward his room, his attention was caught by sounds coming from one of the convention rooms. That was what the motel called them, although to Mitch, they looked not much bigger than his bedroom. He walked over and peered in, unabashedly eavesdropping. The room was crowded with men, all dressed in what looked like identical suits, a sea of nondescript gray pin-stripe. It was the voice of the man at the dais that had attracted Mitch. It was the voice of a preacher, strong, musical, mesmerizing. He was haranguing the crowd in repetitive phrases. "You're not making money, you're not salesmen, you're not out for yourselves. No, no, no. You're doing the work of the Lord, you're agents of the Lord, you're bringing the word of God to every man, woman and child in this county. And don't you forget it."

My God, Bible salesmen. Mitch scanned their faces, some intent on the speaker, some obviously bored—they'd heard it before. All white, not a black face among them. I wonder, he thought, how many of these good men doing the work of the Lord would murder to hide a black relative. It was ironic, Mitch thought as he headed down the corridor toward his room, that in this country, the smallest amount of black parentage branded you black, while in some countries of Europe, the exact opposite was true: the smallest amount of white parentage branded you white.

MITCH FIDDLED WITH the dials on the television set. The heavy rainstorm was playing havoc with the reception, distorting the image. Specks of colored static flashed across the screen each time lightning struck. When a bolt that lit up the sky outside his room caused it to happen again, Mitch pushed the off button in frustration. He picked up the *Virgil Whig* again. It was open to page three, and there, down amidst the notices of the next Boy Scout meeting and the First Baptist Church sewing circle, was the story Augustus Leon had promised to run:

WRITER RETURNS TO VIRGIL

Professor Mitchel Stevens has returned to Virgil to complete what he says is the final research into a book about Virgil's most famous Confederate soldier, Thomas Clay Washburn. Mr. Stevens, who is finishing the work begun by the late Thomas Cantwell before his untimely death last month, says he has been able to retrace all of Mr. Cantwell's leads to his complete satisfaction. He plans to stay here only a few more days before going home.

196

Not a gem of writing, Mitch mused, but the purpose is served. He dropped the paper onto the bed and reached for the paperback book he was still struggling to get interested in. The waiting game had begun. Mitch and the sheriff had agreed that he should stay put at the Caddo Motel that night and go to the parish clerk's office in the morning. If he ran out of things to do there, he was to go to the local library, which abutted the high school. He and the sheriff would stay in touch via phone; Bochard didn't want them seen together lest that scare off the killer.

Mitch leaned back against the pillows, adjusting his head until he felt comfortable. His glance fell on the chain bolt on the door. Assured that the door was secure, he opened the book and started to read, but his eyelids felt heavy. Drowsy, he closed his eyes. The book fell gently onto his chest, and he fell asleep. It was a fitful sleep. Mitch dreamed that he was running wildly through a bog, his feet heavy with mud and tangled foliage. He kept looking back over his shoulder, aware that someone or something was chasing him but not knowing what. Out of breath, he dropped to the ground, his chest heaving with pain, when suddenly . . .

Suddenly the phone rang. Mitch opened his eyes instantaneously, blinking at the brightness. The phone rang again. He was in his motel room, he realized, coming awake. The phone rang again. Mitch reached over and picked it up, clearing his throat as he did so.

"Mitch, is that you? You sound so funny."

"It's me, Val. I was just dozing." Mitch cleared his throat again. "I'm all right."

"Mitch, what the devil are you doing in Virgil? The hotel in New Orleans said you'd—"

"I had to come back here for a couple of days, just to finish things up. I'll be through in maybe one or two days at the most. And then I'll fly out and join you. I've already checked the connecting flights out of Shreveport. We'll be together soon."

But Val wasn't placated. "But why didn't you let me know,

Mitch? I got worried to death when I didn't hear from you."

"I tried calling, Val, I really did, but you were on location, and I guess you didn't get my message."

"Well, you could have tried again."

"Oh, come on, Val, you know I love you."

"Really? You haven't even asked lately about how my work is going."

"For crying out loud, Val, you know I care about what you do. I've just gotten wrapped up in this thing and lost track of time. So how is it going? You happy with the director?"

"It's okay. It won't be a masterpiece, but all the producer cares about is the box office."

"And your part, did they make those changes in the script you thought were necessary?"

"Some. Enough of them. It'll be a decent film. I won't be ashamed of being in it. It just seems to take forever to make these damn things. And I get so lonely when I don't hear from you."

"Well, it'll only be a few more days . . ." Mitch's voice drifted off.

"Mitchell Stevens, what's going on? You're really not paying attention, are you? You're up to something again, aren't you?"

"No, no, Val," said Mitch, quickly recovering. "I'm just sleepy, that's all. Everything is coming along fine."

"And that business about Tom's death? Is that all settled, or are you still putting your nose where it oughtn't to be?"

"Now, honey, don't get overprotective. It's okay to do that with your son, but not with me. I'm a grown-up guy."

"Since when?"

"Val? Stop it. We're just making each other miserable and it isn't necessary."

"Will you call me when you're through and on your way?"

"Even before that, I promise, honey."

There was a short, dull buzzing on the line. "Val, I think someone's trying to reach me. I better get off now."

"I miss you, Mitch."

"Me, too, Val."

Mitch sighed and pressed the connector down to clear the line, then dialed the front desk. Hollings Carter answered with his usual gruff, "What is it?"

"Was someone trying to reach me?"

"Yeah, Doc J. J. He said for you to call him as soon as you could. He's over to his office. Got the number?"

"Thanks." Mitch pressed the connector down again and then dialed the doctor. The phone rang only once. Dexter picked it up immediately. "Doctor? You called?"

"Stevens, I need to see you," said Dexter, who made no effort to hide the urgency in his voice. "Right away."

"It's almost 10. Can't this wait until morning?"

"This is critical, Stevens. I have to talk with you."

"You want to tell me what this is about?" said Mitch, trying to stall for time, wondering what to do.

"It might not be wise," Dexter said ominously.

"All right, then. How about coming over to my motel?"

"No, I don't think that's a good idea." The doctor paused briefly. "Do you know Cal's Hideaway?"

"No, I've never heard of it."

"It's a bar, a roadhouse, the other side of town from where you are, maybe three or four miles out. Carter can give you directions. Can you meet me there in 15 minutes?"

"Let's make it a half hour. It's raining like hell out."

I wonder what's so urgent, Mitch thought, as he dialed the sheriff's office. Floyd answered. The sheriff, the clerk said, was out at the lumbering camp, but he would radio him immediately. Cal's Hideaway was on the way to the camp, Floyd said, so Bochard would not have far to travel to reach there. It was only after he hung up that Mitch realized he could have asked Floyd for the directions. He picked up the phone and called the front desk. Carter described the route so laconically that it seemed like he begrudged telling Mitch where it was. "Take you about 10 minutes at most."

To give the sheriff plenty of time to get to the roadhouse, Mitch decided to take his time driving there. He dressed slowly, putting on a sleeveless sweater under his sports jacket. He reached deep inside his valise to pull out a light, fold-up raincoat and a collapsible umbrella.

Heading out into the car park, Mitch tried putting up the umbrella, but strong gusts of wind threatened to pull it inside-out, so he ran to his car, sloshing water—and cursing. He got in behind the wheel and slammed the door shut. The rain beat down on the hood and roof. Mitch had to pump the gas pedal several times before the engine kicked over. While letting it warm up, he turned on the rear-window defroster to dry the fog that obliterated his back view, but rivulets of rain made it difficult to see clearly out the glass anyway. Finally, turning the windshield wipers on high, Mitch backed up and turned gradually to get onto the highway. His headlights barely illuminated the surface of the road, which was slick with tiny rivers of water streaming across it.

Driving slowly, Mitch passed through the center of Virgil. The only lights visible, other than the street lamps, were from the rear of the town hall, where the sheriff's office was located. Mitch thought about stopping to see if Bochard had gotten his message, but it was raining so hard that he decided against doing so. Floyd was reliable, Mitch rationalized. Bochard would get his message—and the sheriff certainly was aware of the potential for danger in his meeting Dexter.

Mitch was grateful he was used to the twists and turns of the road. The storm was so heavy he was having trouble seeing through the windshield. There were no lights once he left the center of town. He lowered his window and ducked his head out of it to see ahead of him as the two-lane highway curved to the left. As he did so, he thought he spotted some movement in the side-view mirror, but the image was so distorted by splatters of rain that he wasn't sure whether he had experienced an optical illusion.

Coming out of the curve, Mitch closed his window and reached for a Kleenex from the small box on the seat by his side. He started to wipe his eyeglasses clear of raindrops with his right hand when the car jolted. Mitch dropped the tissue and grabbed the wheel with both hands. The car jolted again. He looked in his rearview mirror but couldn't see anything. Whatever it was behind him hit his rear bumper harder this time, causing the car to swerve toward the verge of the road. Mitch, his eyes darting between the road ahead and the rearview mirror, righted the car just as it was hit again. He was shoved into the wheel, his chest bruised from the sudden shock. "Holy Jesus!" Someone was trying to force him off the road.

Adrenalin surged through Mitch's body. He thought quickly. If he tried to pull away he might miss the darkened road in the rain and crash. If he pulled off to the side and stopped, he risked the possibility that whoever it was behind him might be armed. Suddenly, there was a scraping noise. The vehicle behind was coming abreast of him, trying to force him off the road. Mitch was tossed to the side as the vehicle slammed into the passenger door behind him. He quickly righted himself, turning the steering wheel sharply to the left to avoid the deep ditch, swollen with rain, that his headlights picked up as the car lurched off the road. Mitch braked hard. The vehicle, no lights showing, raced by him and down the road. When it was about 30 yards away, its lights came on, but it was too far away for Mitch to read the license plate or even see what make it was.

Mitch stopped the car. He held a hand over his heart, which was beating rapidly, and rubbed it. He shivered. "Holy Jesus." What had happened was no accident. Someone had been laying in wait for him to come down the highway. Who the hell knew he would be there? Dexter. Floyd. Bochard. Anyone else?

TEN MINUTES LATER, Mitch, still trembling, pulled into the lot behind Cal's Hideaway. There were four other cars parked there, close to the rear entranceway. One, a white Ford sedan, bore MD plates—Dexter's car. Mitch parked next to it, on its left side. He got out of his car and examined the damage to it. The chrome trim had been ripped off and the passenger door bore a deep dent. Ignoring the rain that continued to come down heavily, Mitch walked around Dexter's Ford. There were no marks whatsoever on its right side. Mitch felt the hood. It was only faintly warm. He didn't know what to make of that. If it had been the doctor back there on the highway, was it possible he had driven a different car and then switched to this one? That seemed unlikely, but Mitch was wary. He looked around the lot. Where was the sheriff? Shouldn't he have been here by now?

Still debating whether he should wait until Bochard showed up, Mitch ducked under the overhang of the roadhouse to get out of the rain. The rear door was nearby. A gust of wind pelted him with rain. Mitch reached for the door handle and turned it. He entered the roadhouse, walking cautiously down a short, dimly lit hall and through a swinging door at its end into the bar proper. Almost immediately he spotted Dexter, in the far corner, nursing a glass that was half-empty. The doctor saw him but didn't acknowledge him. Mitch ducked around several tables to reach him, looking around the café as he did so. Several men sat on stools at the bar, talking to the bartender. A couple was at a table in an opposite corner, near a door with a round window in it that apparently led to a kitchen; they were whispering, their heads close together. A lumberjack sat alone at another table, his legs stretched out underneath it, an overturned, empty bottle of beer resting on the table; he was snoring. Where was the sheriff?

Mitch sat down opposite the doctor and waited for him to talk. He was still suspicious that Dexter might have had something to do with forcing him off the road.

Dexter waved to the bartender, then pointed at Mitch. Seconds later, the man appeared at Mitch's elbow. "What'll it be?" he said.

Dexter motioned with his head toward Mitch, who said, "A beer—anything you've got on draft is all right." Mitch searched Dexter's face, trying to discern what the doctor was thinking. Neither man said anything.

The bartender returned almost immediately and put down a glass tankard of foamy beer. After he left, Dexter finally spoke. "I read that piece in the *Whig*, Stevens. I think we should talk."

"What about?" Mitch said icily.

"I get the impression, the idea, from the story, that you've gotten to know just about what your friend Cantwell knew."

"So what?"

"Stevens, we're not enemies," the doctor said. He took a sip of his drink. "I think we're both concerned about the same thing."

"You want to spell out what you mean by that?"

"Look, Stevens, let's cut out this cat-and-mouse game and talk plainly."

"Hey, Doc," said Mitch, holding up his hands, "this is your ball game. *You* asked to see me. *You* said it was urgent. *You* talk plainly."

Dexter looked down at a piece of lint on his suit. He pinched at it until he got it away. "I'm concerned," he began, his eyes still riveted at the spot where the lint had been, "I'm worried, that some things aren't what they seem on the surface." He paused.

"That's still not plain talk, not to me."

"Look, I'm not happy, now that I think of it, with what happened with your friend."

"And what do you think happened to my friend?"

"I don't know—that's the truth." Dexter looked up at Mitch. "I don't think, now that I look back on it, I don't think it was a simple case of heart failure. It was easy to believe it was a natural death, but now . . . I'm not sure."

"And you're a little late also. You want to tell me what you're driving at, Dexter?"

"I will, if you'll be frank with me."

"About what?"

Dexter glanced around. His voice fell almost to a whisper. "About what you found out about—" He stopped abruptly as the front door to the café opened and a woman came in, wrenching a hat from her head and looking around angrily. Spotting the sleeping lumberjack, she marched over to him and swatted him on the head with the hat. He jumped up, flustered, as the woman castigated him, punching him in the ribs and cursing.

"You were saying," Mitch prodded, turning away from the scene.

But Dexter seemed to have second thoughts. "Never mind, Stevens."

Mitch pushed his glasses back on his nose. "Okay," he said, "let's be frank with each other. I'll tell you what I think, and you tell me what you think."

"Fair enough," said Dexter.

Neither man said anything. "So start," Mitch said finally. "You're the one who got me out in the rain to talk."

Dexter took a long swallow from his glass. Putting it down, he wiped his lips with the back of his hand. "It could have been foul play."

"That's a fancy way of saying murder, isn't it?"

"All right, it could have been murder," Dexter conceded, "but it's too damn late to know that for sure."

"Look, I think it was murder, Dexter, but I can't figure out how it was done without the police getting suspicious."

The doctor frowned. "I can only imagine one way. Cantwell took an extra dose of insulin by mistake because he thought his sugar level was too high."

"What would make him think that?"

"He'd obviously tested himself before going to bed. I found the usual paraphernalia a diabetic uses to test his urine. He tested himself, found his sugar content way above normal and injected himself with a dose of insulin to bring it down. And that sent him into shock and killed him."

"Would it? Really?"

Dexter looked around the room. He leaned forward and lowered his voice. "I usually carry in my bag a vial of insulin for an emergency. The local pharmacy closes at six, so I ordinarily stock a few supplies. I don't even think about it. Just toss them in, and sometimes have no call to use anything for weeks.

"I'm missing a dose of Semilente, a type of insulin known as 'rapid-acting regular.' It provides almost instant action, within fifteen to thirty minutes anyway. And its peak effectiveness is anywhere from two to four hours."

The doctor sipped his drink, swallowing hard. "It's my fault. I saw a familiar box and vial in the wastepaper basket and didn't bother to read the labels. Cantwell, according to what he was carrying in his medicine kit, was on long-acting Ultralente, a kind of insulin he would ordinarily have taken in the morning. It goes into action anywhere from four to eight hours and peaks between fourteen and twenty-four hours."

"I'm lost," Mitch said. "What are you saying?"

"I'm saying that when the dosage Cantwell ordinarily took every day was at its peak he suddenly increased that amount with a jolt of the quick-acting insulin from my medical bag."

"And?"

"It sure as hell wasn't me." The doctor took a deep breath and exhaled. "But I would have been the obvious suspect if the sheriff had any cause to investigate further. He could have easily traced that box and vial to me. And I, of course, told him the death was natural."

Mitch played with his tankard of beer, unconsciously turning it around in a circle. "So we're back where we started from, aren't we."

"I got suspicious of what happened to you, too—the food poisoning."

"Where the hell were you that night, by the way?" Mitch asked. "They couldn't get hold of you to come to the Caddo."

The doctor made a face. "I didn't realize it was anything serious. I told the answering service to say they couldn't contact me. I didn't want to have anything to do with you."

"Jesus, are you serious?"

Dexter nodded slowly. "It's too late to apologize—and thank God it didn't turn out like it could have." He put out his hands pleadingly. "I didn't know you had been poisoned, for God's sake. And I didn't think anything of it when I heard about it the next day.

"I've spoken to Pemberton," he went on. "From everything he tells me and what I can surmise as well, you were suffering from a case of arsenic poisoning. Someone, somehow, sprinkled some on your food. Not much, maybe not enough to kill you, but it could have. You were very fortunate."

"My God." Mitch pushed the beer tankard away. "That's insane. If that's what was put into my food—the person who did it wasn't thinking. That would have showed up in an autopsy, wouldn't it?"

"Absolutely," Dexter said. "And an obvious suspect again, if the police were thinking of Cantwell's death as murder and connected that insulin to me, would have been me. I can imagine them wondering why I refused to answer your call for help. Why I let you die." He looked into his empty glass, rattling the remainders of the ice cubes in the bottom. "That's when *I* started to worry. I mean, who the hell would want to set me up like that."

"Who would?"

"No, it's your turn to talk."

"All right, Doc, I'll be honest with you," Mitch said. "You had the opportunity and the know-how. I thought you might be the guilty one."

"I save lives, Stevens, not take them."

Mitch appraised the doctor. He believed him. Dexter wasn't playing games or lying now. "All right. Fair enough." Mitch took a sip of the beer. "Briefly, I've found out about Flora May's background, just like I'm sure that Tom Cantwell did—just as

I'm convinced that you've known all along."

Dexter nodded agreement. "I learned about it a couple of years ago. But I've never told anyone." He drank the water from the melted ice cubes. "I didn't want to see Flora May hurt."

"Are you and she—" Mitch hesitated.

"Lovers?" Dexter smiled sardonically. "Like everybody in town thinks? No, we're not lovers. I once thought—well, I've always been fond of her and . . . No, we're just very good friends."

"And what do you see this all adding up to?" Mitch asked.

"It's pretty obvious to me, Stevens."

Mitch studied the doctor's face. "Will you help?"

"Help you?"

"Me and the sheriff."

The doctor studied his fingernails. "If you need me. I won't hurt either of them, though."

"And who do you think did it?"

Dexter shrugged. "I wish I knew. It's frightening just to think about it." He pushed his chair back and reached behind to pull a raincoat off a peg on the wall.

"Did anyone know you were meeting me here?" Mitch asked.

The doctor shook his head No. "That's the last thing I wanted known."

Mitch sat, his hands cupped around the beer tankard, after the doctor left. What was the next step? He lifted the tankard to his lips just as Bochard dropped into the seat next to him. "Where the hell have you been?" Mitch asked.

"Back there," the sheriff said, pointing to the door with the round window in it. "I watched you from there. I've been here since before you arrived."

"I didn't see your car," said Mitch.

"Off the road, down about fifty yards. Why?"

Mitch told him about being hit and pushed off the highway.

"And Dexter?"

Mitch told him about the talk with the doctor.

The sheriff took off his hat and turned it slowly in his hands.

"I suppose it could have been some dumb teenager playing games with you out on the road there. I don't know how else to explain what happened to you."

"I'm not happy with that theory," Mitch said.

"I'm not either," Bochard replied. He pushed in the crown of his hat. "I want to see your car."

DRESSED IN A blue and white striped bathrobe, Hollings Carter was registering a late arrival at the Caddo Motel when Mitch and Bochard entered. After seeing the damage to Mitch's car, the sheriff had decided to escort Mitch back to the motel and to see him safely to his room.

"Message for you," the surly owner called out to Mitch.

Mitch waited until the new guest moved off before he approached the desk. "The mayor called just as you were leaving," Carter said. "That's all." He started to turn back to the door behind the front desk that led to his own quarters.

"Did you tell him where I was?"

"I told 'im where you was heading," Carter said.

"And?"

"And that's all." Carter closed the door behind him, leaving Mitch and Bochard standing in the lobby by themselves. They looked at each other, guessing each other's thoughts.

"We still have no proof of anything," Mitch reminded him.

Bochard rubbed his chin. "Let's ask Doc J. J. to meet us tomorrow morning. Whether he likes it or not, he's got to help us.

"I think," the sheriff added, "it's time we talked to the Bullochs."

FIFTEEN

"**Y**ou two go on ahead, I'll catch up with you," the sheriff said. "I just want to check something out." He left the gravel path leading to the mayor's house and headed across the lawn to the back of the house. "Play it by ear, stall until I join you. I'll be right along."

"Where're you going, Bochard?" Dexter asked.

"To check the garage," the sheriff called back. "It'll just take a minute."

"I don't like the idea of going in without him," the doctor said to Mitch. "Maybe we should wait for him."

"It's too late," said Mitch, nodding toward the house. The mayor had opened the front door and seen them.

"What do you want, J. J.?" Bulloch looked at the doctor belligerently. "Let's go into the living room." He glared at Mitch as they walked down the hallway. "I've been trying to reach you, mister. I want to talk to you—alone."

"I came to be of help," Dexter said as they entered the living room.

Bulloch ignored him. He turned toward Mitch, his tone menacing. "I want to know what the hell kind of rumors you're spreading about Flora May."

"I haven't been spreading any rumors," Mitch said.

"The hell you ain't. I got a call last night that you're putting it out that my wife has some kind of dark secret, something about her past, something I don't know about."

"Mayor, I don't operate that way," Mitch said.

"Bullshit. You were overheard speaking to Augustus Leon— all about my wife. What the fuck you got to say about her, mister, that you can't say right out?" All the usual Southern good manners had disappeared; what Mitch saw now was raw and dangerous anger. Where the hell was the sheriff?

"Let's sit down and discuss this calmly," the doctor suggested.

"Bullshit. This is my home. You don't tell me what to do in my home, boy. No one does."

"Rhett, we only—"

"Damn you, Dexter. You butt in enough in my life, always hanging around here." Bulloch took a step toward him. "*You* sit down," Bulloch hissed. "I intend to stand."

The sound of the door chimes—three sweet musical notes— sounded incongruously.

"Who the fuck is that?" Bulloch strode down the hall. Mitch and Dexter could hear him shouting from the front door, "What the hell are you doing here, Sheriff?" Was he afraid? Mitch wondered, though he had trouble imagining this red-faced, stocky man being afraid of anything.

"Okay, Bochard, can you say it now, whatever the hell there is to say? Or is this audience not enough?" the mayor said sarcastically as he and the sheriff came into the living room. As belligerent as the mayor was, Mitch thought, he seemed genuinely bewildered.

"Do you know if your wife went out last night—went out in her car?"

Bulloch answered angrily, "What's going on here? What's anything got to do with my wife?"

"Mayor, please. Answer my question." Bochard took off his hat and held it in front of him. Mitch realized that the sheriff was masking his holster, purposely holding his hat in a way that his right hand was close to the revolver. "Was Flora May out in the car last night?"

"Yeah, so what?" Bulloch said.

"In that God-awful storm?"

"I said *yes*. What's the big deal?" the mayor challenged, thrusting his jaw out.

"Do you know why?" the sheriff asked.

Bulloch looked from Dexter to Mitch to Bochard. "Hey, what's going on?" he said, his anger deflating.

"Flora May's car is all banged up on the right side," the sheriff said to Mitch. "It wasn't in the garage. It was stashed away behind an old toolshed with a tarp thrown over it."

"What's that you're saying? Flora May didn't tell me she'd had an accident. Was someone hurt? Is that what this is all about?"

"You'd better sit down, Mayor," the sheriff said gently. "There's something we have to talk about."

Before the sheriff could continue, Flora May came into the room. She went and stood beside her husband's chair, a hand touching it lightly. "J. J., you here? Will someone tell me what's going on. I thought you were going to speak to Mitch, just Mitch, Rhett."

"I volunteered," Dexter told her. "I'm here to help, Flora May."

"Volunteered for what?" Bulloch demanded.

Mitch stared at him, unsure how to begin. He took a deep breath and plunged ahead. "I've found out about Flora May's background."

"What the hell are you talking about?" Exasperated, the mayor looked up at his wife. "Flora May? Do you know what he's driving at?"

She searched Mitch's eyes. "Go on," she said quietly.

"I've found out about your being a descendant of Thomas Clay Washburn—and a slave named Eliza."

"What!" Bulloch rose out of the armchair. "What the god damn are you saying?" He looked back at his wife, who had taken a step back.

"Your wife," Mitch told the mayor, "has . . ." He stopped himself. "I better explain what I discovered."

Astonished, Bulloch listened to Mitch's recounting of his research findings. The mayor slumped back in the armchair, his arms dangling over the handrests, his mouth working but no words coming out. Flora May continued to stand, her face turned downward. "It's a lie," she said so quietly that Mitch wasn't sure what she had said until she continued, "A shameful, sinful lie."

"Flora May," Dexter said gently, getting up and standing beside her. "It's time to tell the truth."

Bulloch looked from Dexter to Flora May. "The truth? What's the truth? That business about Washburn and that Negress, it's all a lot of bullshit."

"Tell him, Flora May," implored Dexter, taking her hand. "Tell him yourself. Don't let it come from someone else."

"May I talk to my husband alone?" Flora May asked the sheriff.

Bochard hesitated. "All right," he said finally, "but I'll be out in the hall—within eyeshot." He gestured to Mitch and Dexter to follow him.

The three men stood in silence in the dimness of the hallway, watching from a distance. Flora May seemed to be pleading with her husband, her voice too low for them to hear. She reached out for his hand. The mayor paused, then took it and kissed it. The two sat down on the divan, Bulloch still holding Flora May's hand as she continued to talk. Mitch turned away, embarrassed.

The mayor finally rose and came out into the hallway. "What are we talking about here?" He ran his hand over his brow. "We're talking about three, four generations ago." He turned to Flora May, who had followed him. The torment on his face mirrored hers. "That's not important anymore."

"No, it's not important, Mayor," said Mitch. "But something else is."

"Damn you, mister," Bulloch said, turning on him. "Haven't you done enough?"

"There's a matter of murder." Mitch looked at the mayor, held his gaze and saw there the beginning of fear.

"Flora May, honey, what is this man talking about?"

"I had to," she started. "The way you feel about the colored—and what would happen to your political career." She reached out for Bulloch. "I couldn't bring myself to hurt you."

Bulloch turned back into the living room, mumbling to himself, "What is she saying? I don't understand what she is saying. What is she saying?"

"She's confessing, Mr. Bulloch," the sheriff said. "She's confessing to murder."

"I couldn't stand in the way of your career, Rhett," said Flora May, standing in the darkened doorway, her face in shadow. Bulloch stared at her. He opened his mouth as if to ask a question, but suddenly, Mitch thought, the mayor of Virgil realized that he couldn't talk his way out of this one.

The sheriff broke the silence. "I'd like to take Mrs. Bulloch down to headquarters for a statement, Mayor. I think you'll want to contact a lawyer."

"Wait!" Bulloch recovered himself. "I'm going with you. I can phone from your office." He turned to his wife. "We'll face this together, Flora May—you and I. I promise. . . ."

Flora May looked at her husband and nodded woodenly, "Well, Rhett, ironic, isn't it?"

They went upstairs, to get Flora May's jacket, leaving Dexter and Mitch in the living room. The two men stood, lost in thought. "She was getting desperate, I guess," Mitch finally said.

"And setting me up like that."

"It probably wouldn't have stuck, Doctor. You know that."

"Sure, but the publicity in a town like this would have ruined me."

"How do you suppose she knew about my going to see you at Cal's Hideaway last night?"

"She must have heard the mayor trying to reach you at the motel." Dexter wrapped his arms in front of his chest. "I just can't imagine Flora May doing anything of this sort. Why, for God's sake, why?"

"It sounds incredible," said Mitch, "but not impossible. It's happened before. The sheriff and I were talking about a similar case in New York just this morning. Driving ambition and racism—it can make for a lethal combination."

"I always thought of Flora May as such a gentle creature." The doctor's eyes started to water. "I can't believe I was so deceived."

Suddenly, Mitch snapped his fingers. "You know what just occurred to me? The rearview mirror."

"The *what*?" asked Dexter, puzzled.

"It's something that bothered me when I tried to figure out who could have murdered Martha Tour Gale," Mitch explained. "Flora May's car was in the repair shop, so I was tempted to eliminate her as a suspect. I forgot, though, that she could use her husband's car."

"And?"

"And when she did, she invariably readjusted the rearview mirror so that she could see out of it. I just remembered. The day after the murder, I got into Bulloch's car with him and he complained about the mirror. She must have used his car to drive to Manton."

"She's obviously a sick and disturbed woman," Dexter said sadly. "And all these years I didn't see it and I protected her."

Mitch felt sorry for the doctor. Dexter would have to live with the knowledge that someone he cared about and tried to help had done so much harm. "A smart lawyer will probably try to get her committed. I suppose that's justice of a sort." He studied his hands. "You know, I didn't come down here for this to happen, not to anyone. But I still see Tom Cantwell's face—his face in that coffin. He died because of this—because she was trying to shield a son-of-a-bitch bigot like Bulloch."

Mitch heard the Bullochs coming down the stairs and walking out the front door. He went over to the window and pulled aside the heavy curtain. The mayor and Flora May were walking toward the sheriff's car. They were holding hands.

Dr. Pemberton's office was jammed with children, most of them crying loudly. One or two, who were huddled in their mothers' arms, looked absolutely terrified.

A black man, his hand newly bandaged, was leaving the doctor's office. Mitch took the opportunity to poke his head into the doorway. "Any chance I could see you for a few words, Doc? I can see you're busy but I just wanted to say good-bye. I have to catch a plane."

Moses Pemberton waved him in. "What's going on here, Doc, those kids outside look terrified."

Pemberton smiled. "All of a sudden, the public health down here gets a bee in its bonnet, and we have to give all the kids shots of one kind or another. They hate needles. Do you blame them? What brings you here, not another case of food poisoning, I hope?"

"No, I just thought that since you saved my life, I'd like to say a personal good-bye and thanks. And tell you, we've caught ourselves a murderer."

"My God, who?"

"The mayor's wife."

"You must be kidding. Why in hell would the mayor's wife want to murder you."

"Because I found out she is part black."

The doctor stared at Mitch. A grin slowly spread across his face, and then he burst out laughing. "I'm sorry, I'm sorry." He tried to stop but couldn't. Tears were running down his face. "I'm sorry, I know it's not funny. I just can't help myself. . . ."

"You'll read all about it in tomorrow's paper." Mitch paused, fumbling with the latch on his attaché case. "Doc, I also wanted to thank you for something else. I haven't been to a church service in more than twenty years for reasons I won't bore you with. But I was inspired by my visit to your friend's church in New Orleans. It was real; there was no phoniness there.

"I can't say it's enough to bring me back, but at least it started me thinking. I thank you for that."

Pemberton reached out his hand. "Thanks for coming by, Mitch. You've helped me, too. I might even consider treating another white man sometime. Who knows?"

"ATTENTION PASSENGERS, FLIGHT 197 to Dallas and connections west now boarding at Gate 2. Flight 197 to Dallas and connections west now boarding at Gate 2. Please have your boarding pass ready."

Mitch shook hands with Bochard. "Thanks for coming to the airport to see me off, Sheriff." He picked up his attaché case. "You were right about the hairpin, you know. You were the first to suspect something."

"A lot of good that did for the Gale woman, or in your case," Bochard said. He paused deliberately. "I thought maybe you'd want to know how she killed Cantwell. I didn't want to tell you over the phone."

"Not really," Mitch said. "I don't want to know, but I guess I should."

Bochard shrugged. "She stole that insulin from J. J.'s medical bag. He was visiting the Bullochs one evening after Cantwell had dinner with them. It was easy as pie. She'd read up on how people with diabetes take care of themselves, and knew Cantwell couldn't tolerate sugar.

"What she did was premeditated, but if you believe Flora May, she didn't mean to kill him, just to get him so sick he'd go back home." The sheriff shook his head increduously. "That's her fantasy, of course.

"She knew Hollings Carter always helped out with the lunch

trade at the motel restaurant. She simply waited in her car in the back parking area until he left the front desk, took the key to Cantwell's room off the hook behind the desk and let herself in."

"How—?" Mitch winced as another announcement blared over the public-address system: "Attention passengers, Flight 197 to Dallas and connections west is now boarding at Gate 2. Please check in at the gate if you do not have a seat assignment. Flight 197 to Dallas will depart from Gate 2."

Mitch raised his eyebrows, waiting to hear whether the squawking would continue. When it didn't, he began again, "How did she manage it? What did she do?"

Bochard smiled wanly. "That was simple, too. She had one of those sugar packets you get at restaurants. She put a few grains in Cantwell's specimen bottle. When he tested himself, the reagent paper reacted to the sugar. Cantwell thought he needed another shot. He kept a supply of insulin in that little room refrigerator. He went to it, reached in and pulled out the nearest box without even thinking twice about it. She'd put that quick-acting insulin up front, where he would find it. Doc J. J. tells me that even if Cantwell had taken one of his normal doses he would have suffered some level of overdosage. But I suppose she wasn't sure that Cantwell normally kept a supply on hand. Anyway, she came prepared."

"Oh, God, poor Tom," Mitch said. "That means he ended up giving himself a lethal injection. He killed himself without knowing it. I don't think I'll tell his wife about that."

The roar of a plane taking off over the terminal drowned out what Mitch said next, so he repeated it. "Did Flora May ever say where she got the step stool from?"

"I didn't believe it when I heard it," the sheriff smiled, "but she borrowed it from a neighbor on the other side of the street. A sort of everyday kind of thing. Open and aboveboard."

"And the neighbor never asked for it back?"

"Would you believe it? The lady said she was used to other

people borrowing things but not returning them for weeks or months on end. It never dawned on her that anything was wrong."

"Flora May took quite a chance with that."

"No, she didn't," the sheriff said. "Not at all. It was meant to look like an accident, and it did. The step stool of itself meant nothing, until you had the presence of mind to look into the cabinets."

Bochard poked his tongue in his cheek. "You realize she had no intention of doing Martha Tour Gale any harm. After Cantwell's death, it wasn't necessary. But when you showed up . . ." The sheriff looked down at the floor.

"It was my fault, wasn't it?" Mitch asked, a pained expression crossing his face.

"Flora May felt she had no choice then," Bochard said. "She had to get rid of her. And then she had to get rid of you, too, what with all the poking around you were doing. She dropped the arsenic into your plate at the picnic while she was serving you. She insists she didn't want to kill you, just get you so sick— well, just like she wanted to get Cantwell so sick he'd go home. That's her story, anyway."

Mitch stared up at the ceiling. "I'm going to have to live with the responsibility for Martha Tour Gale's death, aren't I?" When the sheriff didn't answer, he sighed.

Bochard adjusted his hat, cocking it slightly. "I don't suppose you'll be heading back here sometime?"

"Will I be needed for the trial?"

"I don't think it'll ever come to a trial," the sheriff said. "If you ask me, she'll be committed permanently. And rightly so, I guess. She must have been crazy to think she'd get away with one murder after another. That attempt on your life—the last one, with her car—that was clumsy. A last-ditch act of desperation."

"Well," said Mitch, "maybe if the book is a success, the local Rotary Club will invite me back to give a speech." Mitch smiled ruefully.

The two men shook hands. Mitch began walking down the passageway to Gate 2. He waved briefly at the sheriff, who touched his hat with two fingers in response. Mitch turned away and went through the open door to the plane. Under his arm was a copy of the *Virgil Whig*. A 48-point banner headline raced across the top of the front page, under it a 3-column bank and photographs of the mayor and Flora May:

BULLOCH RESIGNS POST, CITING PERSONAL REASONS

Mayor Will Help Wife to Defend Herself; Says He Is Abandoning Local Politics

And inside, on page four, just below the fold, a much smaller news item:

WRITER RETURNS NORTH

Professor Mitchell Stevens has left Virgil after completing his research into the life of Thomas Clay Washburn, the town's noted Confederate soldier. Before leaving, he said in an interview that he hoped the biography, which was begun by the late Thomas Cantwell, would be received here in the spirit in which it would be written.

Mr. Stevens, a professor of journalism at Metropolitan University in New York City, was headed to Los Angeles, where his wife, the actress Val Stevens . . .

SIXTEEN

MITCH COCKED AN eye open, then quickly closed it. The sunlight was so strong that the curtain was ineffectual against it. It was difficult to stay asleep. Which is just what hotels want, Mitch thought. Get your guests up and out early.

He heard the water running in the bathroom. Val. She had an early call and had to be at the studio for makeup and wardrobe. Mitch grabbed a pillow from her side of the bed and put it over his head, but it was instantly pulled away.

"Hey, aren't you coming with me to the shoot today?" Val stood beside the bed in a bra and panties.

Mitch smirked. "Come on, up and at 'em!" she said, flinging the covers back. Mitch smirked again. "Mitch, come on, I have to be there on time." He reached for her, but she jumped away in time. "Not now. You had your fun last night. Let's go, lover boy. It's now or never." Mitch made a grim face, then smiled and hoisted himself up.

"Lord, save me."

HE FELT IN the way. The day's filming was outdoors, on a back lot that looked like a city street—make-believe storefronts, neon signs in windows, even fire hydrants and litter baskets. Cables were strung everywhere, snaking between tripods holding sun screens. Men and women with earphones jabbered into walkie-talkies. A crew of prop men were hauling a piece of scenery off to one side. A young woman with a clipboard was shuffling papers and marking a script with a glow pen. A sound man and his assistant ducked under a huge umbrella that shielded a tape machine. Two dogs on leashes lay in the shade of a van, their handler filling a bowl with water from a large plastic container. A makeup artist was delicately applying rouge with a paintbrush on the face of a child. Overhead, a crane with a film photographer posed like an aviator behind an enormous camera was slowly gliding down toward a car parked by the curbside. Two men were spraying the car with what looked like mud. Everyone seemed so busy, but nothing was happening. No scene was being shot. This was prep time.

Mitch looked around for a place to stand where he wouldn't be in anyone's way. Over by an equipment dolly was a long table laden with piles of doughnuts, crullers and rolls, pitchers filled with orange juice, and urns of coffee and tea. Some extras were lounging in front of it, munching on pastry. Mitch strolled over and situated himself by the end of the table. With nothing else to occupy him, he started counting heads—20, 30, 40 people—more, he was certain, when you counted the wardrobe personnel, the film editors who would be working on the day's rushes, office workers, and crew. And, it dawned on him, few of them on the lot—a handful at most—were black, or Hispanic, or Chicano, although there were many minority groups in Los Angeles.

Mitch nodded to himself. Not that different from his experience in Virgil. We go down there—I go down there—and chastise Southerners for their attempts to maintain the status quo, when the truth is that things are just the same—well, almost the same—here in Los Angeles, and in New York, for that matter. Limited opportunities for minorities.

Mitch rubbed his lips. He had an idea.

ABIGAIL CANTWELL WAVED a fan desultorily. "Oh, I can't believe how long the summer seemed this year. It dragged on and on so. And so hot. It's still hot." At the end of the porch, her nurse's aide was reading a Bible and nodding her head as she did so.

"It was miserable in California, also," said Mitch. "But I had time to see a lot, and I got to thinking while I was out there—"

"I wanted to write you, to thank you for what you've done, Mitch. The book, I know, is going to be splendid. Tom would have been so proud—proud of you and proud for himself, too."

"It's always been his story," Mitch said. "I've just retraced his steps. But I've got an idea about the royalties—"

"Keep them, Mitch. I told you I wasn't interested in the money. It's yours, you deserve it. You've got all that writing to do, you've laid out a lot of money traveling down there, and I want to pay you back for that."

"No, no, Abigail, that isn't necessary, and that isn't what I mean about the royalties. I had an idea—"

"You and Val could go off on a trip." She smiled at her own suggestion.

"I've got an even better idea, Abigail. How about we set up a scholarship in Tom's name. Take the publisher's advance and whatever we make on royalties—paperback sale, movie option, whatever else we get—my agent is sure we can make subsidiary rights sales—suppose we take all that money, put it into a bank and draw on the interest to set up the scholarship."

"Why, Mitch, that's a grand idea. Yes, I like it. Yes, that's a wonderful idea. For poor people."

"For a needy journalism student, Abigail," said Mitch.

"For a student, yes."

"For a needy minority student."

"Yes, I like that, Mitch." She took his hand in hers. "Tom would, too."